The Good Mother

ORIGINALLY FROM the UK, Karen won the Emirates Airline Festival of Literature Montegrappa Novel Writing Award 2016 with her thriller and now has a three-book deal with Head of Zeus. When she's not writing novels, Karen is busy bringing up her two young children and running her communication business Travel Ink.

The Good
Mother

KAREN OSMAN

ⓐ

First published in the UK in 2017 by Aria,
an imprint of Head of Zeus Ltd.

9 7 5 3 1 2 4 6 8

A catalogue record for this book is available from
the British Library.

ISBN (PB): 9781788541060
ISBN (E): 9781786699015

Typeset by Divaddict Publishing Solutions Ltd.

Printed and bound by CPI Group (UK) Ltd,
Croydon, CR0 4YY

Head of Zeus Ltd
First Floor East
5–8 Hardwick Street
London EC1R 4RG

WWW.HEADOFZEUS.COM

For my boys – Fahad, Zane, and Ryan x

Preface

He lunged at her and, whether it was the amount of wine he'd drunk making him clumsy or he had simply tripped over a chair leg, he came crashing down on the floor. Seeing the knife still in his hand, she didn't hesitate. She turned and ran for her life. Out through the kitchen and into the hallway. She could see it now – the front door was just a few seconds away. She had to get out onto the street where there were other people. Her hand reached for the door handle and she yanked it hard. But it wouldn't open – it was either stuck or locked. She tried again, praying the door was just jammed by the carpet, but it didn't budge. She could see the keychain hanging on its hook to the side and made a grab for it. Shaking, she tried to find the right key from the bunch to open the door. She could hear him stumbling around in the kitchen and knew she only had seconds to spare. Hearing him coming out of the kitchen, she turned to look back. He looked deranged. There was blood where he had banged his head on the floor and as he came rushing towards her, the last thing she saw was the cruel glint of the blade of the knife, and she knew everything was over.

1

Catherine

15 August 2010

Dear Michael,

My name is Catherine and I am a volunteer with the charity Friends of Inmate Rehabilitation. I hope things are as well as they can be.

When I was asked to correspond with you as part of the charity's efforts to help prisoners, I was initially apprehensive. However, I reminded myself that we have a duty to help those less fortunate than ourselves, and I hope that through these letters I can give you a little insight into the outside world. The only information I have about you is your name and offence and I'm aware that you have spent over ten years in prison already. The charity informed me that you will soon be up for parole, which I'm sure you're looking forward to. As a result, they assign people like me to help you prepare for life outside through letters.

So, where shall I start? My husband, Richard, our

daughter, Helen, and I live about two hours away from Durham. Richard works in finance, and I volunteer for various charities as well as working at the local library.

Are you from Durham? I used to know the city fairly well and I always thought it was such a lovely place, especially the cathedral. In fact, I have a lot of memories of strolling through the cobbled streets, and I have walked for miles along the river. We moved to the Lake District just under ten years ago, and we really enjoy life here. When the weather's fine, we spend a lot of time outdoors, walking and hiking, and my daughter loves nature and wildlife, so for her it's ideal.

Do you get to go outside a little each day? I do hope my questions aren't too personal. Perhaps in the next letter, you can tell me a little bit more about yourself? If you have any specific questions, please feel free to ask me. This is the first time I have done anything like this and I'll be honest, I'm not quite sure what I'm doing! I'm hoping you can help and guide me through it.

Catherine looked at the letter in front of her. Then, before she could change her mind, she carefully wrote her signature at the bottom of the page. Leaving the letter to one side, she headed for the kitchen to make tea. Returning, she sat in her favourite chair by the window looking out over the beautiful view. A rugged mountainous backdrop gave way to gentle green slopes. But the rolling hills were not enough to capture her attention; the letter taunted her from its place on the desk. Was she really going to write to a murderer? Her family would be horrified if they found out. She had taken up various volunteer positions in her time but nothing like this. Once she had contacted the rehabilitation centre it had all happened remarkably quickly and, in hindsight, Catherine had been surprised at how easy the process had been. She had thought they would do intensive background checks, but they had simply sent her a list of prisoners for her to review, interviewed her over the phone and asked her if she had a preference. When she saw Michael's profile, she instantly felt a connection. She couldn't explain it – not yet, anyway – but instinctively she knew it had to be him.

As her tea cooled beside her, Catherine forced herself to refocus, taking in the familiarity of her living room. Soft lemon furnishings, echoing the sunlight that filled the room, made it feel spacious yet comfortable. The coffee table, artfully arranged, held a stack of beautiful books, a small bouquet of flowers and a white trinket box, which had been a wedding gift. The bookshelf was home to a variety of cookbooks, novels and travel guides, interspersed with silver-framed photos of family, celebrations and holidays. A plate she had picked up from an antiques fair took centre stage, its blue intricate swirls bringing to mind warm, exotic destinations such as Morocco and Egypt, although she had never been to either. All in all, it was the perfect mix of style and family life that many of her friends had envied over the years. In fact, it was right here in this room that her friend Ruth, while admiring the blue plate, had mentioned the inmate letter-writing charity. When Catherine had learnt that it was in partnership with HM Prison Durham, the seed had been planted.

The living room was one of Catherine's favourite rooms in the house, yet she always had a sense that it lacked a certain something. Over the years she had scoured interior magazines and high-end home shops to find that missing piece: a lamp, a picture, a mirror, but, she hadn't found it yet, and she had a feeling she never would.

Catherine began to feel restless and automatically started to straighten the room: tweaking a cushion, teasing flowers into full bloom, retrieving a stray hair tie – one of Helen's that had slipped under the sofa. She gained great satisfaction from getting things done and took enormous pride in her organisational skills, both at home and in her volunteer work. Yet, despite her efforts that day, Catherine felt distracted and reluctantly sat back down at her desk. She knew she wouldn't be able to settle until she had made a decision on the inmate volunteer programme. She reached out, feeling the crisp whiteness of the letter, her fingers pausing ever so slightly as they traced over the script of today's date, 15 August 2010. She hadn't used her best writing set – that was for special occasions – but she had used the next best thing, which was a quality paper with a pretty floral border of daffodils and primroses. She wasn't sure if such prettiness would taunt him or inspire him (bizarrely, the rehabilitation centre recommended writing on plain paper), but she had decided to take a chance as it was one of her favourite writing sets. Having folded the paper into thirds she placed it carefully into the envelope, its matching floral pattern giving her a pleasing sense of harmony. As she sealed it, her hands shook slightly and she felt the sharp slice of a paper cut across her skin. A small droplet of blood fell and smudged, its rich red stain distinct against the purity of the paper. Catherine covered the smear with a first-class stamp and quickly headed out to the postbox, before she could procrastinate any longer.

2

Alison

He was gorgeous in that silent but thoughtful, studious sort of way. Not Alison's normal type, that was for sure (did she even have a type, Alison thought to herself), and certainly a lot older, maybe between thirty-five and forty years old, she guessed, which to her eighteen years seemed ancient. But her law lecturer – or The Professor, as she had fondly nicknamed him, the Americanism referring to his Hollywood good looks – was in a different league altogether from the beer-swilling, daredevil lads she had met so far at university. Broad, tall and muscular, he was what her mother would call a 'real man', a term most likely inspired by the covers of the numerous romance novels she used to read. His olive skin gave a hint of exciting, exotic foreignness, which was incredibly appealing against the dull, grey skies that so often characterised British weather. Despite his age, he was the type of man you saw in the window ads of Thomas Cook, strolling along the beach, hand in hand with a gorgeous blonde, the prerequisite palm tree framing the picture. Yet, there was also something slightly old-fashioned about him that harked back to a previous decade, as if he was trying to relive the youth of his twenties. Maybe it was the fact that his hair was slightly too long or the way his jacket sleeves were rolled up, revealing his forearms. He was charismatic, though. Alison liked the way he paused a moment before answering a question from a student. If you blinked you would miss it, but that pause spoke to her, as if to convey, "any question you have is important and I'm going to give it serious consideration before answering". He had an intensity that, when directed at you, made you feel like you were the only one in the room.

Her friend Laura – pretty much the only real friend she had made since starting university – would be impressed that she was having such non-intellectual thoughts. According to her, Alison was far too serious for a first-year student and should loosen up a bit and have fun, go on a few dates, for example. Easy for Laura to say, thought Alison. Naturally confident, Laura was one of those girls who didn't seem to be fazed by anything, not even moving hundreds of miles from her hometown of London to start university in Durham. Alison, however, had carried around with her a vague unease since starting the three-year course a few weeks ago. Her fellow students seemed so carefree, spending their days hungover but happy, and not too fixated on the work. Every dorm room she passed, students were in and out of each other's rooms, watching TV, listening to music, and generally getting to know each other. Everyone said the first-year results didn't count anyway but Alison felt that she would have to study really hard to have any chance of graduating with even a 2:2. This was an alien concept to her. She, who had always been in the top three performing students at school and sixth-form college without really having to try too hard, was now facing some stiff competition.

Alison thought of her schooldays wistfully. While not considered one of the 'popular' girls, she had an active social life, was on various sports teams and committees, and had a great group of close friends that she had known all the way from primary school to sixth-form. She sighed. This was just another of the many unexpected things about university. When she first heard that she had secured a place on the law course at the prestigious institution, she was thrilled – her mother had almost gone there and it was considered one of the top universities in the country. And while she had bravely insisted to her parents on leaving home and moving into the halls of the college so she could experience student life completely, she was secretly relieved to have her family close by in the same city, if only to do her washing and provide supplies and moral support. So it was with much excitement that she had looked forward to her new life. The three-year course meant she would graduate in the millennial year, 2000, and that felt like a good omen in itself. But within weeks, Alison realised that the course was much harder than she could have ever anticipated. It wasn't just the intellectual rigour required – the lecture style of teaching was radically different from what she was used to and the students often had a lot of time for their own study, which required huge amounts of discipline and independent learning. She was also used to having familiar relationships with her teachers but the university lecturers seemed busy and remote, sealed in their offices, their closed doors making her reluctant to knock.

One of the things she did like was her room, which was in the college of St Hild and St Bede, a traditional building perched at the top of a hill. The stone arched windows in her room formed a window seat overlooking Bede Chapel and in the distance, the square, grey buildings of HM Prison Durham. It was a warm and cosy room and she had made it her own with her sunflower-covered bedspread, bedside lamp and Jack Vettriano posters. Her desk was next to the window seat, and between study sessions she would often sit and look out, the view exposing a marked discord between the gentle curves of the hills and the sharp corners of the prison building.

Alison forced herself to refocus on what The Professor was saying, rather than the way his body moved as he paced up and down, delivering his lecture. Reams of notes later, her head full, she knew she would have to review what she'd written later in the hope that it might make more sense. As the students left the class, Alison felt disconcerted to see everyone chattering away to each other. Topics floated past her ears: the coursework that The Professor had set that day, evening plans, what to have for lunch. Yet, she didn't hear anyone complaining about finding the course difficult. She wondered what she was doing wrong. Why was she finding it so hard? She thought of asking for some help but dismissed the idea immediately. It wouldn't make a good impression so early on in the term. What if the Faculty discovered that she was struggling? Would they kick her out? She thought of her mother's note she had received that morning along with a care package.

Your father and I are so proud of you, Alison, and I'm not ashamed to admit that we tell everyone about your achievement! I swear Betty next door must be fed up of hearing about it! You worked so hard to get your place and we know you're going to make a success of this new chapter in your life as well. The University of Durham is an incredible institution that will stand you in good stead for the rest of your life.

If only her mother knew, thought Alison to herself. Troubled, she walked along the cobbled streets to meet Laura from her history lecture. She was one of the first people Alison had met when moving into halls. In that definitive way she had come to identify as being 'very Laura', the friendly stranger had knocked on Alison's door, introduced herself and told her life story all within the first fifteen minutes of their meeting. It was obvious that Laura had been one of the 'popular' girls in school. Bright, vivacious and confident, with an open, relaxed attitude, she made everyone she came into contact with feel comfortable. Laura had been brought up in the capital, and her exhilarating childhood made Alison feel that her content but provincial upbringing in the small city of Durham was slightly on the boring side. Theatres, nightclubs, shows, fancy restaurants, Laura had experienced it all, but it was related in such a humorous manner that it didn't come across as showing off – simply, that was her life and she didn't know any other way. She was very friendly and suggested that the two of them go along to the Freshers' Week event that evening together, the traditional college initiation being something Alison had dreaded attending on her own. Alison's shyness sometimes led people to believe that she was aloof and, after years of having the same group of school friends, she wasn't entirely comfortable when it came to meeting new people. As it turned out, the evening was a lot of fun. Within minutes of arriving, Laura had attracted a crowd of fellow freshers and they spent the evening having a laugh, playing silly drinking games and generally getting to know each other.

After that night, Alison and Laura became firm friends, bonding over hangovers, eating breakfast together, meeting up after classes and going out in the evenings. Alison was happy to have made a new friend so soon, especially one so popular. Laura was a social butterfly and seemed determined to make the most of university life, joining a whole array of clubs and societies. She made friends quickly, not just in St Hild and St Bede but also in other colleges, as well as on her history course, and she was always planning the next get-together. Alison often wondered how Laura found the time to study. While Alison clearly put in more hours in the library, the apparent lack of work didn't seem to affect Laura's results, She could produce a two-thousand-word essay the night before it was due and get a decent mark, whereas Alison panicked if she didn't have at least three days to research and write her assignments. Considering how different they were, Alison felt pleased that Laura had chosen her to spend so much time with and it was a nice to know that she was only down the corridor.

That evening, Alison and Laura were planning to go to the library together. Alison had to finish an essay, which was due the next day, and she also wanted to start drafting ideas for some upcoming coursework.

'Hey, how's it going?' Laura greeted her. 'How was class?'

'Not bad, thanks.' Alison's cheeks flushed slightly as she thought of The Professor, hoping her friend wouldn't notice. She would think it hilarious if sensible, strait-laced Alison had a crush on her lecturer and she knew she would never hear the end of it.

'Sooooo,' Laura said, in the drawn-out way that Alison

had come to know very well. 'The library, huh?'

It was a tone that told her Laura had something much more exciting in mind than going to the library to work.

'Now I know we had plans,' started Laura, 'but how does this sound? There's a social at the Student Union tonight at eight – what do you think?'

'But what about the library?'

'I know, but I thought this might be more useful.'

Alison raised one eyebrow at her, meaningfully, not needing to voice her scepticism but not being able to resist.

'Since when does drinking your own body weight in vodka become useful?'

Laughing, Laura brushed away Alison's concern.

'No, really! You're going to like this one, I promise. It's a student and faculty social so you get to mingle with the staff and chat to them about the course. There's one member of staff from each faculty. C'mon… it'll be great, and much more fun than an evening at the library. I can't believe I even agreed to that in the first place!'

Laura said the word 'library' as if it was the most boring place in the world.

'Well…' Alison paused, a slight hesitation rising in her throat at the thought of all the work she had to do. 'How about we do a couple of hours' work and then go to the social for one drink?'

'Really?' replied Laura. 'Is it worth going all that way to the library just for an hour?'

'Yes!' Alison replied, laughing. 'And I said two hours, by the way – not one! Come on, let's go before you find something else to distract me with!'

Happy to have got her way, Laura linked arms with her friend.

'Me? I would never be distracting!' she said, a picture of innocence. 'But if we could just stop off at Superdrug on the way, I need a new lipstick. A girl has to make an impression, you know.'

Alison laughed. 'Trust me, you don't need anything else to make an impression.'

*

By the time the girls finished their work, had a bite to eat, and arrived at the Student Union, the social was well under way. It was busier than Alison anticipated and everyone seemed to be in deep conversation. Laura had disappeared to the bar to get some drinks so Alison tried to make herself look as inconspicuous as possible – not an easy feat at five foot eight, and carrying a large bag of books. Alison moved closer to the wall, accidently bumping someone with her bag. Muttering apologies, she found a quiet corner and sidled into the chair, hoping Laura wouldn't get caught up in conversation at the bar.

Soon wishing she had never agreed to come, Alison pulled out one of her textbooks and tried to look as if she was reading it.

'Mind if I join you?' a familiar male voice said beside her.

She looked up and saw none other than The Professor. He was wearing a black jacket, white shirt and jeans, and she could see the end of a red scarf peeping out of his bag.

Glancing around, she double-checked to make sure he wasn't talking to anyone else.

'Of course,' she replied. 'Have a seat.'

'Alison, isn't it?' he asked.

'Yes – Alison Owen – I'm in your law class.'

'That's right,' he nodded.

The next few seconds seemed to last an eternity as Alison tried to come up with something interesting to say.

Eventually, he noticed the book she was reading and, probably just to fill what seemed to her to be an almost excruciating silence, he asked how she was finding the course.

'It's going well,' she lied. 'I'm finding it really interesting.'

'Are there any parts you're struggling with?' he asked, indicating the book.

'Well, chapter eight was a bit hard-going but I managed it in the end,' she stammered. 'The question I had, though...' she trailed off. Trying to locate the chapter, she fumbled and accidently tore the page as the book dropped to the floor.

Cheeks burning, she made a grab for the book, trying but failing to compose herself. Just at that moment, Laura turned up with drinks.

'There you are,' she announced. 'I've been looking all over for you. What are you doing tucked away in the corner?'

Suddenly noticing The Professor, Laura exclaimed, 'Oh, sorry!'

Alison wasn't surprised when he stood up to leave. He nodded at Laura, then turned back to Alison. 'Well, Alison,' he said, 'it's nice to meet you personally – I remember reading your application and being very impressed with it. If you need any help, my door is always open. In fact, come and see me next week about that question you had.'

'Thank you,' Alison managed to say.

And with that, he disappeared into the crowd, leaving Alison with her book and pride in tatters.

'Ooh, he's gorgeous,' said Laura after The Professor had left. 'Is he one of your lecturers? How lucky are you! He does realise, though, it's 1997 and not the eighties anymore?'

Cheeks still burning, Alison felt inexplicably cross on his behalf at the minor criticism.

Peering closely at her, Laura caught on. 'Check you out – you're all of a fluster. You like him!' Laughing, Laura started to make kissy, kissy noises while Alison tried to feign nonchalance.

'Don't be stupid,' she said. 'Of course I don't. He just caught me off guard, that's all, and it is very warm in here.' As if to emphasise her point, Alison removed her jacket, but Laura wasn't having any of it.

'Well, well, well, you *are* a dark horse! How old is he? He looks like he's nearly forty – sooooo old! But he does have something about him, doesn't he? Not that I can blame you – the boys in our year still need to grow up, if you ask me.' Laura adopted a worldly air. 'Did I tell you that Steve dared me to finish two pints in one go? He thought he could outdrink me, but of course I showed him!'

Alison had no idea who Steve was but she was happy that the focus was off her.

'Really? Did you do it?' asked Alison, her curiosity getting the better of her.

'Of course I did!' cried Laura. 'I'm a pro and now he knows it.' Abruptly changing the subject, she continued, 'Come on, let's go and mingle. There's a guy I want you to meet who I think would be perfect for you.' And at the pull of her arm, Alison followed her friend gratefully towards a group of students.

3

Kate

Kate could feel the sweat dripping down her back. Her hastily gathered ponytail had come loose and escaped dirty-blonde strands stuck to the back of her neck. With no time to put on any make-up, she knew her face was probably beet red, the dark circles under her eyes exposing her fatigue.

It was an unusually hot day for the North-East, and she had spent a frustrating morning shopping, getting her elder child kitted out for school. At five years old, her daughter knew exactly what she wanted and everything she wanted was the most expensive. And, of course, whatever she wanted, her three-year-old sister also wanted. So Kate had spent most of the morning using her negotiating skills – which were so well developed she could be a politician – to placate her daughters while ensuring there was enough money left over for the weekly food shop. They had been out since nine that morning in an attempt to beat the crowds, but it was still hectic as mothers – most with their children in tow – prepared for the upcoming school year. To make matters worse, the school uniform shop had run out of stock of some of the items, forcing her to traipse across to the other side of town, loaded with shopping bags and her two very reluctant girls.

With the folded buggy in one hand and the bags of shopping in the other, Kate constantly cajoled her daughters while directing a silent stream of swearing at the broken lift, as she struggled up five flights of stairs to reach their flat. The slight throb above her eyes signalled the onset of a headache, which threatened to turn into a migraine if she didn't take some paracetamol soon.

It was only noon but the three hours had felt like three days. All she wanted to do was lie down with a cool drink and close her eyes, but with lunch still to be made, the washing to do, and trying to settle her younger daughter down for a nap, a lie-down was not very likely. Kate had decided to come home to eat rather than spend money on food in a restaurant, but not for the first time she wished she had simply taken the girls to a cheap fast-food place. However, she was determined to give her children the best and that included a healthy diet. She sighed. No one had told her it would be this hard. Well, she corrected herself, they had, but she hadn't listened. It wasn't just the physical demands of running around after children; the emotional energy needed was overwhelming. Love, guilt, worry, happiness, stress and fear made for a tumultuous cocktail of emotions, which saturated her days and infiltrated her nights. She loved her children deeply – she would take a bullet for them – but she felt constantly depleted and rushed, with no time to replenish. This feeling had increased after her second child. It was more than double the work. Her elder daughter had been a much easier baby. It didn't help that her younger daughter was a difficult sleeper and often woke up during the night. Over time, she had slowly given up and simply brought her into her own bed. It was the only way to get some sleep. Her husband wasn't much help either. He worked long hours, had a long commute, and when he got home he was too tired to do very much apart from eat his dinner, which he normally did while reading the newspaper, and go to bed.

However, from next month, her elder daughter would be in school, Kate thought happily. She had done as much as possible at home to teach both of her children, and the free playgroup at the local church was a godsend. But now she could focus on her younger daughter who, possibly in awe or perhaps slightly overwhelmed by her older sibling, often got lost in the fray. Kate was uncomfortably aware that she had a different relationship with each of her daughters, and while she didn't have favourites, her relationship with her elder daughter was unquestionably easier. Her younger child was quieter and perhaps not as confident as her big sister, and Kate hoped she would flourish with a little more focused attention. She had already planned some outings for just the two of them. Most of them were free, such as a visit to the park, and walks along the river to feed the ducks. But she had also been saving a little of her housekeeping money each week and decided to splurge. She'd bought tickets for the large soft-play area in Newcastle, and had invited her daughter's playmate Emma and Emma's mother, Susan. Kate had mentioned nothing to her daughter except that she had a surprise for her, and although it was costing a pretty penny once you added the train fare, the snacks and the food, the look of excitement on her young face was worth it. Kate increasingly needed those cherished moments with her children, and the scrimping and saving often meant she went without. She couldn't remember the last time she had bought something for herself. While she didn't regret having her children for a second, she did wonder what her life would have been like if she hadn't become pregnant so young. She was only eighteen at the time, and while many of her friends had babies, Kate had had other plans. It had been the late 1970s, after all, and women had a lot more options than their own parents had back in the day. Or she did have, until she met her husband. At the time, she simply couldn't get enough of him. He turned everything she thought she wanted – university, a career – on its head. Within a week, she was in love. Within three months, they were inseparable, and within six months, she was pregnant. The pregnancy was a shock for both of them, but to his credit, he had done the honourable thing: told her everything was going to be all right, proposed, and married her. That whole year had been a maelstrom of passion and new beginnings, and at the time, Kate had felt it was romantic. They were in love with a baby on the way. What could be more perfect? It was only on the morning of her wedding, when her mother asked her if she was sure marriage was what she wanted, that Kate had felt a sliver of anxiety.

'If you're not sure, love, tell me,' her mam had said. 'Marriage is for life and with a child on the way, it's not going to be easy. Your dad and I will always look after you. There are other options, you know. It's such a shame to give up your place at university after you worked so hard for it.'

Kate had brushed away her concerns, along with the brief unease she had felt. 'I'm ready for anything. As long as I have him by my side, I'll be happy!' she responded naively, kissing her mother on both cheeks.

Kate grimaced as she remembered those words. As always,

her mother had been right. It was hard. Kate remembered bringing her second daughter home from the hospital. She had felt so happy when she'd brought her elder daughter home, so she couldn't understand why she was crying all the time with her second. And the exhaustion was something else entirely. Kate became lost in her memories as she recalled trying to cope with a toddler and a newborn. There were days when she literally didn't know how she was going to survive. She could never get them to sleep at the same time so she rarely napped during the day, and at night, she was feeding every three or four hours. Her husband did what he could but as she was breastfeeding, there wasn't much he could do. In addition, her elder daughter, after being the centre of attention for so long, had severe jealousy issues. She had imagined that the little girl would be helpful, but it got to the point where Kate couldn't turn her back for a second without her daughter taking advantage of the opportunity to try to pinch the baby.

Her mother had visited her just after the birth but in a two-bedroom flat there was little room. However, after hearing her daughter cry down the phone one morning from sheer exhaustion, she had got on the train and stayed for three weeks. Kate remembered her mother sleeping on the couch, not complaining once how uncomfortable it was. It had been the lifeline she needed. Her mother took her toddler and the baby out for a walk in the morning, letting her get some much-needed sleep. Eventually, Kate got into a routine and everything settled down but she still remembered feeling overwhelmed by it all. After her mother left, and at her encouragement, slowly Kate had started accepting offers of help and letting friends and neighbours pop in to watch the baby for an hour or help with the washing. Normally,

Kate prided herself on being able to do it all, but during those months, she had no choice. It was either accept the help or go insane. It sounded dramatic now but that's how it had felt at the time. And now, a few years later, she still treasured those friendships. She still visited her neighbour in the flat upstairs who had brought her a home-made casserole on the very day that the fridge was completely empty because she hadn't been able to get to the shops, never mind cook something. She still gave Margaret, next door but one, a bunch of flowers on her birthday, never forgetting how she had done a week's washing and ironing in a day when Kate was running out of nappies. All in all, Kate felt she had come out stronger and with better friendships, but she still wouldn't want to go back to those early newborn days. It was one of the reasons she had insisted to her husband that they have no more children.

And while it had become easier, it was still difficult. In the five years she'd been married, any illusion of romance had long since disappeared. Her husband worked all hours, they barely spoke to each other, and they were both exhausted. When was the last time they had gone out for a drink? When had he last asked how her day was or told her she looked pretty? Kate couldn't remember. Not that she did look pretty, she thought ruefully. Lack of sleep had taken care of that. These days, if they did talk, it was about money, or rather the lack of it. When he had lost his job, it had taken a huge toll on them, both financially and psychologically. They couldn't pay the rent or the bills, and even the basics, such as food, were a struggle to afford. Kate didn't sleep properly for weeks worrying about it, and to this day she wondered how her husband had managed to sleep so soundly each night. In the end, she had gone to her parents for help. Kate knew her husband still hadn't forgiven her for asking them for money – he said she'd made him look an incompetent fool – but she didn't know what else to do. He just seemed so remote and unreachable. For the six months he was out of work the strain was unbearable. Eventually, he had found another job, but it wasn't as well paid as his previous one – which hadn't been especially lucrative to start with – and it wasn't as close to home. By that point, Kate was just relieved to have him out of the house. The tension between them had become tangible. For all their troubles, she still loved him, but they were so far apart now, divided by stress, resentment and exhaustion, and she simply didn't know how to fix their marriage. They could go out for a meal and have a little time to themselves, but these days they wouldn't be able to afford the meal, never mind a baby-sitter, and Kate didn't want to take advantage of her friends, who'd already done so much.

They would have to address the situation soon. They couldn't go on like this; it was starting to have an impact on the girls. Kate felt weary at the thought of it. Why should she have to take the initiative? Why did everything fall to her? She knew he hated his job, but in this economic climate he should be grateful to have one at all. For a moment, Kate imagined being able to leave the house for just one day and sit behind a desk in an office filled with other adults. She imagined the ringing of phones, the clicking of typewriter keyboards, people's voices as they talked about different clients. And blissfully, the absence of children – no crying, no wailing, no 'Mummy!' twenty-four hours a day. No having to come up with exciting new games because she didn't have the money to buy the latest My Little Pony figures and Care Bear cuddly toys. Kate could hardly imagine it: to have a whole day to yourself, where you could be absorbed in something other than childcare. On certain days, she would swap places with her husband in a heartbeat. She took a deep breath and made a mental note to try to find the time to talk to him. Along with the million other things she had to do, she thought grudgingly. Perhaps on Saturday night when the children were in bed, she could cook him a nice steak. If she caught him between his first and second beers, he should be relaxed enough to have a chat. A surge of frustration ran through her again that she had to plan ahead to try to get a conversation with him. How had things become so complicated? She remembered a time when she could have talked to him about anything. A time when he made her feel safe and that he would do anything to make her happy.

Sighing, Kate dragged her thoughts back to the present. She didn't have time to deal with her marriage now. Her to-do list was getting longer by the minute, and she also had to come up with something for dinner that didn't involve frozen pizza. Grabbing a knife, she quickly buttered some bread and made cheese sandwiches for the children. She was chopping salad when she heard a scream, followed by the sound of crying in the children's bedroom.

'Mummy,' one of them began to wail. 'She hit me.'

'Mummy! I didn't! But she took my new pencil case!'

Kate sighed and waited a few moments to see if they would sort it out themselves. When she had found out she was pregnant the second time, everyone had talked about having a boy so she had 'one of each'. But for Kate, while she would be happy either way, she was particularly pleased when they found out they were having a second girl. She had thought same-sex siblings would get on better because they would have more in common. How wrong she had been. The girls fought all day long.

Walking into the children's bedroom, Kate took in the

scene. Her younger daughter was lying on the floor with her head in her arms, holding on to the pencil case for dear life, sobbing so hard it would seem the world was about to end. Her elder child, on the other hand, was parading about in an old curtain pretending she was a queen and demanding the sought-after pencil case back immediately. She had called the guards already, she grandly informed her mother. While the pencil case was rightly her elder daughter's, Kate sympathised with the little one. She too just wanted to lie on the floor and sob because she wanted things she couldn't have. But it wasn't going to get lunch made or the washing done. She knew it was going to be a long day, and not for the first time did she imagine what her life would have been like if she had heeded her mother's words.

4

Catherine

Catherine woke up to silence, instantly alert. It was so unusual in her house that she immediately thought something was wrong. Normally, Helen would have her music blasting from her iPod or Richard would be talking loudly on his mobile phone. He liked to pace while holding the wretched thing to his ear. He told her it helped him think, but it put Catherine on edge watching him march around like that.

She padded downstairs and was greeted with the smell of fresh coffee and bacon, and her husband and daughter chatting quietly, enjoying their breakfast. Pleasure – and another feeling she couldn't quite put her finger on – welled up inside her as she took in the idyllic scene.

'Good morning,' she said, smiling.

'Morning, love, how did you sleep?' Richard asked her this every day. Just one of the many mechanical things married couples do when they have been together for so long, Catherine thought.

'Fine,' she responded. 'You?'

'Yes, good thanks – there's coffee in the pot and bacon in

the pan. You just need to pop a couple of slices of bread in if you want some toast.'

'Thanks.' Catherine kissed the top of his head, grateful that while they had been married a long time, not everything was perfunctory. He knew she didn't operate well in the morning without a strong cup of coffee and a bite to eat. Helen hadn't inherited her father's 'jump out of bed and be chipper' personality either. Instead, she took after her mother and tended not to interact much until after breakfast. Both Catherine and Richard had learnt early on to give her the space she needed and even now, in her late twenties, she was more like a non-communicative, moody teenager in the mornings, only really coming to life around 10 a.m., which was why Catherine was so surprised to see her chatting happily to her father.

Catherine moved to the kitchen, her only focus being the coffee pot, and poured herself a generous cup. When anyone asked why she refused to drink instant coffee, she told them it was because of the aroma. As she breathed it in deeply, Catherine thought to herself that there was nothing like the smell of freshly ground beans to turn something ordinary into something worth getting up for. And recently, she felt that she needed more and more incentive to be able to face each day. After a few grateful sips, the wheels of her brain started to turn and she began a mental list of the things she had to do that day. It was Thursday, which meant a committee meeting for one of the charities she volunteered for, and a quick shop for the weekend so she wouldn't have to battle through the crowds on a Friday.

As she helped herself to the bacon, the flap of the letterbox rattled, indicating the postman's arrival. Catherine checked the clock on the microwave. He was early today – usually he arrived when Richard had already left the house and was on his way to work. Hurriedly, she put her breakfast to one side, and went to the front door. She had been checking the post each day, wondering when, and even if, she would receive a letter from Michael. It had only been two weeks and the rehabilitation centre had warned her that, in some cases, it took at least a couple of months to receive a response, and it could be a short one at that. Yet today, there it was, a light blue envelope, its Durham postmark just visible amongst the bills and circulars. Quickly snatching it up, she slipped it into her dressing gown pocket before scooping up the rest of the post. As she glanced through the letters, she could see most of them were for Richard.

'I'm going to take a quick shower,' she said as she handed him the bundle, the letter from Michael still safely hidden in her pocket. 'I may be a while as I need to wash my hair,' she added, grinning. It was a running joke between them about how much time she took in the shower. 'You'll probably have left by the time I'm finished. See you tonight.'

'What about your breakfast?'

'I'll finish it later.'

'Really? That's a first! Normally, you can't move until you've had something to eat! OK, love. I'll drop Helen off to her interview on the way.' Of course – Catherine had forgotten that Helen had an interview that day. So that was why her daughter was a little chattier this morning – the excitement and nerves of a job interview.

'See you later, and good luck,' she said, kissing Helen goodbye.

'Bye, Mum.'

As she leaned over to Richard to kiss him goodbye, he put his arm round her waist and Catherine stiffened as she heard the letter in her pocket crumple under his embrace.

Extracting herself, she turned, her hand in her pocket, feeling the thin paper between her fingers as she walked towards the bedroom. Conscious of his eyes on her back, she tried not to hurry. She went into their en-suite bathroom, and locked the door behind her. Sitting on the covered toilet seat, she took a deep breath to calm herself. She hadn't mentioned to her family that she had written to Michael. There didn't seem much point if she wasn't even sure he was going to respond. It wasn't necessarily a lie, more of an omission, she told herself. Why shouldn't she have a secret? Her family didn't need to know everything about her, did they? But still, it was an unfamiliar feeling. Pushing the guilt aside, she slipped the envelope out of her pocket, and tried not to rip it open. Slowly slipping her finger under the flap, Catherine felt the anticipation increase in intensity as she unfolded and smoothed out the letter. No floral patterns here, but the handwriting was cursive, neat and legible, with some of the letters having a stylistic flick.

September 2010

Dear Catherine,
Thanks for the letter – it was such a pleasure to receive something so personal and learn a little about your life. I can imagine it's incredibly nerve-racking being in communication with a convicted murderer. As you can imagine, I don't really get many visitors (apart from my solicitor and even those visits have stopped as I recently fired the last one) and rarely any post, so when your letter arrived last week it was a real treat.

I have been inside since 1999 so yes, over ten years and it's true what they say: you can get used to anything. The food's not bad and they let us watch TV every week. You're right about my upcoming parole – if my good behaviour continues for another year, my parole date is likely to come up sooner rather than later, so that's something to work towards.

I am originally from Durham – or rather, from a small village just outside the city. I moved around various prisons and holding cells initially but I have been in Durham Prison for several years now.

Saying that, it took me a long time to get used to being here and sometimes I don't even recognise myself. I used to live a pretty normal life – I worked in education and enjoyed it. In my spare time, I used to play the guitar, but that's all a different life now.

Michael

Catherine swallowed down her disappointment. For some reason, she had expected more. Not even a page long, the letter was brief, to say the least, but she couldn't say she hadn't been warned. And she hadn't had to wait long for a reply – that was a good sign surely, she thought. Slipping it back into her pocket, she reassured herself that it was only his first letter and, slowly, she would be able to get him to open up. What did she expect? She was a stranger to him – she would have to be patient. She would write back to him in the next few days.

Having taken a shower, Catherine got dressed, pulling on her favourite jeans, a white T-shirt and a pale pink V-necked jumper. She didn't bother to check herself in the full-length mirror: she knew what she looked like as this was her regular uniform for a Thursday. She had never had a problem with her weight – certainly not in the last ten years, anyway – and as a result, at almost fifty, her figure looked at least several years younger. Her philosophy of keeping as busy as possible and eating food to live rather than for pleasure was better than any diet. With her light blonde bobbed hair and tall, slim elegance, she was saved from the full-blown envy of other women by her face. Her life was etched there, every line and wrinkle reflecting her history, but while it was ageing, it also gave character, making her somehow more likeable, more approachable. Peering into the handheld mirror, Catherine applied her expensive anti-ageing cream, which Ruth had talked her into buying. Catherine idly wondered if it did any good. A fine layer of foundation, a touch of mascara and blusher, a quick blow-dry of her hair and she considered herself ready to face the day.

Catherine retrieved the letter from her dressing gown pocket and went into the kitchen. As she expected, it was empty, the hastily gathered plates and cups on the kitchen counter the only signs that Richard and Helen had been there. Having emptied and rinsed their dishes, Catherine placed them in the dishwasher before making a piece of toast. She sat down at the table, her breakfast in front of her, distractedly picking at her food as she read the letter once again. This time, she decided, she would use her best paper.

5

Alison

Despite spending endless hours in the library, as the end of the first term approached, Alison still felt she was floundering and out of her depth with the workload. With lecture-style teaching and a large number of students, the learning experience seemed alien and isolating. Their heads bent over their notepads, students wrote furiously as the lecturer droned on and on about the principles of law. It was all very theoretical. Alison had spent the previous summer imagining the course to be much more dynamic: outings to watch proceedings in courtrooms; role-playing; analysing high-profile cases in groups. She had envisaged waking up every day passionate and eager to learn more about how she could help and change people's lives for the better. Now, she silently chastised herself for it, being such a cliché. Instead, each class just seemed to get harder and harder, no matter how much studying she did, and the boredom was, at times, excruciating. Perhaps her life-long dream of working in law wasn't for her after all? In the last few weeks of the first term, with the pressure of course-work deadlines and tests, she was spending twelve hours or more a day studying. Sometimes she would wake up with her head on her desk around two in the morning, various notes stuck to her face, and when she went to review them, she found she had little recollection of making them the night before.

While Alison still had breakfast with Laura, between lectures and study sessions, she just didn't have as much time to see her friend, and their lazy coffee breaks and lunches in their free time slowly dwindled to once every few days. When they did catch up, Laura would chatter non-stop about all the activities she was involved in: rowing, dance classes, socials, and various events she attended. Alison could barely keep up. How did she find time for her work? Perhaps her course in history wasn't as demanding, thought Alison, trying to reassure herself. But deep down, Alison knew the real reason. She was struggling because she wasn't clever enough. She was struggling because she was used to being a big fish in a small pond at school, and now she was in a much more competitive environment and losing ground both academically and socially. She hadn't really made any friends on the course and she knew she relied heavily on Laura for her social life, but the more time went on, the harder it seemed to make the effort. On her course, groups had already formed and Alison was either too shy, or too exhausted to try to involve herself. There didn't seem to be room for anything else except making sure she got through the workload. Her fear of failing increased day by day and the only way she seemed to be able to conquer it was by spending more time in the library, note taking and re-reading up topics she'd failed to grasp in the fast-paced lectures. The endless hours began to take their toll and she would often catch herself drifting off. She knew she wasn't being effective with her work but she couldn't stop herself. The library became like a security blanket and she believed that as long as she was amongst the caverns of books, she would somehow get through the course.

*

One morning, having woken up late after studying until the early hours the night before, Alison found her favourite jeans were in the wash, so she grabbed another pair. However, the university diet of alcohol and cheap takeaway food had taken its toll, and as she struggled to do up the zip she realised just how much weight she had put on in less than a term. With no time to change, she secured a thick elastic hairband through the buttonhole and looped it over the button, giving her a much-needed extra few inches, then covered the gap with a long jumper. It wasn't very comfortable but it would have to do. Typical, Alison thought as she grabbed her bag. Today was an important day and she had planned to dress carefully. During the last week of the first term, students were invited for review sessions with their lecturers. Alison was dreading the sessions. She had six appointments in total and had booked them all in one day, in order to get them over with quickly. Finally ready, she hurried to the law department, walking quickly to reach the first meeting on time. She was only halfway there, when she felt the first splashes of rain on her face, then she realised she had forgotten her umbrella.

*

As each appointment drew to a close, the message was clear: she had a strong work ethic but was an average student and unlikely to be in the top tier of graduates. Of course, none of the lecturers put it in so many words, but she knew what they were saying and could infer the meaning behind their feedback. It started with the first meeting at 9 a.m. with Dr Asher. She was an astonishingly dry woman whose tone of voice never seemed to moderate. Many students dreaded her class, particularly after a big night out, as her monotonous voice induced a feeling of such sleepiness that students often dropped off. Alison had never seen so many people wearing sunglasses indoors as they did to Dr Asher's classes.

'Good morning, how very good of you to join me,' said Dr Asher as Alison, late, with hair plastered to her scalp, entered her office. Ignoring her typical sarcastic disdain, Alison apologised. Outside, the drizzle threatened to turn into a torrential downpour.

Alison sat opposite Dr Asher on a hard, uncomfortable chair, feeling the makeshift band of her jeans cut into her. As she raised her arms to smooth the frizz out of her damp hair, she felt the slight ping of the elastic holding her jeans together pop open. Alarmed and unable to move, Alison rested her bag on her lap.

Dr Asher didn't waste any time on small talk. On her desk, Alison recognised her submitted coursework, the black markings interspersed with splashes of red. Handing the document over, Dr Asher cleared her throat.

'Here's your coursework – just an average 65 out of 100, I'm afraid. While the arguments were solid, they could have been strengthened by additional details that you had missed out. Take this section for example...'

Alison barely heard the rest. She was still trying to come to terms with the grading. How was that mark even possible when she had spent so much time on the essay? Her eyes threatening tears, she kept her head down, trying to take in the feedback while focusing on the paper so Dr Asher wouldn't see her fighting her emotions. After about thirty minutes, Dr Asher had finished going through her work and it was clear the meeting was over. As Alison stood up murmuring her thanks, one hand trying to discreetly hold her jeans together, her only thought was to get out of the stark office as quickly as possible. As a result, she didn't hear Dr Asher's comment that it was only the first term of the first year and that she felt Alison would have a bright future in law. Alison only heard her own thoughts reverberating in her ears – those of failure.

Out in the corridor and frantically searching for the ladies' loo for a little privacy to fix her jeans, Alison fought the tears as her gut twisted with the realisation that her worst fears were becoming real. Her brain tried to process the word 'average'. Academically, she had never been average. She had never had to work so hard for such low results. Staring at herself in the mirror, she tried in vain to reassure herself. That's just one meeting; the next one will be better, she thought. Reluctantly, she headed to her next appointment and, despite being told she was a hardworking, promising student, all her marks were average across all modules. She found herself becoming angry and the more review sessions she attended, the angrier she became – with herself, with the education system, with the lecturers, even with Laura, who had had her appointments last week and who was, inexplicably, on track for a first-class degree. Alison felt incredibly tired, as if the whole term had been for nothing and all those long hours of study had been a complete waste of time.

Bitter, she swung her bag over her shoulder. She just had

time to pick up a sandwich before her last appointment. As she waited in the queue to order her lunch, the day's newspaper caught her eye. Curious, Alison moved the paper towards her for a better look. Glancing briefly at the headlines, she read:

Evans Conviction Overturned
Wednesday 3 December 1997

Andrew Evans, convicted in 1972 of murdering school-girl Judith Roberts, has sensationally had his conviction overturned after serving 25 years in prison. Evans contacted—

'Who's next, please?'

A tut behind her indicated she had slowed the impatient queue with her reading. Hurrying to the till, she ordered her sandwich to take away, slipping the newspaper in her bag as she did so, trying to imagine what it would be like to spend so many years in prison. With her sandwich in hand, Alison ambled reluctantly to her next appointment. Checking her diary, she had forgotten this session was with The Professor and her thoughts ran back with embarrassment to their last meeting at the Student Union, where she had been so clumsy. The door was ajar and after gently knocking and hearing the customary 'Come in', she entered his office. As she looked around, she was thrown off guard. There was a small but comfortable-looking couch, a tartan-patterned reading chair near the window and various artworks hanging on the walls. Potted plants, some in full bloom, were dotted around, and several shelves of books lined one wall. In the corner, asleep on a cushion, was a black and white cat. The office was more like a living room than a workplace, and for just a moment she felt the tension seep from her shoulders. While her home was less than an hour away on the outskirts of Durham, the restful room induced such powerful feelings of homesickness and loneliness, she felt unsteady on her feet.

The Professor had his back to her and was reviewing some papers. Without turning round, he motioned for Alison to take a seat on the sofa.

Gratefully, she perched at one end, carefully placing her book bag on the floor.

'Sorry about that,' said The Professor, taking a seat opposite her in the armchair. 'Once I get into an essay, I like to finish it.' Smiling, he peered over his tortoiseshell glasses at her.

'So, how are you?'

And to Alison's horror, she burst into tears.

*

Later, when this scene had already been scorched in her brain for almost a year, and she was in so deep she didn't know how to get out, she knew that that moment of shared intimacy – of open vulnerability – was the start of it all. The desperation, the incredible highs coupled with the almost unbearable lows, the excitement of the unknown. She was on the scariest rollercoaster in the world, but unable to get off.

6

Kate

'For Pete's sake, Kate, will you just give it a rest? We don't always have to talk everything to death, you know! All I want to do is eat my meal in peace and relax after a long week at work.'

Kate flared up at her husband. 'I've had a long week, too. At least you get a break in the evenings and at the week-ends – I'm on call 24/7. With very little support from you, I might add.'

'Oh, I'm sorry it's so taxing spending so much time with our children—'

'That's not what I meant and you know it,' retorted Kate, burning with anger at the sarcasm dripping from his voice. 'I just want a conversation with you – why is that so difficult?'

'Maybe it's because I'm working all God's hours, commuting two hours a day, and for what? For what?' he said, shouting now. 'For you and the kids, that's what! And what thanks do I get, eh? A bloody steak that's not even cooked properly!' He pushed away his plate in disgust and Kate watched with dismay as the steak landed on the carpet.

For some reason, the waste of the expensive meat upset her more than his refusing to talk to her. She could have bought several days of cheap cuts for the price of that one steak, and here he was wasting it because of his temper.

'Keep your voice down – you'll wake the girls,' said Kate through gritted teeth.

'I'll do what I damn well want in my own home, which I pay for!' he retorted, raising his voice even more.

Kate somehow found the strength to turn away. If she said or did anything else, it would only make him shout louder and the noise carried so far in these flats. Kate repressed an almost primal urge to scream.

The evening hadn't started off well. She had put the girls to bed slightly earlier than normal but they wouldn't settle. So instead of being able to give her full attention to preparing the evening meal, she was in and out of the girls' room trying to get them to sleep. Kate knew she wasn't the best cook – a fact that her husband used to think was charming when they first lived together after their wedding. These days, she could usually rustle something up but she still needed to focus, and multitasking was out of the question if she didn't want the food to burn or a pan to boil over. She usually bought inexpensive cuts of chicken and turkey and she had hesitated for just a fraction when she saw the price of the prime steak. But it was his favourite and she wanted him to be as relaxed as possible. However, as she watched him bite into the meat, she realised she had overcooked it and it was tough and chewy. She had also misjudged the mood. Stupidly, she had decided to plough on anyway. Why hadn't she just left it for another evening?

Anger and frustration seeping through every pore of her being, she headed to their bedroom. There was nothing for it but to get into bed and have an early night. How Saturday nights have changed, she thought sadly. Sinking under the covers, she remembered how they used to go to the pictures. They both had a passion for films and Kate had loved everything about those dates, from the darkness of the cinema where they would snuggle up to each other, regardless of who was around them, to the interval when he would always treat her to an ice cream, its cold vanilla creaminess flavouring their kisses. She turned over onto her left side, trying to make herself comfortable. Pausing, she listened intently. It was quiet but she could still hear it. Getting up, she stood outside the girls' door to see if they had been disturbed and heard the soft crying of her younger daughter. She clenched her fists, trying to quell the desire to hit something. Quietly, she went into the room and rocked her tearful child back to sleep, whispering that everything would be all right. As hot tears slid down her own face, she didn't know if the reassurance was more for herself or for her daughter.

*

'Mummy!' Someone was pulling on Kate's arm. 'Mummy!' the voice whispered, now even more insistent. Kate opened her eyes to see her elder daughter dressed in her new school uniform. Even half asleep, Kate could see that the buttons on the pinafore were mismatched and the tie was slightly askew, but otherwise her little girl had done a pretty good job of getting herself dressed.

'What time is it?' Kate mumbled, groping for her alarm clock, afraid she had slept through it. It said 5.37 a.m. Relieved, Kate lay back on the pillow. Looking at her daughter, she couldn't help but smile.

Normally, it was a lengthy battle to get her up and dressed, yet here she was on the first day of school, ready to go, two hours early. Kate wondered fondly how long the enthusiasm would last. Quietly getting out of bed, so as not to wake her husband, Kate put her finger to her lips and gently led the little girl out of the room. Once in the darkness of the living room, she assessed her options. She could try to put her daughter back to bed; she could put the TV on for her and go back to bed herself, or she could make a cup of coffee and sit with her daughter, who was now jigging on the spot, bursting to talk about her upcoming first day at school. Realising the latter was the only choice, Kate tried to imagine the enormity of this event for her daughter. She had looked forward to starting school all summer, telling everyone and anyone who would listen that she was starting 'big school' in September. As Kate put on the kettle and scooped the Nescafé into the cup, her daughter chattered away in exaggerated whispers.

'Mrs Allsopp said the playground has a new slide, Mummy!'

'I know, love, I was there when she told you,' replied Kate, thinking back to the half-day school visit for new pupils.

'Mrs Allsopp also said we can paint – every day if we want to!'

'Well, I'm not sure about every day but, yes, I'm sure you'll be doing lots of painting.'

'Nope,' her daughter responded confidently. 'Every day.' Kate smiled at such certainty.

'Aaaaaaaand… my new pencil case is going to be the best one in the class!'

Despite being granules and not the real thing, Kate took her first delicious sip of the steaming liquid. She was thankful she had agreed to the pencil case, even if it was the most expensive. With a magnetic clasp, individual compartments and swirls of pastel pinks, it certainly was the business and it was the only one her daughter liked. Her daughter often had to go without, so to be able to treat her to something she really wanted was a lovely feeling.

Today marked a memorable chapter in the little girl's life but it was also an important milestone for Kate herself. The house would be quieter, the days would be calmer, and Kate experienced something she hadn't felt for a long time: a sense of freedom.

Leading her daughter over to the sofa, Kate scooped her up in a cuddle and leaned back into the cushions, listening to her excited whispers. As the sun rose, dispersing the gloom of the night with its watery rays, for the first time in a long time, Kate felt hopeful.

*

The family didn't have a car – her husband cycled to the station and commuted by train – but luckily the school was just close enough to walk. It was a good twenty minutes away and probably wouldn't be pleasant in bad weather, but today the skies were clear and Kate sent a silent prayer of thanks that they wouldn't arrive wet through on the first day. Pushing the buggy, which also held her daughter's new school bag with one hand, and holding her elder child in the other hand, Kate was surprised that they made the walk in record time, thanks to her daughter practically skipping the whole way there.

'Hello!' Mrs Allsopp greeted them at the door of the classroom. Turning to her daughter: 'You must be starting school today!' she said with a warm smile.

'I am!' announced the little girl. 'I have a new pencil case!'

'Do you? Well, I can't wait to see it! First, though, hang your coat and your bag up over there in the corner and join the rest of the class.'

She ran off with barely a backward glance and Kate didn't know whether to be relieved or sad that her daughter had not even said goodbye.

'Kate, good to see you. How are you?' Not waiting for a response, Mrs Allsopp continued, 'If you have any queries, feel free to have a chat with me at any time. Though, she looks like she's going to settle in nicely, don't you think?' Kate followed Mrs Allsopp's gaze to where her daughter was busily going through a toy box with her classmates.

'Yes, I'm sure she will! She's been excited for weeks!'

'She'll be fine; I have a great day planned for them. I'll see you at school pick-up?'

While Kate was not quite ready to leave her little girl just yet, she felt Mrs Allsopp was keen to get her class started.

'Yes, of course! See you then.'

Kate cast a last look at her daughter before heading out of the classroom. Her first-born was off on the start of many adventures and she wouldn't be there to protect her. Kate felt a catch in her throat. Turning away from the classroom and towards the reception area, Kate looked around her.

It had all changed since she'd attended the school twenty years ago, but the smell of chalk, paint and musty blackboards remained the same, taking her back to her own school days. Even the old notice board in the main entrance was still there. Kate scanned the general notices before her eyes fell on a green flyer that was offering free creative writing classes at the adult community college in the next building. *Every Tuesday from 7.30 p.m. to 9.30 p.m., taught by Mr Barnes.* Kate had always loved writing. She'd written hundreds of letters to pen pals when she was growing up – childish scribbles to Canada, Germany, France and America, a chronicle of the simplicity of childhood. Even today, she still relished the feel of a pen in her hand, the flow of ink, gliding across the page. It reminded her of an ice-skater leaving a trail of beautiful ice patterns behind her. And while she was more likely to be writing shopping lists these days than creating a work of fiction, the very act of putting pen to paper still gave her an element of control and satisfaction. Kate looked at the flyer again, imagining how wonderful it would be to have a couple of hours a week to herself to do something she enjoyed. Turning to leave, she hesitated. Why couldn't she attend the classes, she thought to herself. They were free, and the girls' would be in bed so they wouldn't even know she was gone. As long as her husband was home, then she could easily attend.

Kate turned it over in her mind, rapidly planning the schedule in her head. If the class started at 7.30 p.m., she could have the girls fed, bathed and in bed easily enough by 7.00 p.m. and it would still give her enough time to walk to the class.

But what if one of the girls woke? Well, her husband would have to deal with it. He wouldn't like it, but maybe it was time he started helping out a little more in the evenings, Kate thought determinedly.

In a moment of rare spontaneity, she signed her name and added her phone number to the sign-up sheet. To hell with it, she thought, remembering their argument and the wasted steak. Why should he care anyway? He'd probably be happy that he had the house to himself for a bit and didn't have anyone nagging him.

'Come on then,' she said, looking down at her younger daughter. 'Let's get our day started! Shall we go to the park?'

Stepping out into the September sunshine, Kate felt a surge of self-determination. She would attend the classes. After five years of dedicating herself to her family, a couple of hours a week were really nothing in comparison.

7

Catherine

15 September 2010

Dear Michael,

Thank you for your letter and responding so quickly. I am writing this letter at my desk, which looks over our garden. Today is a fine day weather-wise. Autumn is one of my favourite seasons – I have always considered it to be more of a fresh start than the more traditional January. I think it has something to do with the school year – when I was a girl, nothing used to please me more than the promise of a fresh clean notebook and buying all my school supplies. It's funny the things you remember and carry on to this day. Even now, I like to buy a fresh notebook every September! You mentioned you were a teacher – did you have that exciting back-to-school feeling or was it more of a dread going back to work? I would have liked to have been a teacher myself – unfortunately things didn't work out that way, but I'm heavily

involved in the local school. I'm part of the Education
Committee Association and dedicate a lot of time to
running and attending meetings and organising all the
activities. As I mentioned in my last letter, I'm also a
volunteer at the local library. I'm a big reader so to
be amongst all those books several times a week is a
wonderful feeling. My husband doesn't understand
it – he's more of a television person! Finally, I also do
a lot of charity work – mainly children-associated.
All in all, my days are kept quite busy. And now of
course, I'm a volunteer writing to you.

Catherine paused, her pen hovering over the paper. It
had taken a huge amount of effort to write something about
herself, but she knew if she was going to get him to open up to
her, she would have to take the lead and initiate it. Catherine
considered herself a very private and self-contained person but
she knew she had to share things about her life. Talking about
her family to a criminal was especially difficult, but in her gut
she knew it was the only way. Taking a deep breath, she picked
up her Mont Blanc pen – a gift from Richard – took courage
from its comforting weight in her left hand, and ploughed on.

My daughter Helen is grown up now but she still
spends a lot of time with us. She has been studying for
the last few years – a BA, an MA, followed by a Ph.D.
– but like so many post-graduates, she is struggling
to find decently paid work in this economic climate.
She lives with us to keep her costs down, and while
both my husband and I love having her around, I
sometimes suspect she finds it annoying!
I can only imagine how difficult it must have been

to get used to life on the inside. I read somewhere that some inmates – especially those who have been inside for many years – struggle to come to terms with so much freedom once they're released. It must be a very strange feeling. I understand that these letters are supposed to help with the start of rehabilitation and I do hope they lend some insight to life today.

Shifting positions in her chair, Catherine continued.

So enough about me – if you're comfortable, I would really like to learn more about you. What is your routine? Do you volunteer for any particular jobs there? And, this may be a strange question, but have you made any friends in prison? I understand I'm still a complete stranger to you, so please don't feel you have to answer if you don't want to. I look forward to hearing from you soon.

Catherine

PS. If you would like me to send you anything specific such as books, newspapers, or toiletries, please just let me know.

Catherine had always considered herself a good letter-writer and she was banking on this skill to establish a good relationship with Michael. Yet, it was difficult to find neutral topics, or to try even to guess what a person in his circumstances would want to read about. Ever practical, Catherine decided that she would do some online research before she had to head out later that afternoon for a dental appointment. Logging online, she wished she had done it earlier. Typing in the search bar, 165 million results came up. She wondered where to start. She clicked on the first link and started to read. It was a good couple of hours later when she lifted her head up from the screen, her brain still trying to process what she had learnt.

She was shocked that, in England and Wales, the number of people in prison in 2009 was almost 85,000 and the UK was still the top incarcerator in Western Europe. And it wasn't mainly men, as she had imagined – the number of women had increased by 44 per cent in the last decade. Catherine could barely bring herself to read about the number of children in prison but she was determined to learn more, so she pressed on. Not only were there children in prison, but there were also over 160,000 children with a parent in prison. Catherine struggled with the reality of it, becoming hyperaware of her comfortable middle-class life. Yet she had always had a deep sense of empathy and she felt something shift inside her as she read about the number of children born in prison. She dug further and when she came to information about re-offenders, she felt her heart quicken as she read that an astonishing 47 per cent of adults are reconvicted within one year of release.

Straightening up in her chair, Catherine felt a surge of anger at such a possibility. Now she realised just how important it was to connect with Michael. The thought of someone else suffering at his hands was unbearable. In her next letter, she would be more careful with what she said. So engrossed was she in her thoughts that it was several hours before it struck her that she had missed her dental appointment. It was only when the phone rang that she realised the time.

'Hi,' said Richard. 'How was the dentist?'

'Oh, hi,' Catherine responded. Hesitating, she tried to come up with a plausible excuse. 'Actually, I ended up not going—'

'Well, that's a relief, I suppose,' interrupted Richard. 'Did they cancel? I'm guessing you'll have to reschedule.'

For once, Catherine didn't mind that her husband's daily phone call was hurried and distracted. Not wanting to correct his assumption in case he asked what she had been doing, Catherine quickly responded, happy to be on truthful territory.

'Yes, I will, absolutely. In fact, I was just about to call them when you phoned.'

Changing the topic, Catherine asked, 'How's your day going so far?'

'Not bad – busy. It was just a quick call to check in. I'll see you later.'

'OK, bye.'

Her husband was not a huge talker on the phone. In fact, he wasn't a man of many words in general. Years ago, when they used to socialise a lot more, Catherine had got frustrated when she arranged dinner with other couples as she often had to do the talking for both of them. She tried to recall what they used to talk about. With his background in accounting, he was a very practical man and she suspected the younger generation would consider some of his traditional ways almost sexist. Yet, he was also surprisingly fun and she remembered that it was this aspect of his personality that was appealing. He was a family man at heart, brought up on solid values. With Richard, you would never have to worry about his having an affair or spending all their savings. Yes, there had been issues – of course there had, they had been married a long time – but overall he had made sure his family had everything they needed. He had never wanted her to work a single day since she met him. Not that he had a problem with her working, he just wanted her to enjoy motherhood without the stress of having to work as well. Looking back, she hadn't regretted that decision but she did love her voluntary and charity work. In fact, she liked to be kept busy in general. Being a housewife hadn't really suited her and she'd done it for a few years, but she had been keen to keep learning and Richard had encouraged her. As she felt herself slide back into the memories of the past, she sharply interrupted her own thoughts. Richard wasn't perfect but he was a good husband and after so many years of marriage she could still honestly say that she loved him just as much now as she did in the beginning – in fact, probably more. There weren't many couples who survived marriage these days. The divorce rate was high, and she could understand why. Marriage was hard. It took courage to forgive and forget, and that was just the little daily annoyances. And then, of course, there were the major challenges: the arrival of children, money worries, parents-in-law, boredom and so on. They all took their toll and she knew they had both experienced times when they could have easily walked away. But ultimately, it wasn't in Catherine's nature. She wasn't the type of person to give up. Sometimes, the only option was to fight back, whatever the consequences.

8

Alison

The break over the Christmas holidays was a relief for Alison and she spent much of her time sleeping. She hardly went out at all apart from a little last-minute Christmas shopping. She felt depleted, drained, especially in the mornings when her limbs felt so heavy it was difficult to get out of bed. Some days she would manage to rouse herself just enough so she didn't give her parents cause to worry too much. She could sense their concern and surprise that she was so withdrawn, but she simply didn't have the energy to pretend. Her mum, clearly happy to have her home, bustled around bringing comfort foods of chunky vegetable broths, warm roast beef sandwiches and meaty stews. She helped Alison unpack her bags, did her washing, and asked questions about her university life.

Alison responded as best she could, telling her about Laura, the socials, and the students. But she never mentioned her results from the first term. She felt flashes of humiliation as she remembered the feedback she had received and she pushed it to the back of her mind. But the anxiety was always there in the pit of her stomach, a seed in the earth, its roots growing slowly but surely. There seemed to be no solution; she couldn't work any harder and she didn't want to tell anybody how difficult she was finding the course for fear of being the odd one out as nobody else seemed to be finding it challenging. Durham University had been her dream and her parents had been so happy when she had got her place there. She couldn't disappoint them.

After the first week at home, Christmas Eve dawned crisp and clear. Alison woke up earlier than usual, and the glimpse of the blue sky through the gap in the curtains, so unusual for this time of year, caught her attention. Padding across the floor in her socks, she drew back the curtains and took in the view of her childhood. Neighbouring houses – home to people she had known all her life – presented a pretty contrast to the snow-capped hills of the North-East. A touch of frost glazed rooftops and gardens, and while the trees were bare, leaves long lost to autumn, birdsong welcomed the weak but determined warmth of the sun. Unexpectedly, Alison felt a rush of mixed emotions: happiness at the sheer beauty of a scene that was so familiar to her, sadness that she had moved on to a new stage in her life that wasn't going as well as she would have liked, but perhaps most importantly, a sense of hope. Alison reminded herself that 1998 was just around the corner – it would give her a chance for a fresh start at university. Feeling better than she had in days, Alison slipped on her dressing gown and went to make coffee for her family.

*

For many people, Christmas Eve was full of traditions, and

for Alison and her family, it was no different. Early in the morning, she and her sister went shopping with their father to the market to buy the vegetables, pick up the turkey, and have a bacon bun breakfast together in a café, while her mother had a lie-in and a rest before the cooking, arrival of visitors, and general preparations started in earnest.

Since her teenage years, it was also traditional for Alison and her school friends to go out in the evening. A group of six, the friends had met at primary school and had remained close all the way through secondary school and sixth-form college. In their early teens, they would all meet up at someone's house and when they were older, they would go into town to the pubs and bars. This year was going to be extra special as they were all catching up with each other's news after being away since September. With so much shared history and experience, it had been an emotional goodbye as the friends had departed for different university cities: Edinburgh, London, Bristol, Lancaster and Nottingham. Alison was the only one who had decided to stay local and she was eager to know how her friends were getting on. They had been planning the Christmas Eve night out for a few weeks and everyone was really looking forward to it.

That afternoon, Alison reluctantly looked in the mirror. It wasn't a pretty sight – pale, pinched, and without a scrap of make-up, she didn't look like herself at all. She noticed a small stain down her front, probably from lunch, and her hair, scraped back in a ponytail for days now, needed a good wash.

Stripping off the offensive T-shirt and dumping it in the washing basket, Alison headed to her wardrobe. Selecting a pair of jeans, a fitted red top and the highest-heeled boots she could find, she laid everything on the bed. Something was missing. In her parents' bedroom, she rifled through her mother's collection of handbags until she found the one she was looking for – a small diamanté clutch. Placing it next to the outfit, she saw it looked just right. Then she washed her hair, put on a hair mask, and took a long soak in the bath.

By seven o'clock she was ready. It had taken all afternoon but she was pleasantly surprised by the results. She had done her hair so it fell in long waves, and carefully applied her make-up – not too much, but she knew her eyes were her best feature so she emphasised them with a smoky shadow, eyeliner and lots of mascara. With a last look in the mirror, she almost didn't recognise herself. As she said goodbye to her parents, their look of relief was unmistakable. They even forgot to remind her not to be in too late. As she wished them a Merry Christmas, she felt a whisper of her old self returning.

*

It had been such a fun night. Alison had forgotten how easy life could be with friends who had known her for years. Drinks and conversation flowed easily and she found herself laughing and joking about their school days, long before university, when everything seemed a lot simpler. Over the evening the friends had been to several pubs and, feeling tired and a little tipsy, Alison almost didn't make the last stop, a sophisticated wine bar, which had recently opened. But her friends begged her to come and as she was having so much fun, she thought, why not? One last drink and then she would head home. Linking arms for warmth, the girls sauntered off down the street without a care in the world, singing Christmas carols and debating whether to stop off at the chip shop. When they arrived at the wine bar, the place was packed and they squeezed through, singing and dancing, much to the crowd's amusement, drawing attention to themselves and loving every minute of it. Drinks appeared and they merged into the sea of revellers to enjoy the rest of the evening.

An hour or so later, and by now slightly unsteady on her feet, Alison was ready to go home and she weaved her way through the bar to get to the loos before getting a taxi. On her way back, she caught sight of a familiar face and it was a moment or two before her drink-addled brain realised who it was. The Professor smiled and walked over, wishing her a Merry Christmas. Despite her tears at their last meeting, he was gentlemanly enough not to bring up that fact that he had sat with her for forty-five minutes handing her tissue after tissue.

'Hello,' Alison said, smiling, the wine making her bold.

'Hi, how are you?'

'I'm fine – better, thanks.'

'That's good to hear. Merry Christmas!'

'Merry Christmas!'

And with that, she said goodbye to her friends and headed out into the sobering cold, feeling ridiculously happy.

*

Thirty minutes later, her elation was plummeting as quickly as the freezing temperatures. There wasn't a taxi in sight and she was a good few miles from home. Her feet were starting to throb from the height of her boots and Alison decided to walk in the direction of the bus stop, hoping to catch a taxi on the way. Another fifteen minutes later, and she was shivering, trying to keep warm in the bus shelter. She chided herself for being so ridiculous as to think she could easily pick up a taxi on Christmas Eve. She was just about to go to the phone box to call her parents for a lift when a sleek, black car pulled up beside her. The smooth hiss of an electric window, and a voice called out, 'Fancy a lift?'

She knew who it was, but she peered in anyway just to be sure. The Professor was leaning over, already opening the passenger door. Without thinking, Alison quickly got in, enjoying the warmth of the heater as it defrosted her hands. He leant over to adjust the warm vents in her direction and Alison could smell his scent – a mixture of fresh air, aftershave, and the festive atmosphere of the bar. It was as intoxicating as the wine. She leant back and closed her eyes, savouring the relief at being on her way home without having disturbed her parents. After a few moments, she opened them and saw his handsome profile watching her, the car not moving. Smiling, he put the car into gear and they glided off, the engine quiet, the only sound coming from the low volume of the Christmas carols on the radio.

Somewhere in the back of her mind, she acknowledged the moment. It felt like the calm before the storm. They didn't speak but in the secluded privacy of the car, the atmosphere felt charged. Later, Alison realised that moment had been pivotal – the actions she took then would have consequences. If she had even imagined for one moment just how catastrophic those consequences would be, she would have run for her life.

9

Kate

It was Tuesday and Kate was running behind schedule. She had promised her husband that he wouldn't need to do anything if she went out to her night class, as the girls would both be fast asleep. But since she'd picked up her daughter from school, both girls had been difficult and now, at 6 p.m., she was still trying to get them to finish their dinner. She knew she still had a long way to go to get them both settled and asleep within the hour.

'I don't want it. It tastes horrible,' pouted her younger child.

'Just two more spoonfuls of carrots and then you're done,' countered Kate.

'No!'

Forget terrible twos, what about terrible threes, Kate thought to herself. If she heard the word 'no' one more time, she thought she might scream.

Sighing, she gave in and gathered up the dishes, scraping the carrot into the bin. She hated wasting good food and she just knew that in an hour her daughter was going to be hungry again, exactly at the time she should be fast asleep. Kate wondered if children were specially programmed to know when you had plans for yourself so they could sabotage them.

Putting the dishes in the sink, Kate hoped she would find the time to wash them. If there was one thing that her husband hated, it was coming home to a sink full of dirty dishes.

'OK, girls, time for your bath,' she said, trying to muster the energy to sound like having a bath was the most fun thing in the world.

'I want to play with Mary-Beth!'

Kate pretended not to hear.

'Come on then, let's go,' she said, lifting her daughter down from the table. 'Which toys do you want to take into the bath with you?'

'Mary-Beth! Mary-Beth! Mary-Beth!' she chanted.

Mary-Beth was her younger daughter's rag doll and went everywhere with her. She'd lost it once and, to the toddler, like so many things, it had felt like the end of the world. In an effort to find Mary-Beth and to console her daughter at the same time, Kate had turned the hunt into a game of hide-and-seek, searching the house from top to bottom. But the doll was nowhere to be found. Her daughter was inconsolable and Kate had kicked herself for making the rookie-parenting mistake of not buying a second one as a back-up. In the end, having no choice but to leave the girls with her husband, she had spent the afternoon traipsing through the rain, going to the places they had visited that morning to see if anyone had handed the doll in. After scouring the supermarket, the park and the pharmacy, Kate found Mary-Beth in the post office.

'Oh, yes,' replied the postmistress, when Kate had wearily

enquired about the lost doll. 'I found it tucked behind the leaflet stand. I kept it safe, as I know how important a doll can be to a little girl. I wondered who it belonged to so I'm glad you came back for it – just in time, too, as I was about to close.'

'Thank you so much,' replied Kate, the relief evident in her voice.

'It's no problem, dear. I have two young granddaughters so I know what it's like! You look exhausted, would you like a cup of tea? I was just about to put the kettle on to give this rain a chance to ease off a bit.'

Cold, wet and desperate for a hot drink, Kate could have wept at the simple kindness.

'Thank you very much but I best get this doll back before World War III breaks out. I've left both my daughters with my husband so goodness knows what I'll get back to,' she joked.

'All right pet,' said the postmistress, whose nametag read 'Margaret'. Around fifty-five years old, with her trim figure and well-fitted navy-blue cardigan, Margaret reminded Kate of her own mother. 'Take care getting home now. This downpour looks torrential to me.'

Kate grimaced as she looked through the window.

Peering over her metal-frame glasses, Margaret's eyes met hers.

'Are you OK, dear?'

'Yes, of course,' smiled Kate. 'Just gearing myself up for the weather!'

Margaret gave her a knowing look. Patting her arm, she said, 'It does get easier, pet, I promise.'

In that moment, all Kate wanted to do was to stay in the warmth of the post office and soak up the comforting reassurance of the older woman, to be told that everything was going to be all right: her children, her marriage, her finances, her life.

*

Kate ran a bath for the girls – and Mary-Beth – and as a special exception, decided she would let them watch TV for half an hour before bed. Normally, TV was for weekends or when they were ill, but she needed a little time to get ready. She didn't normally bother with make-up but she was sure she had some mascara and foundation in one of her drawers, and there was some lip-gloss in the bottom of her handbag which she could use. Her jeans were a few years old and slightly dated but she had a top that she had bought two years ago and hadn't yet worn, meaning it was unlikely to be covered in spaghetti hoop stains. Hurrying the girls, she got them into bed and by seven o'clock she was dressed and ready to leave.

*

Practically running, Kate suppressed her resentment at not being able to afford a car. It was pouring with rain and her umbrella was fighting a losing battle against the elements. She was late because her husband had missed the train and was in a foul mood because of it. Claiming he'd had to deal with a last-minute difficult customer, she had made no comment about the beer on his breath as she said goodbye. He'd obviously had the time to stop off at the pub for a quick one on the way home, she thought, annoyed. It rankled that she had asked him to be on time that evening and he didn't respect her enough to do even that. Quickening her pace, she finally entered the community college gates. The flyer had stated classroom 2A but as she went through the corridors, she struggled to find it. The place was deserted and she wondered how many people would turn up to an evening class on a night like this, when it would be so much more preferable to stay at home, warm and dry. All of sudden, she was nervous. What was she thinking? It was years since she had done anything even remotely academic. She had given all that up several years ago for marriage and children – a different life altogether. She bargained with herself: if she didn't find the class in the next five minutes, she was going to walk back home. As she turned the corner, she saw a group of five or six people heading into a classroom. That must be it, she thought. Checking the sign outside the classroom door, Kate followed them inside and gratefully took a seat at the back. Looking around her, she saw it was a mixed bag of students. Most of them were older than her, most likely reaching retirement age and looking for a new hobby. In fact, Kate seemed to be the youngest in the class. Once again, she wondered if she was just wasting her time.

*

Glancing up at the clock Kate saw that two hours had passed already. Then, taking a moment, she realised her shoulders were relaxed. Her body, so used to constant movement, had settled into itself, unfurling as the rhythmic strokes of her pen glided across the paper. For the first time in a long while, she was using her mind for something other than shopping lists and scheduling play dates. It was a strange, but not unwelcome, feeling.

Absorbed in her own thoughts, she didn't hear Mr Barnes the first time. Afterwards, she wondered how many times he had had to say her name before she realised he was talking to her.

'How did you find the class?' he asked. He was standing in front of her desk.

Kate looked up and got a closer look at the teacher. He was slightly younger than she was and she guessed him to be in his early twenties. His self-assurance was casually worn, reflecting a life of few hardships. Although he looked forbidding, in black jeans and a black leather jacket, this was offset by an amiable charm. She hadn't paid too much attention when he had first walked in. In fact, she had thought he was one of the students at first, as he was so far removed from her stereotypical idea of a teacher. But now she noticed his dark, granite-grey eyes. There was an intensity there that drew her in, yet at the same time made her wary, despite his attempt to be friendly. Glancing away, she began to pack up her things, noticing that most of the other students had already left.

'Really good, thank you.'

'Seems like you were inspired,' he said, as he thumbed through the sheaf of A4 papers covered in her script.

Wondering if he was being sarcastic, Kate looked up at him but saw only friendliness.

'Yes, the topic of escapism was a good one. I had a lot of ideas.'

'I look forward to reading them,' he replied, taking the papers from her.

And then he was gone, leaving Kate to wonder why hers was the only paper he had taken from the class.

10

Catherine

It always started the same, which made Catherine wish the first part of the dream would go on for ever. Like in a film set straight out of Hollywood, she was sitting on the riverbank with Richard, enjoying a picnic she had made herself of freshly baked rolls, salad, fruit, cheese and a crisp bottle of wine, with nothing more to do than watch the sun's rays bounce off the water. They weren't alone: there were numerous families picnicking, making the most of the good weather. She lay back lazily, serene from the wine and the food, resting her head against her husband's shoulder. Out of the corner of her eye, she watched the children, including her own, paddle amongst the rocks and stones on the banks of the river. The English countryside of the North-East was at its best. Humming with the warm arrival of summer, it was vibrant with life, showing off its beauty, not yet aware that a precious cycle of life would soon abruptly come to an end.

As she leant against the comforting bulk of her husband, her eyes started to close. The lazy feeling was irritatingly interrupted by an arrow of instinct, demanding vigilance from her as her family played in the water. Like a patient trying to resist the effects of anaesthetic, the more she tried to remain alert, the more she felt dragged down into an unwelcome darkness. She tried to tell Richard to make sure he stayed awake but she could only manage a murmur, which he couldn't hear. A part of her, somewhere deep inside, experienced a flicker of unease, which she quickly extinguished. Surely she deserved a few minutes' rest. No longer able to resist, she fell under the spell of sleep.

In her dream, she slept and woke up, and that was when the terror began. What had once been the stunning countryside of her home had now twisted and turned into something barren and bare, the river flowing not with crystal-clear water, but with a thick, scarlet liquid that bled over its banks, rushing towards her as she scrambled to her feet. She was alone and the candle of unease that had briefly flickered was now a raging bonfire. The river was molten lava: hot and overflowing. It burnt the tips of her toes and she scrambled up the bank, trying in vain to climb the nearest tree. But its trunk was unaccommodating and her strappy sandals, which had seemed like the perfect choice for such a relaxing day, sealed her fate, as the burning lava slowly edged up her legs, sweeping her up in its path and pulling her downstream. As Catherine turned her head towards the shore, the last thing she saw was her family standing on the dry shores of the bank, silently watching.

*

Catherine had experienced the nightmare – or various versions of it – so many times she now had a routine. She would quietly get out of bed, wash her face, change her nightclothes and drink a cold glass of water. Despite being used to the after-effects of the horror, her hands still shook as she took the glass and drank greedily. It felt cold and refreshing against her sweating skin and she sat at the kitchen table for a few minutes, focusing on the various bits of paper, letters, keys and the minutiae of everyday life. She used them to drag her thoughts back into the present. Out of habit, she started a to-do list for the next day, the soothing strokes of her pen slowing her heartbeat. Next she checked her diary, making sure she had remembered everything for the week ahead. They were small things, but she felt that they gave an element of control, and it was her way of guiding her mind back into focus, away from the remnants of the dream. It also gave her the courage to climb the stairs and get back into bed. As she lay there, she felt trapped by her own mind. Not even sleep could provide a few hours of complete respite any more. But she knew, given time, that the panic would subside and she would eventually drop off into a fitful sleep.

*

Richard had long ago learnt to ignore Catherine's midnight wanderings. At certain times, especially during the summer, they seemed more frequent than others. He knew they were often preceded by nightmares, but whenever he asked, Catherine told him she was just hot and needed some water. He never told her that she cried in her sleep. He had mentioned it once but she had dismissed it so abruptly, he never brought it up again. Over the years of their marriage, their communication had had peaks and troughs. As a couple, they had phases when it felt like they lived separate lives – he going to work and she doing her various activities for the school and community, their only bond being their daughter. She wondered if Helen knew she was the glue that held the sometimes fragile pieces of her parents together. Maybe that's why she still lived at home, Catherine thought the next morning as she made coffee. She hoped that wasn't the case but couldn't quite convince herself that it wasn't. She was close to her daughter but they had never shared the most intimate of secrets. Helen was not an open book, and she liked her privacy. At the same time, it would feel strange to Catherine to talk about her marriage with her daughter. In fact, she didn't feel comfortable doing it with anyone. She had been brought up to believe that you didn't air your dirty laundry in public.

When she had met Ruth, almost ten years ago now, she remembered being shocked at how open she was. She had opinions on everyone, from her own husband to her local butcher, and she didn't care who heard. Catherine smiled to herself as she remembered their first meeting, soon after she and Richard had moved to the Lake District. Ruth was her neighbour and had stopped by to welcome them to the area. In her hands, she held a basket of local goods: thick, apple and pork sausages, home-made jams, apples freshly picked from the orchard, and one of the area's pride and joy – Cartmel Sticky Toffee Pudding, which Catherine and Richard had shared that evening. Not usually tempted by dessert, she could still remember the first taste of the pudding, its comforting warmth deliciously balanced by the chill of ice cream.

While Ruth was an undeniably generous woman, Catherine suspected the real motivation for her visit had been to get the lowdown on who had moved into Bramble Cottage. Reluctantly, Catherine had invited her in for a cup of coffee, and had spent the next hour listening to Ruth as she explained, in great detail, who was who in the village. Despite Ruth's almost award-winning skill for talking, over the years Catherine had come to rely on her much more than she would care to admit. Yes, she could be slightly overbearing, but she was also warm, generous and funny. Without knowing it, Ruth had helped Catherine settle into her new life in the countryside and she started to look forward to her visits, her offers of help and her chitchat as a way of breaking up the days. Catherine knew that Ruth occasionally got frustrated with Catherine's own lack of sharing. Women's friendships were often built on shared confidences, knowing intimate details about each other's lives, yet over the years Ruth and Catherine had comfortably established themselves as talker and listener respectively and, for the most part, it suited them both. Ruth was slightly younger than Catherine. Her two sons had both moved away: Matthew was overseas in the army and Luke worked in London in retail. Much like Catherine, she had dedicated her life to raising her children and they were her pride and joy. Matthew wrote to his parents monthly, and Catherine knew Ruth looked forward to the letters immensely. She would then keep the letter in her handbag, sharing with neighbours and friends little snippets of his life as he travelled the world, so different from the calm, peaceful rhythms of the Lake District where he had grown up. Luke dutifully called his mother every Sunday afternoon at three o'clock and Catherine had got used to putting the kettle on at four thirty, ready for when Ruth would come over and excitedly share his news. Both 'boys', as Ruth still referred to them, were unmarried and, to their mother, each was living an intriguing life in places that Ruth had only dreamt about visiting. Ruth had been to see Luke in London once, for a weekend, and while thrilled with the hustle and bustle of the capital, the shows, the restaurants, the shopping and, most of all, seeing Luke, Ruth had confessed on her return that she was happy to be home in the peace of the Lakes.

They were also both women who liked to keep busy so they would often plan a morning out: a walk in the nearby woods, a trip to the garden centre, a visit to a particular boutique in one of the nearby towns. More often than not, they would treat themselves to a cup of coffee and a toasted teacake or, if they were feeling a little more indulgent, a pub lunch of roast beef or lamb on a cold day, and a ploughman's platter if the weather was warm. Occasionally on the weekend, Richard and Ruth's husband, James, would join them, but Catherine suspected that Ruth preferred it when it was only the two of them, just as she did. After almost ten years, although unspoken between them, Ruth was Catherine's closest friend. But despite the years of friendship, or perhaps because of them, Ruth had become used to Catherine's need for privacy, reverting back to her own chatter when Catherine became evasive about certain subjects. And for this Catherine was grateful. There were some things that were simply too dark to share.

11

Alison

January 1998 arrived, and with it a new term. As Alison packed her bags, trying to squeeze in as many of her Christmas presents as possible, she felt a flicker of excitement at the thought of seeing The Professor again. Dropping her home on Christmas Eve, he had given her a very respectable kiss on the cheek before she got out of the car. She could still feel the brush of his stubble. When they saw each other again, what would he say? What would he do? A million questions raced through her mind as she zipped up her bags. Her parents were dropping her off in the car, and as she got in the back seat, her thoughts swirled with possibilities.

*

Despite what Alison had imagined, their first meeting was a huge disappointment. His lecture was the first of the week at midday, and she had spent most of the morning getting herself ready for it. Taking almost two hours to do her hair and make-up and carefully choose her clothes, she almost felt like she was going on a night out. By the time she left her room, she had practically convinced herself it was a date. But of course, the reality was very different. He barely acknowledged her as she entered the class, took her seat and opened her notebook. She tried to catch his eye but The Professor was very much in business mode, writing on the board and reviewing his notes as the class settled down to begin. Disheartened, Alison thought to herself that he might approach her after the lecture, which seemed to last an eternity as she tried to concentrate.

Finally, the hour was up and at 1 p.m., the students raced out of the lecture hall, eager to get something to eat to assuage their hangovers. Alison had planned to linger in her seat, hoping The Professor would do the same, so that they could talk alone. But he had packed up and was out of the class with the rest of the students before she even had time to gather her things. She tried to console herself by reasoning that it was the first lecture of term, so it was bound to be a hectic time, but she still battled with the wave of disappointment that engulfed her. Had she imagined everything in the car that night? It was possible – he hadn't actually done or said anything to indicate he had feelings for her. Maybe she'd drunk more wine than she thought and got it all wrong? But deep down, she knew that the kiss, even though it was only on the cheek, had lingered. She knew that she hadn't imagined his fingertips brushing hers as he changed gears. And most of all, she knew that the last look exchanged between them before she got out of the car was one of promise.

*

Alison walked back to her college, her head bent low against the bitter, bracing wind. The biting temperatures cooled her simmering mood, and as she walked she turned over in her mind the various possibilities. Perhaps The Professor had simply been busy? Wasn't it possible that he was even, perhaps just maybe, looking for a sign from her? Could it be that he was in his study right now, wondering why she hadn't approached him? She hadn't even greeted him! No wonder he had rushed out – he was probably cross with her that he had been ignored. Cheered slightly by the thought, Alison crossed Elvet Bridge, her gaze drawn to the River Wear. Its calm waters had never failed to soothe her, but she still felt restless, dissatisfied by the outcome of the long-anticipated meeting. Perhaps she could take The Professor up on his offer and stop by his office, on the pretext of having a few questions about the course? She would go towards the end of the week she decided, once the initial flurry of the new term had settled down.

Pleased at having been so decisive, and her mind now able to focus once more, Alison wrapped her scarf more tightly around her neck and headed back to the sanctuary of her room. It was only once she was back in the warmth that she realised it was the first lecture she had attended where her first thoughts hadn't been how difficult the subject was and how much work she had to do.

*

Alison didn't have too much time to dwell on the situation. As the week progressed, she was busy getting back into university life. There were classes to attend, study sessions to prepare for and books to read. In between, she caught up with Laura and occasionally went to the student bar in the evening. Unlike Alison, whose highlight had been a night on the town on Christmas Eve, Laura had spent her Christmas holiday skiing in the Alps. Her whole family had gone for a fortnight, and with days spent on the sunny slopes, afternoons in front of the fire drinking hot chocolate and evenings with a glass of champagne over dinner, it sounded incredibly glamorous to Alison's ears.

'You will have to come with me next year! I told my family all about you and they're desperate to meet you,' exclaimed Laura, as they walked to the library together.

'Thanks, I would love to,' replied Alison, wondering what her parents would say and how she would even afford it. Her family was a long way from being poor, but she doubted they would want to splash out on a skiing trip and all the gear when they had other payments to make, such as her accommodation and living expenses. Besides, who knew who she would be celebrating Christmas with next year?

'You can borrow all my old skiing gear,' continued Laura, as if reading her mind. 'I got new stuff this year, anyway.'

Alison smiled her thanks at the offer and thought, not for the first time, how different their childhoods had been.

'So what did you get up to over the holidays?' asked Laura, changing the subject. 'Let me guess – you studied!'

Alison made a wry face at the thought. Laura was always on at her for studying too much and not enjoying the more social side of university life, but if last term's test results were anything to go by, she clearly needed to study more, not less. When she had eventually confessed to Laura how disappointed she was at the end of the first term, Laura had dismissed the results with a wave of her hand and the confident announcement that the results didn't go towards your final degree anyway, so what was the point of worrying about it? Not for the first time, Alison wished she had Laura's laid-back attitude – it certainly made life easier. Strangely, Alison had felt comforted by her words and even though she was still working long hours, the panic had subsided a little, at least enough to actually take in and remember what she was reading.

'Not much,' Alison responded. 'Spent time with my family, saw my school friends, went out for drinks on Christmas Eve... you know, the usual stuff.'

Alison wondered whether to tell her about bumping into The Professor over the holidays and quickly decided against it.

*

It was that coming Friday that Alison eventually plucked up the courage to go to The Professor's office. Going through the same hair, clothes and make-up rigmarole to get ready, she hoped this time it would be worth it. She had attended her morning lectures and was planning to casually pass by during the lunch hour, knowing it would be unlikely he would have any appointments or classes. As she walked through the law building to his office, her palms became sweaty and she could feel her heart racing. Arriving at his door, she noticed it was slightly ajar. She took a deep breath and was just about to knock, when through the crack she noticed a woman with her legs crossed, perched on the edge of his desk. Trying not to notice how shapely her legs were, Alison heard soft laughter, and was just about to retreat, when her heavy book bag slipped off her shoulder and banged against the office door, moving it open. The unknown woman, whom Alison now recognised as a post-graduate student – and a very pretty one at that – and The Professor both turned to her in surprise.

'I'm so sorry,' Alison stammered, realising that it looked as if she had been eavesdropping. 'I was just about to knock when my bag fell ...' She trailed off, aware how feeble she sounded. 'I'll come back at another time...'

'No problem,' the post-grad announced. 'I think we were finished here anyway, weren't we, Doc?' And with a suggestive smile and a wink at The Professor, she hopped off the desk, flicked her hair behind her, and in seconds she was out of the door, leaving both Alison and The Professor with the lingering scent of her perfume.

12

Kate

Kate was brushing her hair when her husband came up behind her. 'I haven't seen you with your hair down for a long time,' he said.

Glancing at him in the mirror, Kate looked up in surprise. 'Really?'

'You should wear it down more often, it looks nice,' he commented.

Kate didn't have time to respond before he left the room, but the exchange left her feeling slightly peculiar, perhaps because it was so rare these days for them to talk, never mind compliment each other. Their marriage had changed a lot over the last couple of years. There were small things at first: saying goodbye without a kiss, the daily lunch-time phone call becoming once every few days and then becoming extinct, her birthday being marked by just a card rather than a thoughtful gift, although that was more likely due to lack of funds than anything else. Kate tried to think when they had started taking each other for granted. She couldn't remember, although she did remember when things started to go really wrong. Her husband's job loss two years into their marriage had made a huge dent in their relationship and she still wasn't sure if they would ever recover. For six months, she had tried to support him, to be motivating and encouraging. She bought the newspaper every day and circled potential opportunities for him to apply for, and in the first few weeks he also seemed optimistic. He even said it was the motivation he needed to get into a job he really enjoyed. But as time went on, it was clear it wasn't going to be easy. Job vacancies – when there were any – were being given to more qualified candidates. It didn't seem to matter about experience, of which her husband had a decent amount, it was all about qualifications. Without a degree, it was difficult to get even a foot in the door.

As their meagre savings started to dwindle, he became more and more withdrawn. He stopped applying and spent his days at home watching senseless daytime television. In what had been terrible timing, Kate was pregnant again and was exhausted looking after an active toddler. With her husband always at home, it felt like she had another child to look after and her patience was in short supply. The final straw came when she was balancing the cheque book and discovered they wouldn't be able to pay next month's rent. When she told him this and how worried she was, he barely acknowledged her. In fact, he brushed it off and simply told her not to panic and he would handle it. How could she not worry? What would happen to them if they couldn't pay the rent? She didn't want to have her worries dismissed, she wanted a plan. In the end, she felt she had no choice but to go to her parents and ask for help. They loaned her the money to pay the rent for another three months, as well as some extra for food and bills. When her husband had found out, he had lost his temper. She had never seen him so angry and, what was worse, the anger was directed at her because she had gone to someone else rather than letting him deal with the problem. But he wasn't dealing with it, was he, she remembered shouting back. He just sat on the couch twiddling his thumbs, that's what he was doing. The argument was one of the worst they had ever had, and to this day she still shuddered at the thought of it. Resentment had erupted from both sides like a series of explosions and the silence that followed was eerie and haunted, respectful of the destruction it had caused. Communication was already difficult and the argument had made things even worse. When Kate's father had then found her husband a job, and he had turned it down as, according to him, his pride wouldn't allow him to take any more handouts from his father-in-law, Kate was dumbfounded with shock. She could no longer speak to her husband as her throat physically constricted. She had taken part-time work where she could, but with a child to care for, one on the way, and little work experience, she struggled to find something with even minimum wage. In the end, her husband had found a job by himself, even if it was two hours away. But Kate had never really forgiven him and she had never forgotten the time she had to ask the cashier to put some items back at the supermarket because there wasn't enough money in her purse. Her face still burnt at the memory. But she was also angry that her husband had insisted on doing things his way, leaving her to pick up the pieces. She was the one who had kept going, kept looking for solutions. Her children were her life and she would have done anything for them, pride be damned. Yet, he didn't see it that way and his stubbornness, which she felt had put them all in danger, was a difficult pill to swallow.

Knowing that the memories had the power to take over her mind, Kate pushed them away and zipped up her jacket against the cold as she went to meet Jan, a friend she had made at the writing class. One of the retirees, cheerful, optimistic and always looking for a new hobby, Jan freely admitted she had only attended the writing course because the pottery class was fully booked. She had recently finished her administration job at the local hospital after thirty-five years, and it was easy to see why she had been so popular. Jan was a talker and loved to make jokes. She didn't take anything too seriously and was the life and soul of any gathering. Kate suspected that Jan found the quietness of the writing class difficult to cope with at times, but for Kate it was two hours of pure bliss. She could let her thoughts wander and she found the process of brainstorming different topic ideas relaxing and therapeutic. Mr Barnes – soon to be Dr Barnes, he had told the class, as he was finishing up his Ph.D. – had arranged for flasks of hot water so they could make themselves tea and coffee, and Irene, who had joined the class in an effort to meet new people after the death of her husband last year, always brought a tin of home-made goodies.

Kate had also started reading again after Mr Barnes had told them that the best writers were also the most avid readers, and now she was working her way through some of her favourite classics. Little Women was currently on her bedside table. It brought back so many memories of her childhood, snuggled up in bed, listening to the wind howling outside, enjoying the pleasure of pure escapism. Why in the world did I stop reading? Kate thought. What else have I stopped doing that I used to love?

'Hello, stranger! Remember me?' said a familiar voice, interrupting her thoughts.

'Sorry, Jan. I was lost in my own world for a moment. How are you? Did you do the homework?'

'What do you think?' giggled Jan. 'I was going to do it last night – no, really I was,' she insisted at the look of doubt that crossed Kate's face, 'but then my Trevor said, "Let's go out for a drink," and I said, "Well, just the one then," and before I know it, it's midnight, and of course, I have to sleep, you know how I am when I don't have my eight hours, and then today I had the grandkids over because I promised Melissa I would take care of them, and then at six o'clock, when I'm giving them their tea, Trevor says to me, "Weren't you supposed to be writing something?" So what with one thing and another, I forgot and now I'm going to have to come up with an excuse!'

Kate laughed. It wasn't the first time Jan hadn't done the homework and her excuses were so outrageous that no one in the class, including Mr Barnes, took them very seriously. The class was free to attend, after all. Besides, Jan made it easy for everyone to get to know each other and her funny quips and unique take on life meant she was well liked.

'So,' inhaled Jan, pulling on her cigarette and linking her arm through Kate's. 'What was the homework again, pet?'

'Basically, we had to come up with a character and write a character profile,' explained Kate.

'What! What does that even mean? It would have taken me ages!'

'I know,' replied Kate. 'It took me a while but once I got into it, it wasn't too bad.'

'So who was your character?'

'Ah, that would be telling. You'll have to wait until we get inside.'

'Ooh, I'm curious now,' said Jan. 'Anyway, it's bound

to be good. Barnsie loves all of your work.' Kate laughed at the nickname; only Jan would be able to get away with something like that.

'Not all of it,' replied Kate in protest, although secretly she was pleased at the praise. And it was true – Mr Barnes had said she had promise.

'I bet you were a right swot in school, weren't you?' joked Jan. 'Were you the teacher's pet, Kate?' she asked with a twinkle.

'I suppose I was in some classes,' chuckled Kate. 'Especially English and languages. One teacher wanted me to go to university to study literature,' she recalled. 'If I was the swot, though, let me think … hmm, I bet you were the class clown!'

'Oh, Gawd – how did you guess? It was all such a long time ago. I was saying to my Trevor just the other day, back then you couldn't get away with as much as you can today, but I do remember pulling a few pranks. The secret was not to get found out otherwise the nuns would be after you!'

Changing the subject abruptly, Jan asked, 'So, what happened?'

'What happened?' echoed Kate.

'To university?'

'Oh, that. A man happened,' replied Kate, disguising the scorn in her voice with good humour.

'Men!' announced Jan. 'They ruin everything! Although, I have to say, I am rather fond of my Trevor. He couldn't cook his own tea to save his life, though.'

Laughing, the two arrived arm in arm to the class where they found Mr Barnes already there, preparing.

'Ladies! How are you this evening?' he said, warmly greeting them.

'Very good, thank you,' replied Jan, her beseeching tone already present to Mr Barnes' well-versed ears. 'But unfortunately—'

'Let me guess, Jan. You didn't manage to do the homework?'

'Well...'

'What happened this time? Your dog ate it? You put it in the washing machine? Tell me, I'm intrigued,' said Mr Barnes, a smile playing on his lips.

'Ah, Barnsie, no need to be like that. I really do try, I promise! It's just with looking after my Trevor and the grandkids, and don't even get me started on my Melissa – a grown woman, she is, Mr Barnes, I tell you, and she still comes home with her washing—'

'And you do a great job, Jan,' he said quickly, interrupting what was about to become a full diatribe of her life. 'Don't worry, I'm just joking,' he added with a wink. 'You can listen to the others as they outline their characters. I'm sure you'll get some inspiration.'

'Aw, thanks, Mr Barnes.'

'How about you, Kate? Did you find some time?'

'Yes, I did. It took me longer than I thought but hopefully I've come up with someone credible.'

'Great! I'm sure it's going to be amazing.'

With a conspiratorial wink, Jan dragged Kate to their seats at the back.

'Told you so! Swot,' whispered Jan.

'Troublemaker,' whispered back Kate.

Stifling their giggles like two school children, they collapsed into their seats as they waited for the others to arrive.

13

Catherine

10 October 2010

Dear Catherine,

I'm sorry it's taken me a little longer than last time to write back – it's not like I have the excuse of being busy! (Sorry – jail humour – you become immune to it eventually!) Your letter was so newsy and interesting, I wanted to take the time to try and match it. There's not a lot to write about in terms of daily life here but I guess to someone who has never been inside, it could be intriguing. As a Category B prison, our routine is fairly restricted, although not as restricted as Frankland (Category A) where I was initially placed. Here, we're allowed thirty minutes outside each day but the majority of time is spent in our cells. We're confined for ten to eleven hours a day. Every Sunday, a priest comes to the prison and we're allowed to pray with him. It's ironic that it's now become one of the highlights of my week. A lot of prisoners turn to prayer *and religion inside – most probably because there's not much to do and it's another opportunity to interact with someone from outside.*

I also spend some of my time in the prison library. My nickname inside is Brains because I'm able to read – you'd be amazed how many prisoners are illiterate. I once read somewhere 60 per cent of inmates in the UK are below the literacy threshold. I'm lucky in that way, as reading has always been a great outlet for me and it gives me a bit of respite from this world and entry into another.

I'm not sure I would call the inmates here 'friends' but you certainly build up some type of relationship, if only for protection. The people locked up in here are really insane – serial killers, for example. As long as I've been here, there have always been various incidents between inmates, but you learn quickly. It's definitely been one of my most difficult lessons in life, and the fear never really goes away – it's hard to trust people.

Thank you for the offer by the way – books, newspapers and stamps are always well received. Your last letter was great and I enjoyed reading it. I hope in this letter I have answered your questions.

Michael

Catherine sat back in her chair, holding the letter between her thumb and forefinger. She tried to imagine being locked up in a small cell for so many hours and felt a flicker of claustrophobic panic at the thought. She imagined being stripped of her clothes, searched, and given a prison uniform and an identification number. She imagined being shown to her tiny cell, the thick, steel door slamming behind her and the key turning in the lock with an almost unendurable click. She imagined sitting on the thin mattress, nowhere to look except the four grey walls. What would you think about if you had so much time, Catherine wondered. Would you think about your crime? Would you think about survival? Would you think about the people who had gone before you in the same room? Possibly. She knew what she would think about, though. She would think about whether the crime committed had been worth it or not.

*

Catherine knew quite a bit about HM Prison Durham, mainly because it was such a dominant building in the city, but also through her Internet research. The prison itself was full of interesting history. It was built in 1810, and between then and the 1950s, there had been ninety-five hangings, three of which were women, and the majority were for murder. Catherine wondered how she would feel if capital punishment was still legal. In another life, she would have been horrified by the notion but these days she wasn't so sure. With age, she had discovered that not everything was black and white. Closing her eyes, she envisioned being a spectator in the noisy crowd, watching the condemned as they awaited their fate. Being dragged through the passage from the prison out into execution area, eyes covered, the convict's remaining senses heightened to the sound of the baying audience and the smells of the city. Justified? It would depend on your perspective, thought Catherine grimly.

It had been a few days since she had received Michael's letter before Catherine felt ready to write back. Reading the letter again, her attention was caught by one particular section:

I'm not sure I would call the inmates here 'friends' but you certainly build up some type of relationship, if only for protection. The people locked up in here are really insane – serial killers, for example. As long as I've been here, there have always been various incidents between inmates, but you learn quickly. It's definitely been one of my most difficult lessons in life, and the fear never really goes away – it's hard to trust people.

She wondered what kind of incidents had happened to Michael during his time inside. Had he discovered broken glass in his food? Had he endured beatings or threats? With only books and TV shows to draw from, she had no idea, and she doubted she would be able to find out, unless he volunteered the information. She also found it curious that he had mentioned the *other* prisoners as being insane, almost as if he wasn't one of them. Did he think because he had killed only once, he wasn't as bad as his fellow inmates? The part she could easily empathise with was finding it hard to trust people. They had that in common.

Catherine looked outside the window. Her desk, where she did most of her paperwork, overlooked the garden. The October sky was dark and overcast, with a slight drizzle. Normally, she hated this weather; damp and gloomy, it dragged her down. But as she switched on the lamp, the atmosphere matched her thoughts as she picked up her pen and began to write back.

Dear Michael,

I'm happy to hear that you have found some solace in prayer. I lost my faith many years ago and have chosen a different path for my spirituality but I can imagine it must be very helpful for you. And any connection with the outside world must be a benefit. Does the priest visit you for confessional purposes or simply to pray?

Durham is a city often in my mind. My memories are quite varied but I used to enjoy the walks along the river and the little coffee shops. Now, in the North-West of England, we still have the countryside around us, but the temperatures are a little warmer than in the North-East. My husband got a job here several years ago and since then we have made it home. I have not been back to Durham since. Maybe I'll return there one day – who knows?

The library sounds like a welcome distraction from your cell. I have always loved books and use them to relax and escape from daily life. My favourites are thrillers and historical novels – I really enjoy a good page-turner! If you have any recommendations let me know. I was shocked by your statistic of 60 per cent illiteracy. That's incredibly high. I do hope those people have the opportunity to learn while spending time on the inside. The website showed there were several courses available for inmates to learn new skills and trades – I'm presuming as part of their rehabilitation. I'm also interested to know if you get volunteers who actually visit the prison.

At the moment, I'm preparing for Christmas. While not as busy as it used to be when we were a young family, it's still a hectic time as we often get a lot of visitors, weather permitting. You may think I'm a bit of a control freak preparing so early but Christmas shopping in October is much more bearable than December!

Catherine paused wondering at the sense of including such a special holiday in her letter. It must be a painful time of year for all the inmates. But the letter-writing volunteer programme had advised them to talk about daily life, keeping it light-hearted and chatty, so she kept going.

It becomes harder and harder each year to think of unique gifts so I like to plan well in advance, often going into Manchester or Leeds for the day, as there's so much more choice. I know my husband is desperate for an iPad so I may get him that. For my daughter, I tend to get a mixture of small gifts such as books, pyjamas, perfume and so on, and then something a little more special like a watch, but I will have to come up with something new this year – any ideas much appreciated! And, of course, I often make the pudding around now as well.

I have included some writing paper and stamps in this letter, so I do hope you receive them. I look forward to hearing from you soon,

Catherine

As Catherine sat back, she tried to imagine being in prison for Christmas. The last few years she had had so many visitors and guests over the festive season, she thought ironically how she might enjoy a little solitude. She couldn't quite remember when it had started but she would guess that for at least the last few years they had had family and friends over to stay, and not just for a few days, but often for two or three weeks. While it kept Catherine busy, a state she always welcomed, she often collapsed with exhaustion afterwards. She didn't know why she invited so many people. Well, she did know really, but she didn't want to admit to herself that three was quite a sad little number for such a social season.

14

Alison

Over the next few weeks, Alison tried to put The Professor out of her mind. When attending his lectures, she always made sure she was the last one in and the first one out, and during class, she kept her head down and her pen moving. But every so often, her cheeks flamed with embarrassment as she recalled the intimate moment she had interrupted between the post-grad and The Professor. Her plan abandoned, Alison had muttered that she would come back later and fled the room. What had she been thinking? Of course he wasn't attracted to her. She'd clearly had more wine than she had thought that Christmas Eve; in her drunken haze, she had imagined everything and now felt very foolish.

But halfway through the term, The Professor managed to catch her as she slinked into the class, and asked her to come to his office after the lecture. She wasn't feeling the best, having overindulged the night before and woken up with a pounding headache and a touch of paranoia. Alison's thoughts reverberated as she wondered why he would want to see her. Was it her last paper? Had it not been good enough? While her marks hadn't improved, she was still retaining a solid average score, so she hoped her most recent submission hadn't been a complete failure, especially as she had spent a lot of time on it. But what if she had misunderstood the assignment? By the end of lecture, Alison had got herself in such a state that she was convinced she was going to be asked to leave the course. Panicking and frantically trying to work out how she would explain to her parents that she had failed, she hurried to his office.

'Come in, come in,' said The Professor when she arrived. 'Take a seat.'

Once again, Alison was reminded of home as she sat down in the comfortable armchair. She noticed the black and white cat wasn't there today.

'So, how are you?' he enquired pleasantly.

'I'm fine, thanks. How are you?' replied Alison, wishing he would simply get on with it. She wasn't in the mood to be patronised with small talk.

'Good, good.'

He paused for a moment and Alison got the feeling he was trying to think of the best way to say his next words. Certainly, it couldn't be the best part of the job, thought Alison, but to draw it out like this was a bit unfair.

'So, I know it's a bit unorthodox but I wondered if you would like to catch up for a coffee?' he tentatively suggested. 'Perhaps next week? We didn't really get a chance to discuss how you're finding the course at the last social at the Student Union so it would be good to catch up in a bit more of a relaxed setting.'

Alison stared at him in disbelief. Was he actually asking her to meet him one-on-one?

'Sure, of course,' she responded, the relief making her

eager to agree to anything. 'When did you have in mind?'

'How about Wednesday evening at seven thirty? We can meet in town on Elvet Bridge and go from there.'

'Sounds good.'

'Great, great – look forward to seeing you then.'

Alison had the feeling she was being dismissed so she picked up her things and left the room, shock and surprise mingling with relief, which caused her to laugh aloud. Noticing people looking at her strangely, she hurried out of the building, barely registering the fact that the proposed meeting was out of office hours.

*

As it turned out, Alison and The Professor didn't end up going for coffee. Instead, he suggested a pub that Alison had never heard of, which was strange because she knew most places in the small city. It was not frequented by students but locals, and when they arrived it was filled with a much older crowd. Taking her first sip of wine, and trying not to smudge her carefully applied lipstick, Alison tried to act casual. He had a way of making her feel at ease, though, and as one glass turned into two, she became more relaxed and she found that they actually had a lot in common. They were both from the city of Durham and loved their hometown, as well as being avid supporters of the same football team. Before long, Alison was telling him about her dream of attending the university to complete her degree to become a barrister.

'I'm not sure where the idea came from,' she responded when he asked what made her want to go into law. 'There's no backstory. I suppose it's just always been there as a part of me. Almost like a calling,' she added, slightly embarrassed at how ridiculous she sounded. But it was true – it had never crossed her mind to study anything else. She had done her work experience at the local solicitor's office and it simply confirmed what she knew already: that she didn't just want to be a solicitor; she wanted to be a barrister. She hadn't actually admitted that part to anyone but it felt good to say the words out loud.

'Impressive,' The Professor had said when she told him. 'It's incredibly competitive but I'm sure you'll do well.' Incredulous, Alison beamed at the praise, a welcome change from the average feedback she had received so far. Seeing her surprise, The Professor delved a little deeper. 'Alison, you have great potential – why do you look so shocked?'

Alison debated her next words carefully. 'I'm not shocked, as such, just…' She tried to find the balance to convey her disappointment at the course without letting him know how much she was struggling with it. 'I suppose I had imagined the course to be a little different – something a little more practical, I guess…'

The Professor burst out laughing. Seeing her dismay, he quickly reassured her. 'Don't worry; I'm not laughing at you, I promise! It's just if I had a pound for every time I heard that, I'd be a rich man!'

Relieved, Alison smiled. 'Glad I'm not the only one, then!'

'You're not, that's for sure. I've been working here for a while now and every year I see the same disappointment. It's not always the glamorous career people dream of.'

It was incredibly subtle but there none the less: a note of bitterness in his voice that indicated that teaching law was perhaps not The Professor's first choice. Maybe, he'd dreamt of becoming a barrister too, thought Alison. Dying to ask but not wanting to embarrass him, she let him talk.

'People study for many reasons: because their parents told them to, because they want to implement change and, of course, because they want to help people,' he said, his emphasis on the last reason showing his disdain for the overused reason. 'But rarely do people realise just how dry the law can be with the everyday work being largely administrative. Few truly make it to the top as Partner and if they do, they soon become disillusioned with the long hours. But you, Alison,' he whispered to her, 'I sense something in you that's going to take you straight to the top.' Enthralled, Alison leaned forward. 'I see something in you that I haven't seen in a student for a long time.' Alison held her breath, eager to hear what it was.

'Passion,' he whispered.

*

The pub became a regular meeting spot for them, although the arrangement was always last minute and Alison never knew which day it was going to be. As a result, if she was out with friends, she would have to make something up in order to leave them and go to meet him. Eventually she started declining invitations from friends as there were only so many times you could have food poisoning. It never crossed her mind to say no to The Professor's invitations. He had become a lifeline for her, and in her mind he was the answer to all her negative feelings; doubt, loneliness and insecurity all disappeared when she was with him. Besides, he always apologised for the last-minute requests to meet, citing his workload. She did wish, though, that they could meet in a different location. The pub was on the outskirts of the city and several racing greyhounds and their owners often made up the patronage, the dogs' sleek bodies curled up around the bar stools of their trainers. There was the customary regular, known as 'Ol' Jim', who had his own spot at the bar, slowly drinking his pint. Alison had never heard him utter a word, yet through some unspoken agreement, whenever he ambled in, his gait slowed by arthritis, his bar stool would be vacated by whichever unsuspecting drinker had claimed it. There was a pool table at one end, although Alison had never seen anyone play, and the air was filled with tobacco smoke from cigarettes and the occasional cigar. The Professor seemed to know the barman – a tall, wiry man with a grey comb-over, his wrist weighed down with a heavy, gold-linked chain. He never acknowledged her presence but he usually had a word or two and a nod for The Professor. He always led her to a table towards the back, away from the bar, either in the corner or behind the cigarette machine. The first time he had taken her there Alison had been so nervous she had barely noticed her surroundings, but each time they came, she saw a new layer of grime. On one occasion, she even spotted dog dirt, no doubt because the trainer of the guilty greyhound was too inebriated to see to the dog's needs. Alison had trouble finishing her drink that evening.

By the time the Easter holidays came round, The Professor was in Alison's thoughts almost constantly. She had tentatively asked questions about elements of the course she was struggling with and found his answers easy to understand. As a result, she became more confident about the workload and, although the syllabus was still challenging, she at least felt she was making some progress.

But it wasn't just the course they talked about. The Professor had travelled extensively before coming back to Durham to take up a role at the university, and to Alison, who had only been to Europe, it was a doorway into a new world. He described beautiful temples in Thailand, his awe at the Great Wall of China, and the exotic chaos of Cairo. His travels had taken him across the Middle East and Asia to India, Indonesia and Jordan, and it was clear it had been a very special time for him. He encouraged her to consider taking a year off after graduation and, from his descriptions, she was sorely tempted.

Without quite realising it, she had become dependent on their irregular meetings. Alison expressed her dismay one evening in the last week of term.

'I can't believe the Easter holidays are here already. I'm going to miss meeting up with you. Who's going to answer all my questions now?' she teased.

'Well, there's no reason for us to stop, is there? We both live in Durham so it should be easy to meet, even in the holidays.'

Elated, Alison smiled at him. 'I would love that,' she said.

'Oh, I almost forgot,' said The Professor. 'I got you something.'

Alison took a deep breath in. She had never received a gift from a man before. Unwrapping the box from its paper, she discovered inside a mobile phone. 'Oh, wow! This is amazing!' She was genuinely excited. She had wanted one for so long and had pleaded with her parents but to no avail, not when there was a perfectly good phone box just in the hallway. Then she remembered her manners. 'I can't accept this, though – it's far too expensive!'

'Of course you can,' he laughed. 'I know it's a bit extravagant, but with the holidays coming up I wanted a way to stay in touch.' He winked.

As they left the pub, the darkness shrouding them, he kissed her on the cheek. 'I'll call you,' he promised.

Practically floating on air, she greeted her parents with much excitement when they came to collect her, although she had to keep the phone hidden in her bag to avoid their questioning. The Professor had already messaged her to say have a good break and she had enjoyed the thrill of typing back her own SMS. At home for the Easter holidays, she told her parents all about university life and how much she was enjoying it. They were clearly reassured to see her returned to her normal self and the first few days were a busy blur of unpacking, family meals and outings. Motivated, she then made a start on the workload in preparation for the next term, determined not to be put off by the large, almost ominous, stack of books that needed to be read. As she got through each chapter, Alison checked her new phone almost constantly, but after a few days at home with no calls or messages from him she began to worry. Why hadn't he been in contact? As the days passed, she became more despondent and struggled to concentrate on her studies. She became withdrawn and uncommunicative, staying in her room, her law books, now untouched, on her desk, taunting her. With the phone clutched in her hand, Alison got into bed and read her novels, trying to block out images of The Professor. What was he doing right now? Was he meeting the pretty post-grad student? Taking her to dinner...? Sleeping only fitfully at night, she dozed on and off during the day.

By the tenth day, Alison was not just depressed, she was angry. How dare he do this to her? But what if something had happened? Maybe he'd had an accident and was in hospital? Maybe she should contact him and check? The idea took hold – anything had to be better than this constant wondering and waiting. Typing and retyping, it took her a whole thirty minutes to get the message right. She wanted to come across as bright and breezy and not in the least like she had been waiting by the phone for the last ten days. Nor did she want to sound pushy. In the end, she typed:

Hey, how are you? Haven't heard from you, so just thought I would check in.

Pressing 'send', she waited apprehensively. Whenever Alison met him, he usually had his phone with him, so she expected him to respond fairly quickly. However, several hours later, she was still waiting. She felt like she was going slightly mad.

Finally, as she was getting ready for bed, her phone beeped and she frantically grabbed it. Opening the message, it read:

Sorry, got caught up with work, all good, see you soon.

That was it.

Furious and frustrated, Alison threw the phone against her books and, tears streaming, she flung herself on her bed. She knew she was acting like a child but she couldn't seem to help herself. Angry with him, but most of all with herself for wasting so much time at the expense of her studies, she had no idea how she had gone from being an A-grade student with an exciting future to such a desperate wreck. She was painfully aware of just how much time she had spent waiting for him to contact her when she should have been doing more to prepare for next term. Why had she let him do that? It was like she wasn't in control of her own mind.

Over the next few days, Alison became more and more

sullen and by the time the Easter holidays were over and she was preparing to head back for the third term, she was barely talking. Her mother tentatively broached the subject, two days before she was due to leave.

'Alison, is everything OK?'

'Yes, Mum, everything's fine – why?'

'Well, I'm just a little worried about you – you've been a bit quiet the last few days,' her mother responded, trying to play it down.

'I'm sorry. It's just the work. With third term coming up and the exams, there's a lot to prepare for.'

'I know, love, but you're going to pass with flying colours. You always have.'

Alison tried to smile to reassure her mother, but somehow her words made her feel worse.

'I'm sure I will – I'll just be glad when the exams are over, that's all.'

'Of course you will. But don't worry about anything. If you need to come home at any time, just call us, and your dad and I will come and pick you up.'

Alison gulped. 'Thanks, Mum.'

The next day Alison's phone beeped.

Hey, sorry I've been AWOL – fancy a coffee this afternoon?

Having stared at the text in disbelief, Alison put the phone under her pillow, determined to make a point by not responding. Five minutes later, unable to resist, she had typed out her message:

Where and what time?

That afternoon was one of the most amazing times of her life. He had told her how sorry he was that he hadn't been in touch but his mum had been ill and he'd spent the holidays taking her to various medical appointments. In between, he had had a lot of research work to do, which had needed to be submitted by a certain deadline and he'd only just managed it in time.

'I shouldn't have left it so late in the first place,' he laughed. 'But as you may have noticed, a certain someone was distracting me last term!'

Alison's heart soared. So, there was a proper explanation after all. She should never have doubted him. The cosy meeting she'd interrupted with the pretty post-graduate student flickered across her mind, but it quickly dissolved with his reassurances.

As they left the coffee shop, The Professor reached for her hand. Alison felt her heart explode at his touch. Apart from the odd peck on the cheek, which didn't count in her opinion, this was the first time he had made such an intimate gesture. There could be no doubt now of his intention and as they walked through the quiet cobbled lanes of the city, Alison had never felt happier. As the afternoon sunlight gave way to dusk, they continued walking, their fingers still interlinked. By unspoken agreement, they ended up on the bridge overlooking the river. As the darkness shrouded them, and the last of the ripples of the river disappeared, The Professor gently turned Alison to face him.

Caressing her cheek, he looked into her eyes. 'What is it about you, Alison?' he whispered.

Alison didn't know what to say. Struggling to maintain

eye contact, she leant into his chest, her heart pounding with anticipation. With one arm around her, he used his free hand to lift her chin so that their eyes locked once more. It was at that moment, as their lips met, Alison knew, without a doubt, she had fallen deeply in love.

15

Kate

Despite Kate's initial concern that she was one of the youngest on the writing course, she had found – if not friendship, then something close to it – in her classmates. Mr Barnes included a time for discussion in each of the sessions, and as the weeks went on, everyone began to open up a little bit and share parts of their lives. There were eight of them in total: herself; Jan; Irene; Harry and Joan, who were married and looking for a shared hobby to enjoy together; Patrick, who worked in a bank during the day but pursued his dream of becoming an author at night; and Elizabeth and Mary, two spinster sisters who were so close they were able to finish each other's sentences.

'So I hope you've all prepared for our discussion today, the topic of which is regret. Now I know what you're thinking, Jan,' said Mr Barnes, cutting her off before she could comment. 'I can hear the wheels of your brain turning as I speak – "But, Barnsie, isn't that just a bit pessimistic?" The class laughed at his impersonation of her. Jan grinned.

As the laughter died down, he continued, 'Perhaps. But it's such experiences that can really inspire us in our writing.'

Nobody said a word. Kate looked around. Even at the tender age of twenty-three, she still held on to the long-held Northern tradition of keeping your feelings to yourself, so goodness knows what the older members of the class were thinking. *There's no need to air your dirty laundry in public, pet,* her mother would say to her.

As if he realised what she was thinking, Mr Barnes said, 'Now, I know it may be difficult to explore and share some of these feelings on such a personal topic, and of course, you're more than welcome to sit this one out if you're not comfortable. However,' he paused and cleared his throat, 'it's our greatest challenges and regrets in life that have the power to unearth our deepest emotions.'

He let his words sink in to the circle of students around him, who started to shift uncomfortably in their chairs. When no one responded, he said, 'Why don't I start?'

As Kate listened to him talk about a time of regret when he was a teenager and had spent six months bullying a younger boy, she looked around the group. They were all listening intently. Slowly, like flowers unfurling their petals, each member took his or her turn to share a story of regret. Kate had been planning to talk about not staying in touch more often with her parents. She still called them once a week and visited with the children when she could but she didn't spend nearly enough time checking in on them, especially as they were getting older. Instead, when her turn came, Kate found herself sharing her regret over not taking up her university place. 'It was difficult, really,' she told the class. 'I had a baby on the way and a new marriage, and at the time it just didn't seem important.'

'And you regret not going?' Mr Barnes asked.

'Yes, I do. I could have made it work even with a baby. My parents offered to help but at the time I was too loved up and naive to see it.'

'Well, it's still not too late,' commented Jan. 'You're still young, love, and let me tell you, that makes all the difference!' The murmurs and nods of heads from around the room told Kate they all agreed with Jan.

'Thank you, Kate. This brings me nicely on to the next part of tonight's session,' said Mr Barnes. 'And you'll be relieved to know that you don't have to share it with the class,' he added, winking. 'So, just on your own for a few minutes, think if there is anything you can do today about that regret. Of course, you can't go back in time and change it but perhaps there's something you could do on a smaller scale. For some of you,' nodding at Kate, 'this course may be the start. For you, Harry, it may be writing a letter to the children or the grandchildren of the soldier you couldn't save in the war. For you, Patrick, it may be just a case of calling that girl who you let slip through your fingers. Whatever it might be, you don't have to do it, you just have to think about it and let the thoughts settle in your mind. How can you incorporate these ideas into your writing? How can you leverage the power of emotion that such actions may bring to the surface?'

*

Walking home with Jan after class, Kate let the thought of regret float around in her mind as her friend chattered on. It was an interesting proposition that while you may not be able to undo the regret, there was the possibility to fix it.

She didn't think she would be able to go to university now, but what if there were some other night classes available? Perhaps she could invest in a couple and see if she could get a few qualifications. Kate examined her emotions: excitement, nervousness and apprehension. She made a mental note to see how she could include these in her writing.

'I quite liked the homework today,' said Jan, interrupting her thoughts.

'I'm sure you did. Is that because it doesn't involve writing anything?' Kate quipped cheekily.

'Ha-ha, yes, maybe! My Trevor will be relieved, that's for sure. He keeps saying his tea is burnt because I'm so distracted by all the homework we have to do!'

'Still,' said Kate, 'it was weird, wasn't it, having to share our feelings like that? I was planning on saying something completely different.'

'Really?' replied Jan. 'I think everyone enjoyed it. Mind you, I used to hear all sorts in the hospital. I kept telling the supervisor, "I just work in admin, Mr Drake," but it made no difference to him. "Get out there, Jan," he used to say. "And cheer some of them up." I have to admit, I did like to go around and have a chat with some of the patients, especially the long-staying ones. It's surprising what comes out of people when they're at death's door.'

Realising the turn the conversation had taken, Jan announced, 'Honestly, that Mr Barnes! He's a good-looking chap, isn't he, but he hasn't half got into my head with his depressing talk tonight!'

Kate laughed. 'Don't worry, Jan. By the time you get home, you will have forgotten all about it. Isn't Trevor baby-sitting the grandkids tonight?'

'He is that. I'd better scoot. I'll see you next week, pet.'

'Bye!'

Walking the last half a mile to her own home, Kate was pretty certain she wouldn't be able to forget. She felt more motivated than she had in a long time. In fact, she may just have a look at the newspaper and see what courses were available. Perhaps Jan was right. Perhaps it wasn't too late after all?

16

Catherine

Dear Catherine,

It sounds like you're very busy in the run-up to Christmas! It was never my favourite time of year, to be honest, even before I came here. The cold weather, the busy last-minute shopping. In fact, most of the time I used to spend the Christmas holidays working. I didn't really have family close by to visit – I had friends who I would go out and socialise with in the pub but that was about the extent of it. There was never a girlfriend special enough around at that time or if there was she was busy with her family. Well, there was one particular girl who I could have seen myself with, but that's all over now. I didn't even used to bother putting up a tree. In hindsight, perhaps I would have made more of an effort if I'd known I would end up in here. Your family celebrations sound lovely, and the home-made pudding I'm sure will be delicious. There is an opportunity here to volunteer in the kitchens, and a few years ago we had an inmate who was a chef. We bribed him heavily to volunteer during Christmas so we would get a half-decent meal on the day! He's gone now, released a couple of years ago and from what I hear, lucky enough to be working again as a cook. He's working in a homeless shelter as opposed to a fancy five-star hotel, but it's better than nothing.

If I do get released on parole, I'm not sure what I would do. Probably just try and keep my head down and stay out of the way. Durham, as you know, is a small city, and an unforgiving one at that. I'm not under any impression that life on the outside is going to be easy. If I'm lucky enough to be released, it will be another journey that I have to survive. Sorry to sound so philosophical. As you can imagine, we have a lot of time to think and sometimes it's not always a good thing. Many inmates who are released have very little support with the exception of their old crowd, who often tend to be criminals themselves and so the vicious circle begins. Of course, my situation is a little different but I believe this is why the letter-writing programme exists to help convicts have a more moral form of support. I have to say I can see why you have been approved for the job. It's not an easy one, and not one many would do so willingly and voluntarily. If I haven't said it before, thank you for reaching out.

Michael

Catherine reread the letter. She had a sense that it was different from the others. There was a rawness to it that made her pause, an honesty that she hadn't quite anticipated. And there it was again – Michael's reference that he wasn't the same as his inmates, almost as if they were beneath him. She had a feeling that this was a critical point in their correspondence and her response would either make or break the trust so carefully nurtured between them. Catherine checked the time. It was just after 10 a.m. She was supposed to be popping over to Ruth's for coffee in half an hour but this seemed so much more important. Making a snap decision, she picked up the phone and dialled.

'Hi, Ruth, it's Catherine.'

'Hello there, how are you?'

'I'm fine thanks but I just wanted to let you know that I can't make it this morning. An urgent request has come in from the school to put together a report so I need to work on it and send it to them today.'

'That's fine, Catherine, I'm around tomorrow.'

'Thanks, Ruth. Sorry about the late notice.'

'No problem. You do so much for the school – I hope they appreciate you!'

Laughing, Catherine said her goodbyes, eager to get off the phone before Ruth pulled her into a long, gossipy conversation.

As Catherine put the kettle on, she felt a mild sense of discomfort at the white lie she had told her friend. Pushing it aside, she took her coffee, sat down at her desk and reread Michael's letter again. Taking some scrap paper, she decided to draft the letter first. It took several attempts before she was happy with it. This required her best writing paper, she decided, as she pulled the rich, thick, creamy paper from its box. Clearing her desk, she began to write.

Dear Michael,

I received your letter this morning and felt compelled to write back immediately. I'm so glad to hear that I'm helping by reaching out to you, even if it's only slightly. After so long in prison, it must be daunting to try to come to terms with your upcoming parole and the prospect of release. You're right – this volunteer role is part of a bigger rehabilitation programme and the centre has a lot more to offer, so I feel sure when the time comes they will help you as much as possible.

I have always been a big letter writer, so writing to you is something I enjoy. I'm sure that there are many people who would be reluctant to write to a Category B prisoner, but for me I saw it as a challenge because I truly believe that I can make a real difference in your life, both now and when you're released.

Of course, I'm aware of your conviction for murder and I would be lying if I said it didn't affect me. I can imagine what the victim's parents would think of me being in regular contact with you. As a mother myself, I can easily empathise with how much they would struggle to understand, but I honestly believe that by reaching out to prisoners, people can start to put things behind them and move on. I don't mean 'to forget' – one could never forget, of course – but at least start the process of overcoming the grief and dealing with it. Although it would be painful, I feel sure they would understand and that it's all for the *greater cause. Ultimately, each of us lives with what we have done or what we are about to do and we bear those consequences for the rest of our lives. Nobody is perfect and we can only do the best we can, with what we know.*

I do hope these words offer some kind of comfort and reassurance to you. I believe that you have over-come the most difficult part and while the future is still unknown for all of us, I feel optimistic that you will find closure very soon.

Catherine

Catherine placed her pen down slowly. She was taking a risk by moving away from the easy-to-digest topics of daily life and moving into a more intimate realm, but it was a risk she was willing to take. Besides, she had a gut feeling that he would appreciate the honesty in her writing and that it would deepen their relationship, encouraging him to trust her. And while the rehabilitation centre warned all volunteers not to get too personal, Catherine was not one to do things by halves. Her aim was to ensure that she prevented Michael from reoffending, and as she sat back down at her desk and folded the paper into the envelope, she strengthened her resolve to do everything in her power to achieve that.

17

Alison

Since their first kiss, things had progressed rapidly with The Professor. Texts flew back and forth under the pretext of help with coursework, but these soon developed into more intimate messages. They didn't see each other again until Alison returned to university for the third term a few days later. She was a little apprehensive about attending his class, but with so many students there, she had no opportunity to do anything except grab a seat and start writing. It was only after the class, when all the other students had left, that The Professor approached her and asked how she was doing, telling her to stop by his office during her free periods. She felt a frisson of excitement as he discreetly put his hand on her lower back. Alison didn't hesitate and started to do this at least once a week, and while they always talked about the course, conversation inevitably went off in other directions. Despite meeting during office hours, he was just as intimate with her, which, to Alison, seemed to be a bit of a risk. What if someone barged in?

'Would it make you feel better if I locked the door?' he laughed, when she resisted his kiss.

'Yes, it would, actually! Anyone could come in!'

'Ah, well, that's the thrill, isn't it?' he said to her, ignoring all her protests and gathering her in his arms.

Laughing, she threw caution to the wind and allowed him to kiss her. But soon, he did start locking the door, which made Alison relax a little more. After months of feeling remote and cut off from university life, she began to feel connected again, and that finally someone understood her. Whether it was the warm, cosy feel of the office or just the fact that he was attentive, those office visits became like a retreat for Alison – much more so than the meetings in the grimy pub. Whatever else was wrong in her life, as long as she had that hour in the warmth of his office and with his understanding gaze, she could manage anything, even the next two years of university life.

Laura noticed the change in her and quizzed her endlessly about what was happening. Alison wasn't socialising much in the evenings but they still had breakfast together and, being neighbours as well as friends, would often knock on each other's doors for tea and a chat. But what was there to tell? That she was seeing one of the faculty members? Alison didn't feel like sharing that part of her life, and besides, she was afraid of the other students finding out. If they did, they may think she had special privileges or that he was too old for her.

So, when he asked her to go for a walk with him rather than meeting in the confines of the pub or his office, she was reluctant. It was just for a coffee and a stroll by the river but she still felt vulnerable. During term time, there were students everywhere – what if someone saw them?

Where was this going? But she wasn't about to risk losing his attention, so she agreed. As it happened, it was early evening by the time they met up, and darkness was falling, so once they had bought coffee, they took the drinks down to the river and sat on a bench. She refused to hold his hand, though. They talked for a while before being forced to walk to keep warm in what was an unusually cold April, and Alison had forgotten her coat. She wasn't going to complain, though. She would follow him to the North Pole if that was what he wanted.

*

The next few weeks passed in a blur of essays, tests and secret meetings. They were now meeting several times a week, either in his office, the dodgy pub or for walks in the evenings, and though these walks weren't the warmest, they allowed them to be anonymous as the darkness concealed their secret. The Professor was an amazing listener and Alison found herself talking endlessly, always seeking his advice, opinions or just general take on life. He made her feel herself again and reminded her that she was intelligent and could succeed in life. Whereas before, she was feeling trapped with the sheer volume of material to learn, now she had an outlet to talk through all her learning and even debated some of the topics. It reminded her of how good she used to be on the debating team at school and why she had decided to study law in the first place. He encouraged her to join the university's debating team – the Durham Union Society – and for the first time in a long while, she felt that there were possibilities.

Gradually, from hand holding to the bliss of that first kiss, their relationship had developed. Alison had had boyfriends before but never anything like this. When she wasn't with him, she was thinking of him, and when she wasn't thinking of him, she was asleep and even then she often dreamt of him. She had always thought of herself as a practical person but she seemed to have no control over her feelings when it came to him. And he seemed to feel the same way, although he was often busy. As a lecturer that was understandable, she thought as she tried to study in her room. She was particularly distracted one afternoon in May as she was going to his house for dinner. This was the first time he had invited her over to his place and Alison could hardly bear the waiting. He had said to come over at seven thirty. She glanced at the clock – five and a half hours to go. She would allow herself an hour to get ready and thirty minutes to walk there, which meant she had four hours to complete her essay, read and take notes on five chapters, and start her research for the next coursework. Glancing out of the window, the outline of the prison stark against the hillside, Alison got down to work.

*

It was only a twenty-minute walk and, despite the chill, Alison could feel herself sweating. The afternoon had dragged but finally, finally, seven thirty had arrived. Well, seven twenty-six, to be exact. Did she look too keen if she was a few minutes early? Alison forced herself to walk around the block a second time, wiping her damp palms on the inside of her coat pockets. What was wrong with her? It wasn't like it was a first date. But she was nervous and she knew why. It wasn't going to his house, or eating dinner, it was what may or may not happen afterwards that was bothering her. What would he expect? Would he ask her to stay over? Should she bring a toothbrush or would that be too suggestive? After much deliberation, she had slipped a travel-sized one in her bag, along with some wipes. Alison had a thing about teeth and the thought of falling asleep without brushing them was horrifying. If he did ask her to stay over, what should she say? There was a part of her that didn't feel quite ready, but there was another part of her that wanted to make him happy so he would never leave her. Arriving at his door, Alison checked her watch: 7.34 p.m. There was no bell, so she knocked three times. Through the glass, she could see his bulk approaching. When he opened the door, she expected to him to hug her as he usually did, but instead he merely stood aside and let her in.

'Hi,' she initiated.

'Hi, how are you?' He sounded slightly terse.

'I'm good, how's everything with you? Did you have a good day?'

Alison was aware she was being overly polite but he hadn't made a move towards her so she kept on talking.

'Something smells good! I'm starving! What is it? Beef?'

'Yup.'

The Professor moved over to the kitchen and began stirring a pot. Following him into the kitchen, she wrapped her arms around him from behind. Feeling his body tense, she let go.

'Everything OK?'

'Sure, I'm just wondering why you're late.'

Alison's mind struggled to understand what he was talking about.

'When?'

'Tonight.'

'Tonight? I wasn't late tonight. You said seven thirty.'

'And what time did you get here? Seven thirty-five. I made everything ready so we could sit down at seven thirty.'

Alison narrowed her eyes. What was he on about? She decided to take a conciliatory approach.

'I'm really sorry about that. I'm here now and it smells amazing.' Hugging him again, she felt his body relax.

Kissing the top of her head, he said, 'Just don't be late next time, OK?'

'I won't.'

Unable to tell if he was joking or being serious, Alison changed tack.

'So, shall I set the table?'

'No, it's all done. Here, why don't you pour some wine and go and sit down, while I serve up?'

Taking the wine, Alison poured herself a slightly larger than normal measure. Taking the glass, she headed into the open-plan dining and sitting area. After the tidy cosiness of his office, his home was in stark contrast. Little attempt had been made to personalise it and the space was bare and unwelcoming. A beige sofa was pushed against one wall while a television sat in the corner. In the dining area, a foldaway table and two chairs had been set up and the mismatched cutlery crisscrossed the cheap white Formica. Overhead, the big light glared harshly in the absence of any soft table lamps. An array of different sized candles littered the windowsill and Alison placed a few on the dining table and lit them. The only similarity to The Professor's office was a shelving unit, stuffed to overflowing with books. Before Alison could browse the titles, The Professor came in holding two dishes of steaming hot beef stew. A man's meal, her mother would have said. Placing the dishes on the table, he switched off the main light, and finally took her in his arms in a long embrace in the flickering candlelight.

*

The wine was making her woozy. The meal had been delicious and they had moved from the table to the surprisingly comfortable sofa. Leaning back against him, glass of wine in one hand, and holding his hand with the other, Alison felt relaxed. They had talked non-stop for most of the evening but now they were silent. Taking her by the hand, he pulled her up from the sofa and wordlessly took her upstairs. All of Alison's fears disappeared as he took her face in his hands and gently kissed her. Her passion rose to match his, as his hands became more urgent, exploring her body. Within minutes she felt herself falling backwards on the bed, the sheer weight of him on top of her. Hearing Alison's breath catch, he quickly lifted himself onto his forearms. 'Are you OK?' he whispered.

'Yes,' replied Alison.

'Sorry, I just can't help myself with you; you drive me crazy.' The last word was lost between her neck and her shoulder as his fingers unhooked her bra. Lifting himself up, he removed his T-shirt then gently lifted Alison's top over her head, before discarding her jeans.

'I want you,' he said simply, as Alison lay back, naked apart from her underwear. Alison felt vulnerable under his gaze, but as he slipped off his jeans she realised just how much she wanted this – wanted him. She wanted to feel the weight of him on top of her and, as she reached out, her uncertainty disappeared under his touch.

*

Afterwards, he had fallen asleep immediately but had woken twenty minutes later. Giving her a quick kiss, he had headed to the bathroom where he had taken a long shower. Alison lay in his bed, uncertain what to do. Should she join him or was this her cue to get dressed and leave? While she deliberated, she could feel her eyes closing, the tiredness taking over her. All of a sudden, the bathroom door opened and The Professor came out. She had expected him to come back to bed but instead he was dressed in casual clothes.

'Do you mind if I work for a bit? You're more than welcome to stay here,' he said. Without waiting for her response, he leant over, gave her a quick peck on the cheek, and whispered he'd be back shortly.

As Alison drifted off, she ignored the flare of disappointment that she wasn't wrapped in The Professor's arms, the two of them falling asleep together. As sleep finally overtook her, she told herself not to be so needy.

18

Kate

It was the last writing class before Christmas and the atmosphere was festive. There was also a slight tinge of anticipation: today was the day that the students shared their writing with the rest of the class. They had been working on their manuscripts for the last few months and while everyone was eager to hear each other's work, Kate wondered if the others felt as nervous as she did. Even Jan was quieter than normal and as she was called up to the front, Kate thought she detected a slight quiver in her hands as she held her manuscript. As it turned out, Jan was as hilarious on paper as she was in person, and at the end of the reading she received an enthusiastic applause punctuated with a few whistles.

'Well done!' whispered Kate, genuinely pleased for her friend. 'I'm so glad you didn't end up in the pottery class.'

Jan grinned, clearly thrilled at the praise. 'You know what? Me, too!'

Mr Barnes held up his hands for quiet. 'Fantastic, Jan! OK, we just have one more to go. Kate – you ready?'

As she caught his eye, Kate was surprised to feel her heart pounding and wondered why she felt so flustered. She got up from her seat and walked to the front of the room. As she turned to face the rest of the class, the noise died down and expectant eyes turned upon her.

Mr Barnes, perhaps sensing her discomfort, nodded his encouragement. 'Take your time, Kate, no rush.'

Taking a deep breath, Kate began.

*

The silence was deafening. In those few seconds, after she had finished her last words and looked up, Kate wondered how she had managed to get it so wrong. And then, all of sudden, there was a thunder of applause. One by one, each of her classmates stood up – even Mr Barnes. Relief surged through her like a shot of whisky, warming her.

'Kate, amazing work! Truly wonderful! You had me on the edge of my seat all the way through,' enthused Mr Barnes.

She could feel herself smiling widely at his enthusiasm. She felt a swell of pride as she made her way back to her seat; it had been a long time since anyone had praised her. Motherhood was a thankless job at times, she realised.

'So,' announced Mr Barnes, 'that's it for this term, and what a fantastic way to finish. You have all worked so incredibly hard. I hope you've enjoyed the class and I look forward to seeing you all after the Christmas holidays in 1985! If anyone fancies a Christmas drink, I'll be in the Dog and Duck.' A cheer went up at that and, as chairs scraped back and people grabbed their coats, Mr Barnes winked at Kate. 'Great stuff, Kate. I hope I will see you in the class next term?'

'I hope so, too,' replied Kate, putting her bag over her shoulder.

'Are you joining us for a drink?' he asked.

'Yes, why not?' she responded. Her husband would probably be in bed anyway. For some reason, she hadn't felt as much tension between them during the last few weeks. In fact, there hadn't really been much of anything between them. Once the girls had gone to bed, she had headed to their bedroom to work on her writing or to read, while her husband ate and watched the television. In the mornings, he was up and out early. Even on weekends, she had started staying at home while he took the girls out to the park for the morning. While he adored his daughters, getting him to take the girls out on his own at the weekend had been a big win for her, giving her some much-needed time and space. She tried not to use the time to do housework and instead focused on doing something nice for herself, even if it was just a cup of coffee and watching a bit of TV in peace. She was painfully aware, though, of her preference for spending time on her own rather than with him. She didn't know which was more dangerous – being angry at each other, or simply not caring enough to have any emotion whatsoever.

*

'Oh my God, Kate, that was amazing!' exclaimed Jan as they walked to the pub a few steps behind the others. 'You have to finish it!'

Kate laughed, high on the adrenalin of her mini success. 'I would love to but I'm not sure when I would have the time with two kids. I don't even own a typewriter!'

'Well, you've signed up for the writing class next term,

haven't you?' responded Jan, drawing on her cigarette.

'Well, maybe, but—'

'So, you can do it then,' announced Jan.

'I'm not sure…'

'Of course you could – how can you possibly think of *not* attending – you have talent!'

'Well, I wouldn't go that far, but…'

'OK, how about this,' argued Jan, unable to let it go. 'If you sign up, I'll sign up too and skip pottery – how does that sound?'

'Ha-ha! That pottery class is never going to happen and you know it! Well… OK, but I need to check with my husband.'

'Bah – he'll be fine.' Jan dismissed that with a wave of her hand along with the remains of her cigarette. 'Anyway,' she added, finally changing the subject as they entered the Dog and Duck, the warmth of the pub drawing them into its embrace, 'let's celebrate your debut!'

As they joined the others at the bar, Jan turned to her. 'I'm just popping to the ladies – need to redo my lipstick,' she said.

Looking around, Kate could see that the pub was busy for a Tuesday evening. It was a popular place despite its slightly rundown feel. 'Can I get you a drink?' asked Mr Barnes. Caught off guard, Kate smiled her thanks and asked for a white wine. She normally drank half a lager but wine seemed more appropriate, somehow.

'So, are you from Durham, Kate?' Mr Barnes asked, making conversation.

'Yes, born and bred! I can't imagine living anywhere else. And you?'

'I am. Durham is very much home for me and I'm hoping to get a job here.'

'Oh, do you have family here then?'

'Just my parents,' he replied, 'but they're getting on a bit now so it's good to be close by. I'm not sure how long they have left, to be honest, but then I guess none of us do.'

'I'm so sorry to hear that,' commiserated Kate. 'It's always difficult. My parents are about an hour away but I don't get to see them too often.'

'Will you see them for Christmas?'

'No, but I will take the children up there on the train for New Year, just for a few days.'

'Sounds fun!'

'Yes, they always enjoy it but it hasn't got any easier as they've got older! Do you have kids?'

'No, I don't but—'

'Sorry about that – the queue took for ever!' burst in Jan. 'It's amazing what women talk about in public loos...' And she was off, their conversation overtaken by Jan's hilarious stories.

As Jan paused for breath, Mr Barnes took the opportunity to ask her what she would like to drink.

'Half a lager, please!'

Turning to Kate, Jan commented, 'Wine, eh? That's a bit posh.' Kate blushed at being caught out while Mr Barnes rescued the situation. 'She deserves it after all her work on her writing this term.'

'She does indeed, Mr Barnes, she does indeed!' Winking at Kate, Jan exclaimed, 'Cheers!' before leading Kate into conversation with the two spinster sisters, Elizabeth and Mary.

By ten thirty, Kate was on her third glass of wine and feeling quite tipsy. She didn't drink that often – children and hangovers didn't go that well together. All three drinks were bought for her and she was conscious she hadn't bought any drinks for anyone else.

'Can I get you a drink, Mr Barnes?' she asked.

'Thanks, Kate! I'm afraid my upbringing as a gentleman would not allow me to accept. However,' he said with a genteel bow, 'can I get you another white wine? Or how about some champagne?' Before she could protest, he had called out to the barman: 'A glass of your finest champagne, sir, for the lady here. She is about to become England's next famous author. What do you think, Kate? Are you ready for stardom?'

Amused, and slightly light-headed, Kate retorted, 'Oh, absolutely! I'll save you a signed copy.' And then with a touch of flirtation added, 'If you're lucky, that is!'

Not missing a beat, 'I consider myself very lucky,' responded Mr Barnes. 'Especially when it comes to beautiful authors with great potential!'

Kate laughed. It didn't mean anything. Everyone was having a good time. The room was warm and lively and the wine was making her brazen. At the same time, she was aware of how close Mr Barnes was and how his hand brushed hers when he leant over to pay for her drink.

'Can I walk you home, Kate?' he asked smoothly. And with that, Kate drew a breath. It sounded intimate and reminded her of when her husband had walked her home after their first date. It was much the same weather: cold and crisp, creating the perfect scenario to keep each other warm.

'Thank you, but I'll be leaving with Jan shortly,' she said, slightly cooler than she had intended.

'Of course! Well, I hope you have a great Christmas and New Year. I also meant to ask you if you wanted to come along to a book club I'm part of? We're always looking for new members and I remember you saying that you had started reading a lot again. The next meeting is 16 January and the book of the month is George Orwell's *1984*.'

'Thank you, that sounds good. Can I let you know in January? If I'm at next term's writing class...' Kate felt foolish. He was only trying to be friendly. There was nothing in his invitations.

'No problem,' he responded amiably. 'Here's my number so if you decide to come, I can give you the details of where to meet. I do hope you make it next term – it would be great to see you develop your manuscript even further.'

'Thanks.' Taking the number, Kate slipped it into her jeans pocket. 'Have a great Christmas, too.'

As he left, Kate glanced after him, not noticing Jan come up behind her.

'Did he just give you his number?' she asked quizzically.

'Yes, but it's so I can make a decision about a book club and whether I'll be here next term.'

Unusually for her, Jan didn't say anything but the slightly arched eyebrow didn't need much of an explanation.

'Come on,' said Kate, suddenly sober. 'Let's get home.'

19

Catherine

It had been six weeks since Catherine had written her last letter to Michael. She hadn't expected a response within the first couple of weeks, but when a month went by and the only post was bills, circulars and Christmas cards, she began to panic that her more intimate approach had backfired. She could feel herself becoming more and more agitated, as Christmas grew closer. She simply couldn't lose him now, after she had worked so deliberately to build a bond with him. She had contemplated writing to him again to see if everything was all right but then worried that it would appear too intrusive. In the end, with Christmas fast approaching, she had sent him a Christmas card – no letter – just 'Season's Greetings', and a small gift, which was a book, *The Fry Chronicles*. She had thought long and hard about the book she would send. She wanted something that reflected today's culture but was also humorous and uplifting. For herself, she chose something dark, treating herself to *The Girl with the Dragon Tattoo*.

Checking her watch, Catherine sighed heavily. After

breakfast that morning, she had driven to Kendal to get some last-minute Christmas gifts. She had already done most of her shopping and didn't really have to go, but she felt the need to get out of the house and keep busy. She was surprised at how much the absence of a letter from Michael was affecting her. She normally enjoyed these excursions. The pleasure of being able to wander as she pleased for as long as she liked, stopping off at Farrer's coffee shop before exploring the indoor market, was usually something she looked forward to, a chance to have a break from the regularity of her daily schedule. However, today she felt irritable and uneasy. The traffic seemed worse than usual, and it was pelting down with rain, bringing a cold chill that seeped through her layers. Despite this being a weekday, the small town was busy, due to the Christmas rush, and Catherine felt herself becoming annoyed as the throng of shoppers quickened their pace to match their hectic lives. While she was in no hurry, she had to admit it wasn't much fun browsing in this weather. Making a snap decision, she popped into a nearby newsagent's, picked up the local paper, and headed to the nearest coffee shop. Lucky enough to find a seat, she removed her coat, ordered, and sat back to browse the paper. She almost missed it, but for the fact that her coffee appeared at that moment, interrupting her turning to the next page. She checked again and there it was, no more than a few inches of column space.

Durham Prison Suicide

A man was found dead in the early hours of the morning at HM Prison Durham earlier this month. The cause of death is believed to be suicide, although no official spokesperson from the prison has confirmed or denied the report. The unnamed man was apparently serving a life sentence for murder. No further details have been released, although his family was informed at the time of the incident. The number of prison deaths across England and Wales has fallen since 2004 with an average of 130 deaths per 100,000. In 2009, the number of inmates who suffered a self-inflicted death was sixty-one.

Almost in disbelief, Catherine read the article again. Could it be Michael? Is that why she hadn't heard from him? Her heart began to pound, her mind racing, frantically trying to remember if there had been any indication in Michael's letters that he was feeling suicidal. She didn't remember anything significant but what if she had missed it? What if she had been so focused on what to write to him, she had been blind to what he was trying to tell her? Running her hands through her hair, Catherine felt her usual calm composure leave her. She felt an urgent need to get home and reread – no, consume – every single one of his letters. She needed reassurance that she hadn't been so thoughtless as to miss his intention to kill himself. If it was Michael, what would the rehabilitation centre think? She briefly thought about contacting the newspaper to see if they had any more information, but she knew they would have printed it if they had. Catching the eye of one of the servers, Catherine asked for the bill, trying not to get frustrated when the waitress insisted on chatting and taking a ludicrous amount of time to give her her change. In the end, Catherine told her to keep the change, even though it was a lot more than a standard tip. Slipping the newspaper into her bag, she headed out on to the street, barely even noticing the now-horizontal rain hitting her face, so intent was she on getting back to the car.

As she half ran, she forced herself to calm down, and made a decision to give it one more week before doing anything. If she still hadn't heard from Michael then, she would contact the rehabilitation centre and see if she could get information that way. In the meantime, she would analyse his every letter if only to reassure herself. She would also cut out the clipping from the newspaper and add it to her already bulging file.

*

Catherine didn't need to wait a week. A few days later, there was the letter on the mat, instantly recognisable by its postmark and hand-written address. She let out an audible sigh of relief. Having quickly hidden it in her dressing gown pocket, she handed the rest of the post to Richard, and hurried to the privacy of her locked bathroom. Her hands shook as she opened the envelope and while she tried to savour the letter, she was so curious she devoured it in minutes.

15 December 2010

Dear Catherine,

I'm so sorry for the delay in writing to you. It's been a tough few weeks. One of the inmates decided he had had enough and committed suicide. It doesn't happen as often as you might think, but when it does, it shakes everybody, even the toughest of prisoners. It makes everyone a little unsettled, including the guards. He was found in the morning during the daily wake-up call. It's not quite clear how he did it but there are various rumours flying around, as you can imagine. No one saw it coming, to be honest, which makes it even harder to take in. There's not a huge amount of dignity in suicide but I can understand when people here feel they have no alternative. It is also something I have contemplated many times just to escape this hell. The strange thing is, he was due for parole in a few weeks – some say he couldn't handle the thought of being in the real world and others say it was the thought of another Christmas without his family. I guess we'll never know, as there was no note. I hope this isn't too difficult for you to read – I just wanted to make sure you had a proper explanation for my delay in writing to you. Thank you for the Christmas card and the book. It was the highlight of the last few weeks and helped keep my mind off things. It's the first time I have received a Christmas gift in a long time, so you can imagine how special it is to me. Our schedule doesn't change too much on the day, but the canteen does serve roast turkey, which we all look forward to. I'm sorry I'm not able to return the gesture but I wish you and your family a very merry and peaceful Christmas.

Michael

Catherine hadn't realised she had been holding her breath, until she released it in one big exhale. She stumbled through the emotions of pleasure, pain and relief all mixing together, before finally settling on worry as the thought crossed her mind that he may also have the same idea to kill himself. He wouldn't. Would he? It was so important to her that she reach out to him. In response, her desire to write back immediately was overwhelmingly strong, but would that be too much? But if she left it till after Christmas, would that seem insensitive? She tried to imagine what she would do if a friend had just had such an experience. Of course she wouldn't wait – she would offer condolences and comfort as soon as she heard the news, so why should Michael be any different? Because he was a murderer? Because he had killed? Because he was familiar with death? It would be churlish not to write and offer support immediately. After all, that was her role here and she took it seriously.

'Bye, love! I'm off now. You all right in there? You've been there for a while, even for you!'

Catherine jumped at the sound of the sudden interruption of her husband's voice outside the bathroom door.

Hastily putting the letter back into her pocket, she opened the door to him. Peering round the door, only her face showing, she joked: 'Sorry, darling, I feel the need for a little more maintenance today than usual.'

As she knew he would, Richard automatically reassured her.

'To me, you're the most beautiful woman in the world,' he said as he kissed her cheek, before heading out to the office.

'See you later!'

'Bye!'

Catherine went back into the bathroom and locked the door. Sinking down again on the side of the bath she cautioned herself to be more careful. Only when she heard the front door slam as Richard was leaving did she head back to the living room to sit at her desk. She didn't start writing immediately in case he had forgotten something and came back. Instead, she sorted through some bills and general paperwork. After fifteen minutes, she removed the letter from her pocket and smoothed it open, trying to iron out the creases from where she had hurriedly crumpled it. She read it again, a lot more slowly this time and, keeping it open in front of her, she started to write a response.

20 December 2010

Dear Michael,

I received your letter this morning and I just wanted to say how sorry I am to hear your news. I did read something in the paper a few days ago, and was quite worried about you, so thank you for letting me know. I have heard and experienced much worse so, no, it's not too tough for me to read. I'm sure it must be incredibly unsettling for everyone there. Perhaps the only consolation is that he will find peace now. The rehabilitation centre made us aware that suicide is not unusual and to possibly prepare for it. I do hope you have the strength to carry on and if you need anything from me, please just let me know. I'm glad you got the Christmas gift and it's helping you through these troubled times. I shall write again in the New Year with all my news, but for now, I just wanted to let you know that I was thinking of you at this difficult time.

Catherine

20
Alison

Alison was spending more and more time at The Professor's house and less time in college. Whenever she did come back – normally, to pick up her post and a change of clothes – she was in and out within ten minutes and managed to sneak around without anyone seeing her. However, one early morning, Laura caught her as she was unlocking her door.

'Where have you been?' she screeched, making her jump.

'Hi,' Alison responded, trying to play it cool.

'Hi? Is that all you can say? I haven't seen you for ages and I've had to start going to breakfast with Lulu down the hall...'

'I'm sorry,' replied Alison, now with genuine feeling. 'I've missed you, too, but I've been busy, studying and everything...' Her sentence trailed off. Alison glanced at the poster on her wall. The Professor had given it to her after their first kiss. It was a print of two cherubs sharing an embrace and a kiss. It was called *L'Amour et Psyché* and it was her most treasured possession. As she looked at the poster, something in her face must have given her away, because Laura looked at Alison quizzically for a moment and then her whole face lit up.

'You've met someone!' she proclaimed with a certainty that was unnerving. 'I knew it. Tell me everything, now!'

And as Laura made herself comfortable on Alison's bed, she knew there was no getting away from this one.

'Er, sort of.'

'What do you mean "sort of"? Who is he? Which college does he go to? What does he study?'

There was no way Alison was going to risk sharing the information that she was in love with her law lecturer, so she did what most people do when they have a secret. She lied.

'Well, he's in a different college, he's studying the same course as me, and he's lovely. But we're taking it very slowly so there's really not much to tell.' Alison was surprised by how easy the lies tripped off her tongue. What had become of her? She never lied, and it wasn't a comfortable feeling.

Laura screamed in delight and hugged her. 'I'm so happy for you! I can tell by the look on your face that you're crazy about this guy – whoever he is! I can't believe you've found someone before me! God, what if I end up a lonely old spinster on the shelf?'

And she was off, and Alison knew then, thankfully, that the attention was no longer on her and they would spend the next half an hour talking about the type of man Laura would like to marry. And while she enjoyed the conversation, she already had the first inkling that their friendship was changing. Alison thought Laura could tell, too. 'Don't forget about me, will you, now that you have a boyfriend?' joked Laura when Alison said she had to get to the library. 'And don't forget we're going to Newcastle for a night out for my birthday. You have to be there!'

'I promise, I won't forget,' responded Alison, and for the first time, she enjoyed the feeling of her friend being in awe of her, instead of the other way around.

*

The end of term was fast approaching and, compared to the last one, Alison felt it had flown by. She was in a whirlwind of classes and secret liaisons, and she felt amazing. The Professor was like her oxygen – allowing her to breathe and survive in the academic world. And the secrecy of it just made it even more exciting. She felt special and not just average any more. Out of everyone, he had chosen her. They talked endlessly about everything, spent whole days in bed, only getting up when they got hungry. Being known as the 'sensible one' amongst her friends, Alison knew she was in dangerous territory seeing a faculty member. While it wasn't illegal, there was a certain protocol and Alison was pretty sure they weren't following it. The age gap didn't seem to make a difference to either of them but there were times when she was conscious of how young she sounded to his ears.

'What do you fancy doing tonight?' he asked one Saturday afternoon.

'Well, Laura, myself and a few others are going into Newcastle for a night out to celebrate her birthday.'

'Really? Should be fun...'

'Yes, I hope so.'

'Of course, I would rather you were here with me,' he said with a wicked smile.

'I know, but it *is* her birthday... I already cancelled on her twice this month.'

'Aah, she won't mind,' he wheedled. 'She'll be fine. She'll be too drunk to notice anyway.'

'I know, but I promised. We already have our costumes and everything.'

'Costumes? What are you going as?'

'Well, the theme is Angels and Devils so I thought I would go as a devil,' Alison replied, her smile suitably wicked.

'Well, I have an idea,' he said. 'Why don't you go home and get your devil costume and give me a preview?'

Giggling, Alison agreed.

She never made it to Laura's birthday.

21

Kate

Kate and Jan's friendship had extended beyond the classroom and Kate often popped round to Jan's for a coffee. Jan's was a busy, welcoming home, where the kitchen table was a hive of activity. Every time Kate visited there was someone there: a kid from the neighbourhood eating a piece of Jan's home-made cake or Trevor and his work mates eating their lunch. More often than not, Jan's daughter, Melissa, was also there with her children, and Kate envied the way Jan took all the chaos in her stride. Kate hadn't really spoken to Trevor that much; he was a quiet man. She knew he had three brothers and that together they ran their family business, but that was about it. Kate also suspected that his business interests extended widely. His friends weren't particularly talkative either. It was not that they were unfriendly, but they were what Kate's mother would call 'slightly dodgy'.

'What does Trevor do for a living?' asked Kate one morning as they sat at the table playing cards while her younger daughter was occupied with crayons and a colouring book.

'Do you know, Kate, I don't really know. A bit of this, a bit of that. He does a fair amount with the dog-racing course and I know he has various investments and business interests. As long as the money keeps coming in, I stay out of it!' laughed Jan. 'But I'll tell you one thing, Kate, if I ever need anything, Trevor knows how to sort it. His family has been in Durham for generations and there's no one he doesn't know in this city and even beyond, in Sunderland and Newcastle.'

Kate laughed. 'You make him sound like the mafia! I can just imagine you as a mafia wife!'

'Me, too!' Jan laughed as well and began to do an impression of an Italian mafia 'mamma'.

'Can you imagine! No, my Trevor's not quite as bad as that, but if you come round one day and I'm dripping in jewels, you know I've killed him and taken over the operation!' she joked.

Taking a bite of cake, Kate sighed, 'If only life were that exciting.'

Jan looked at her sharply. 'You're young, you're beautiful – you have so much to look forward to. You make it sound like your life is half over!'

'No, I don't mean to. I just mean sometimes it's all a bit of hamster wheel, isn't it?'

'You know, when I was working sometimes I used to feel that way, too,' said Jan. 'But one thing you have to remember is that there is always someone worse off than you. That's what working in a hospital does to you – teaches you appreciation. There's always someone battling an illness, dealing with depression, or poverty or worse. It's about taking the opportunities when you can.'

'You're right, Jan, as always.' Feeling motivated, Kate

started to gather her things. 'OK, I'd better get home. I hope you have a lovely Christmas – see you in the New Year?'

'Absolutely. Merry Christmas, pet, and take care getting home now.'

Kate thought about her friend's words on the way home. Age and hindsight were wonderful things but what happens when you just felt stuck? Trying to embrace a more positive attitude, Kate reminded herself that life was never constant and always changing. She just had to be patient. Slowly, things would get better. They had to.

*

Christmas Day dawned bright and clear. Both girls were up early and she smiled at their shrieks as they jumped into bed with her and her husband. 'Merry Christmas, girls!' said Kate, kissing each one of them in turn. Their excitement was infectious. Even her husband seemed more relaxed.

'Who's for pancakes?' he exclaimed to shouts of, 'Me, me, me!'

'When can we open our presents?' the girls cried.

'Very soon – let's just have some coffee and juice and get snuggled into our dressing gowns,' said Kate. 'Why don't you go and see if Santa has left you anything?'

The girls ran on ahead to the living room, while her husband went to the kitchen. As she put on her dressing gown, she noticed her manuscript in her bag, which she had dropped by the chair. The sight of her writing gave her a warm optimistic feeling, and she hugged it to herself like her own personal secret. Today was going to be a good day, she was sure of it. Jan would be proud of her.

22

Catherine

6 January 2011

Dear Catherine,

Thank you for your letter – it's always reassuring to receive them, especially at such a difficult time. How was your Christmas and New Year?

For Christmas, we enjoyed some turkey, which made a nice change. This is my twelfth Christmas inside and probably one of the hardest times. For some inmates it's made more bearable as they receive visitors, although this could just be a reminder of all they are missing so maybe I'm wrong. I have never had any visitors but I think it would be nice to have something to look forward to.

Despite the cold this morning, we did our usual run in the yard and I'm really looking forward to some warmer temperatures. As you may remember, the North-East has a particularly cold bite that can really get into your bones. The slop they call prison food really doesn't help either – on the coldest of days, I really miss good home-cooked food like Yorkshire pudding and gravy and roast potatoes. Watered-down stew and lumpy mash potato are not the most appealing, but I am used to it now.

It's the first time I have ever told an outsider about what goes on in here, and suicide – although it doesn't happen too often – is particularly brutal. It changes the atmosphere of our wing. For me, at least, it brings home just how narrow our choices are. Some inmates see it as the easy way out – some see it as an admirable escape option (it's very hard to get enough gear together to commit suicide) – others see it as a fit punishment, depending on their crime. Either way, I think it gets to even the toughest of men. Perhaps they just hide it well. The only upside is that there is one less inmate – it can get really crowded.

When I first arrived, I honestly thought I had landed in hell. It took a lot of time (and a lot of beatings) to get to know how things work here. It's a different world and you have to be constantly on your guard. You would think that the violence and the constant threat of attack for something as basic as a cigarette would be the most difficult thing to get used to, but it's actually the noise. Sometimes, it's unbearable. It rarely stops and the nights are the worst. During the day, you can keep your mind off things, but at night? Well, that's when people's fears really come out. Sometimes crying, sometimes whimpering, sometimes shouting. I don't think a single one of us has had a good night's sleep in years, and I'm sure many people would argue rightly so. And for many of us, that's our real punishment –

not so much being locked away but the unending void of time we have with our thoughts. I try not to think during the day as I suspect I would end up mad – in fact, a few of us in here probably are slightly mad. So many people take peace of mind for granted, but, for us on the inside, we will never, ever know it again. I think that's what leads some of us to go to such extreme lengths, as we just want to stop the twenty-four-hour horror show that is in our minds.

You're right: hopefully he will have found some peace now but, having killed so many, even in death I'm not sure he deserves it.

Michael

The letter had arrived earlier than usual that morning, taking Catherine by surprise. She had only just come downstairs when she heard the rattle of the letterbox. Helen was almost at the front door to collect the post, when Catherine had panicked.

'Leave the post, Helen, I'll get it.' Her words had come out a little more sharply than she had intended and Richard looked at her quizzically. Helen, still in her morning fog, just shrugged and sat back down at the table. There was probably no letter there, Catherine had told herself but she wasn't prepared to take any chances. But there it had been, nestled amongst the bills. She had had to resist the urge to escape to the bathroom to read it; instead, she had sat down at the breakfast table.

'You sleep OK, love?' Richard had asked, as she handed over the rest of the post to him, the implication clear in his voice that she might need a little more rest.

'Yes, yes, of course, fine.'

She had smiled at Helen, trying to make up for the tone in her voice earlier.

'Do you have a busy day, pet, apart from your interview?' she asked her daughter.

'No, not really. I'm feeling really optimistic about this one though so keep your fingers crossed for me.'

'I always do, love,' responded Catherine, wishing there was something she could do to help her daughter. She had been job-hunting for so long now, it must get demotivating.

Catherine had forced herself to sip her coffee slowly and to eat a piece of toast. As soon as she could, she stood up and went to the bathroom. She didn't see her husband stare at her retreating back, the letter safely in her pocket.

*

It was one of his longest letters yet. Catherine felt she was making headway. Whether it was the suicide or the festive season that had made him open up, she was thankful. She had chosen to ignore the discomfort his last sentence had evoked in her. Perhaps he was right, but she wasn't sure he was the one to be making such judgements. Again, Catherine got the feeling he didn't really accept he was the same as the other inmates. Pushing it aside, as soon as she was alone in the house she started to write back.

10 January 2011

Dear Michael,
    Happy New Year and thank you for your letter.

My Christmas and New Year were enjoyable but hectic. We had guests over Christmas, and then, at New Year, my husband and I went out for a meal with some friends. It's not normally something we do – we tend to stay home, invite people over, have a glass of champagne and do the countdown – but my friend Ruth had suggested it months ago, and at the time New Year had seemed a long way off! It was a very late evening but enjoyable for a change to get dressed up and be cooked for. The food and wine were excellent (it should be for the price they charged!) although I suffered slightly the next day!

Catherine put her pen down and looked at the view in front of her desk, remembering the night. It was so unlike her to drink as much as she had that evening, but lately she had the feeling that she had to make the most of life and enjoy it when she could. You just didn't know what was going to happen in the future. She remembered Richard's surprise and delight when she had pulled him up to dance after the meal. When had they last danced together? Catherine couldn't remember. At midnight, they had kissed, not just a kiss on the cheek, but a long, lingering kiss that held a promise for when they got home. At around 1 a.m., they had got into their pre-booked taxi and, slightly intoxicated, had stumbled up the path to their front door before falling into bed. The next morning, Richard had brought her breakfast in bed along with the papers and an Alka-Seltzer, and they had sat in comfortable silence, nursing their headaches, and enjoying the opportunity to relax. It was one of the very few nights Catherine could remember over the last ten years when she and Richard had felt like teenagers, taking them both back to the early days of their relationship. She appreciated it because she knew better than anyone how a marriage could become stale and uninspiring. Refocusing on the letter, Catherine continued writing.

From your letter, it sounds like you have done well to survive in there. I'm happy that you're one of those who has decided not to take that route. Although, you're right when you talk about the horrors of the mind. It can often be our worst enemy and even when we're in control of our conscious thoughts, our unconscious mind will always bring the truth to the surface.

She had been about to write 'I believe we all get what we deserve in the end...' but was that last sentence too judgemental? Thinking about it, she decided it was. She had already made a very pointed remark about suicide, and after receiving such a long letter from him, she didn't want to scare him off. She needed to address the topic but she had to be more delicate.

Hopefully your fellow inmate will find, if not peace of mind, then at least some relief while atoning for his crime.

I'm sorry to hear that you haven't had any visitors. Unfortunately, I'm not able to visit you in prison (the rehabilitation centre doesn't allow that) but I hope in time your friends and family will come to visit, or at least support you during your parole and potential release. Did they give you a date for the hearing? Let me know if there is anything I can do to help – it's what I'm here for.

There. She had mentioned it. Catherine had been waiting for the right time to ask about his upcoming parole date and she hoped her curiosity hadn't got the better of her too early. But she wanted – no, *needed* – to know. More importantly, she wanted to know the outcome. Was it possible that he would be released after eleven years inside? It seemed such a short sentence for the crime of murder. Catherine tried not to think about the victim but it was too late. She had promised herself that she would only focus on Michael but her thoughts had turned to his actions, and try as she might, she couldn't help imagining the scenario. It made her feel ill. Hands shaking, Catherine took a break from writing the letter, grappling with the various lists on her desk, trying to stop the scenes in her mind from taking over. But it was no use. She imagined Michael lying on his bed in his cell, thinking the same thoughts over and over. Did he feel sick to the stomach like she did? Or did he recapture his crime for pleasure, planning how he would do it again once he was released? He had described his thoughts as a twenty-four-hour horror movie, but some people actively enjoyed horror movies. It didn't mean he was sorry – in fact, it meant nothing. Michael was right about one thing, though: peace of mind was something most people took for granted and Catherine knew that she would do anything to achieve it.

23

Alison

Alison was spending the day in the library and then visiting The Professor afterwards at his place for dinner. Alison had never eaten so well before she had met him. He was an excellent cook and, while his living room and dining room may have been sparse, his kitchen was well fitted out with the latest equipment. He even had a set of chef's knives in their own roll-up soft case. He never kept them in the drawer but always on the counter top, saying that the drawer would blunt them. He had mentioned during one of their conversations that he would have liked to have been a chef. Either that or a writer. Unfortunately, his parents had had a different idea for their son and steered him in the direction of law. The Professor didn't talk too much about his family but Alison knew he was an only child. Although he hadn't said as much, she got the impression that he was the centre of his parents' lives. They lived nearby and he visited them when he could, but she didn't know much apart from that. She wondered if he would introduce her to them. Alison's brain buzzed at the thought of it. What would they think of the age difference? While she knew she looked older than her eighteen years, mainly due to her height, and he looked younger than his late thirties, she knew her own parents would be deeply concerned with the twenty-year age gap.

Arriving at the library, she had no more time to dwell on this. As usual, the workload was heavy and she had a lot to get through if she wanted to spend time with The Professor that evening. Occasionally, they would work together, both at the dining table, taking turns to make tea, which they drank with sugar in it. It took discipline for her to concentrate, though, and she much preferred to work on her own. His sheer presence across the table from her was distracting, and there had been several nights when, work abandoned, they had succumbed to the physical need for each other. While Alison hadn't been a virgin, she had had little experience when it came to sex. The Professor had opened up a new world to her, taking her on an exciting journey. He always set the pace and she was happy to follow, although some of his more adventurous suggestions left her feeling a little embarrassed. He liked to experiment – not just positions but with toys, dressing up and role-play. Sometimes she enjoyed it but other times she would be happy just to lie in his arms and talk. But she wanted to make him happy. In fact, there was very little she wouldn't do for him. She was conscious of how experienced he was and didn't like to think how many partners he'd had before her. When she tentatively asked, he laughed, telling her he couldn't remember as she had obliterated every other woman from his mind. Alison knew it was supposed to be a compliment but somehow it left her feeling a little insecure.

Sensing this, he had turned to her. 'Hey, don't even give it another thought. Those women mean nothing. You are everything to me.' As he leant in to kiss her, she had melted under his touch, and as his hands gently glided over her body, she felt safe in the knowledge that she was enough for him.

*

Arriving at his house that evening, Alison felt tired and stressed. Hours bent over her books had left a series of knots in her neck, and the right side of her back was particularly painful. As she knocked on the door, she moved her head from side to side, trying to stretch out the muscles. A few minutes went by and Alison knocked again. Strange, she thought. Have I got the day wrong? She waited a little longer before taking her phone and checking for any messages.

> Sorry, running 30 minutes late. I left key under the mat at the back x

It took Alison some time to work out how to get to the back of the house. Frustrated, she found it eventually by going through a series of alleyways, a characteristic of the city she normally loved. Letting herself in and slipping the key into her jeans pocket, she gratefully dropped her bag and collapsed on the couch. Closing her eyes, she mustered up enough energy to get back up to make herself a cup of tea. She resisted helping herself to a biscuit, although she was starving. He had promised to cook for her tonight and she was looking forward to it. Her drink in her hand, Alison flipped on the TV and curled her legs up under her on the couch. Thirty minutes later there was still no sign of him. She decided to give it another ten minutes before sending him a text to check. As she was taking her cup back to the

149

kitchen, she remembered the key. She dug in her pocket but she couldn't find it. It must have fallen out somewhere, she thought. Checking the couch, she pulled the cushions off and found that the key had slipped between them. She was just about to put the cushions back when she saw a few coins. Gathering them up, her eye also caught a piece of paper. No bigger than a Post-it note, a telephone number was written on it. Alison felt a strange feeling come across her as she put it with the coins on the table.

*

It was another hour before The Professor came home. As he let himself in the front door, Alison went to meet him in the hallway.

'Hey, I was worried about you. You didn't respond to my text. All OK?'

'Yes, sorry about that, got caught up in the office.' Taking off his coat and hanging up his bag, he began to remove his shoes.

'With one of the faculty?'

'What?' he asked distractedly.

'You mentioned you got caught up – was it with one of the faculty?'

'Yes, something about new coursework requirements. Boring stuff, really. Anyway,' he said, changing the subject, 'how are you?' As he leant in to kiss her on the cheek, Alison could smell the rain on him. The rain, and was that something else? Perfume? She was imagining it. Finding that telephone number had made her paranoid. And it couldn't be that important if it was down the back of the sofa, could it?

'I hope you don't mind, I made myself a cup of tea. I

didn't make a start on dinner as I wasn't sure what you had in mind?'

'That's OK, I grabbed something earlier.'

'Oh, what time?'

'I can't remember now,' he said vaguely. 'It was a busy day. How about you?'

'Yes, busy as well.'

Alison thought it was strange that he would eat something when he had invited her to dinner.

'Then do you mind if I get myself a slice of toast?'

'Not at all, help yourself. You find the key all right?'

'Yes, I did. I somehow managed to drop it down the sofa though so I've left it on the table.'

Alison watched him carefully as he went to pick up the key and the coins and then looked at the paper with the number. Reading it, his face betrayed no emotion. Looking at him questioningly, she said, 'I also found that – I wasn't sure if it was important or not, so I didn't throw it away.'

'Thanks. It's the number of a research institute I'm planning to approach with my work.'

He scooped the coins into his pocket along with the key and the paper. Alison went to make her toast, thinking how odd he was being this evening.

'It's late and I have an early start tomorrow. I'm going to take a shower. Join me upstairs when you've finished?'

'Yes, I won't be long.'

There had been a reasonable explanation after all. Still, doubt niggled at her. He had said the number was for a research institute, so why then was it a mobile number and not that of a landline?

Alison washed her cup and her plate and placed them in the drainer before heading upstairs. She could hear the hum of the shower as she walked along the landing to the bedroom. Did he usually take a shower when he got home? She couldn't remember him doing so before. Questions began to pile up in her brain. She rubbed her neck, trying to alleviate some of the pain. Had he really got caught up in the office? Was the number she found the number of a research institute? She shook her head as if to physically clear the suspicion clouding her mind. She was too tired, that was the problem. Entering the bedroom, the shower still running, Alison saw his phone on the bedside table. For the first time in her life, she was tempted to snoop. It was an uncomfortable thought. When they were growing up, her sister had once read her diary. Full of teenage angst, Alison could laugh about it now but she never forgot that feeling of invasion. She remembered that she had gone to Woolworth's and bought a new diary with a lock, and even to this day she still kept her diary carefully hidden.

Her thoughts were interrupted by the sound of a text coming through on The Professor's phone. Illuminated by a green light, a message from an unnamed contact flashed before her. Sitting on the bed, the phone in front of her, Alison felt her hand reach out towards it. Just then the bathroom door swung open, and The Professor stepped out in a cloud of steam, a towel wrapped around his waist. Pulling her hand back guiltily, Alison was aware of being caught red-handed.

'What are you doing?'

'Nothing,' she stammered, 'I was just checking the—'

'My messages?'

She had been about to say the time, but it sounded false even to her own ears.

Snatching the phone up, The Professor marched back into the bathroom, shutting the door firmly behind him. Alison felt like crying. She had been waiting for over an hour for him, she was hungry, he had smelled of perfume when he came in and he was collecting mobile phone numbers. All of sudden she was no longer so sure about anything.

'What's the problem, Alison?' he demanded. 'Don't you trust me?'

Startled, she hadn't heard the bathroom door open.

'I'm really sorry. I don't know what came over me. You were late, and then I found that piece of paper with the number on it, and my mind got ahead of me.'

The Professor didn't respond.

Feeling the need for reassurance, Alison tentatively asked, 'You're not seeing anyone else, are you?'

Still, The Professor didn't speak. He just continued to get dressed. He looked angry but Alison would have preferred him to shout rather than this frustrating silence. Several minutes passed.

Coming up behind her, he took her harshly by the arm and pulled her to the mirror. Forcing her to look at herself in the reflection, he leant his mouth close to her ear, and simply said, 'Next time you think about checking my phone, think again. And if you ever so much as doubt me one more time, there'll be hell to pay.' And with that, he stormed out of the room, jogged down the stairs and was out of the front door, leaving Alison shaking.

*

It was 4 a.m. before Alison heard the key in the front door. After The Professor had left, she had laid down on the bed, not bothering to take off her clothes and simply waited for him. She couldn't sleep, she couldn't read, she couldn't watch

TV. Relief flooded her that he had finally come back. She started as she heard a crash as a pile of books fell from the hallway table and as his footsteps came up the stairs, his drunken gait gave him away. Turning on the light, Alison got out of bed.

'Ah, there you are. Still here, are you?'

Alison looked at him, where he stood in the doorway, in dismay. He had clearly had more than a couple of pints – his local accent was getting stronger with every word he spoke.

'Been checking any more phones? You still look gorgeous, though, pet, don't you? C'mere and make it up to me.'

He made a grab for her and Alison nearly toppled over as she tried not to be overpowered by him.

'Shall I tell you what I do to naughty girls like you?' His hands were rough against her, impatiently pulling at her clothes to try to remove them.

Alison laughed nervously. 'You're drunk. You need to stop this.' She tried to sound firm but the tremor in her voice gave her away.

'Do I? Are you sure? You usually like it when I'm a bit rough.'

'No, of course—'

Her words were interrupted as he crushed his mouth on hers, the sour reek of beer making her nauseous.

'C'mon, Alison. Make it up to me,' he coaxed. Alison tried to move her arms but the sheer weight of him crushed her, preventing her from moving.

'I know this is what you want.'

Realising, he wasn't going to let the matter go, Alison played along. 'I do! But how about we go slowly—'

His hand over her mouth, he cut her off before undoing her jeans with his other hand. He was on her before she was ready, and tears collected in the corner of her eyes as she tried not to cry out. Gone was his gentleness, replaced with an animalistic, angry energy. He pushed himself into her and Alison tried to relax and enjoy it, but her body simply resisted. Eventually, he collapsed on top of her. As she rolled him to one side, she noticed he was already asleep. Picking up her clothes, Alison went to the bathroom, closing the door gently behind her. Looking in the mirror, the tops of arms showed fingermarks that were already turning into bruises. Leaning back against the coolness of the marble bathroom wall, Alison sank to her knees, tears rolling down her face, fear bubbling just below the surface.

24

Kate

She should never have emptied her pockets. If her jeans had just gone in the wash without her being so diligent, his phone number would have been destroyed and she would never have called Mr Barnes. She had convinced herself that she was simply phoning him to confirm her attendance at the new term of writing classes. But slowly, as one call led to another, Kate realised she had become reliant on his encouragement and compliments. And who could blame her, she thought, as she tried to get the damp washing dry enough to wear. She wasn't stupid. She knew she was enjoying the attention and if it came in the form of a handsome, intelligent man, then so be it, she justified herself. Her husband barely even acknowledged her these days. But still, she felt guilty, especially as she had never mentioned to him the calls to Mr Barnes, and while they had a pleasant family day at Christmas, as a couple Kate and her husband were still poles apart. She had tried her best to make it as fun as possible for the girls, and they seemed to enjoy it. She had saved all year from the housekeeping money to make sure her daughters got what they wanted from Santa. In general, though, it had been a lonely holiday season for her, but as 1985 arrived and New Year came and went, she realised she was looking forward more than ever to seeing Mr Barnes again.

It had started a few days into the year when her husband had gone back to work and she had taken the girls on the train to her parents – a stressful journey in any case, but even more challenging over the holiday period with cancelled trains and delays. The girls loved their grandparents but their house was small and in the middle of nowhere. It was also old and the boiler was so temperamental that they had had to wear their coats and hats indoors.

'Why don't you let me call someone, Dad, to get it fixed for you once and for all?' Kate had asked him when they sat shivering for the second day.

'Robbie will come and have a look at it once he gets back, love,' replied her father, referring to the local plumber. 'He's already had a bit of a tinkering with it. He says the whole lot needs replacing, but I think there's still life in the old thing yet!'

'How much does that cost?' asked Kate, wondering if it was a money issue or if her father truly believed what he was saying.

'I'm not sure, to be honest, but Robbie said he would bring a quote next week. I'll go and give it another bang or two and see if that revives it,' he said, getting up from his chair.

'Well, if you're sure,' Kate called after him doubtfully. She would ring Robbie herself before she left to make sure he was on to it. She couldn't bear to think of her parents sitting in the cold, especially if it was a case of not being able to afford a new boiler. She thought of the money they had given her without question, and remorse rose to the surface.

'Mum, do you need a hand? Anything I can do to help while I'm here?'

'No, love, of course not. We manage well enough, your father and I. It's enough to have you here with the girls. They have grown up so fast!'

'They have,' Kate agreed.

'Right, girls, shall we go and do some baking? That will keep us warm, won't it?'

'Yay! Can we make fruit scones again?' said Kate's elder daughter.

'We can indeed,' replied her mother, 'and I think we have some jam and clotted cream to go with them.'

Her mother and daughters trooped out, leaving Kate alone in the living room. She sneezed, feeling a cold coming on. Rifling in her jeans pocket for a tissue, she discovered the number Mr Barnes had given her. Her husband hadn't called her once while she had been away. Feeling the need to talk to someone – anyone, about anything other than boilers and the weather – Kate called out to her mother.

'Mum, I'm just going for a breath of fresh air – will you be OK here?'

Popping her head round the kitchen door, her mother replied, 'Of course – go and get a bit of a breather. Could you just do me a favour and pick up some milk from the shop on the way back? Thanks, love.'

Kate put on her boots and stepped outside. Luckily there was a phone box right next to the shop.

*

'Hello?'

'Hello, Mr Barnes, this is Kate.'

'Kate?'

'From your writing class?'

Kate cringed at having to remind him. This had been a mistake – he didn't even know who she was.

'Ah, Kate! The famous author-to-be! How are you? I didn't expect to receive your call. How was Christmas?'

'It was good thank you – how about yours?'

'Well, you know, quiet. Glad it's over with, really.'

'I just wanted to give you a quick ring to let you know that I will be attending the second term of the writing class.'

'Well, that's the best news I've had all day.'

Kate glowed at the compliment. 'Thanks – I'm really looking for to it.'

'Me, too – your writing has such promise. But it's not just that – I'm really looking forward to seeing *you* again, as well.'

Kate didn't know how to respond.

'I'm sorry, perhaps I'm being inappropriate. I just felt there was something special about you and wanted to get to know you better, that's all.'

'Thank you, I think...' Kate responded tentatively.

Mr Barnes laughed. 'You sound so surprised, Kate! You shouldn't be – surely you attract attention wherever you go?'

Was he flirting with her, Kate asked herself. It would seem that way.

'You flatter me!' responded Kate, laughing, relieved to resume a more jokey style of conversation. 'Anyway, I'd better get back but I just wanted to let you know about the class.'

'Get back? Where are you?'

Kate mentally kicked herself. 'I'm at my parents' house with the girls.'

'Well, have a great time. Shall I give you a call when you're home and you can let me know about the book club? I have your number from the class registration.'

'Yes, of course, that sounds good. Bye!'

And just like that, Kate had another reason to speak to him.

*

'So, you're still coming to the book club with me?' Mr Barnes had asked for at least the third time, on their last phone call the day before. Kate was now back at home and her elder daughter had returned to school for the new term.

'Yes, I'm going to try. As long as the girls are in bed and fast asleep. It starts at eight o'clock, doesn't it?'

'Yep. What did you think of the book?'

She had read the book over Christmas, picking it up from her local library just before they closed for the holidays.

'Incredible,' Kate responded. 'And frightening at the same time.'

She could feel his smile down the phone as he spoke. 'It's the second time I've read it and it still makes the same impression on me.'

Was it a mistake going to this book club with him? It sounded so innocent but she felt that certain something – what was it – anticipation? Possibility? Kate searched for the right word in her head as she recalled their conversation…

'Mum!'

Kate snapped out her reverie at the sound of her younger daughter's voice. 'What are we going to do today? I'm bored.'

'We can go to the park, if you like?'

'We went to the park yesterday.'

'I know but I'm sure you'll enjoy it again today – it's a fine day.'

Kate had recently noticed that she didn't like leaving the house for too long in case she missed Mr Barnes's call. The park was just a few minutes away, a quicker option than trekking all the way into town or getting the train to Newcastle. Such outings could take up to half a day or more. Kate wondered when she had started putting her own needs ahead of her daughter's.

'Let me just finish this washing, and then we'll go, OK? We might just stop off at your favourite sweet shop if you're lucky,' placated Kate.

'Promise? Last time you said we would go out but you were ages on the phone.'

'I promise. Come on, go and get your shoes on and your big coat. Don't forget your hat and scarf.'

As Kate loaded her younger daughter into the buggy and opened the front door, the phone rang. Both of them froze. Her daughter's big eyes looked up at her mother, and in the moment Kate's heart broke.

'Come on, you, let's go. The phone can wait.'

Relief crossed her little girl's face, and Kate vowed to put an end to the calls. It could lead to nowhere good. She would attend the classes but she would cancel the book club, and she would ignore the phone when it rang. Satisfied with her resolution, she marched out with her daughter, determined to show her the best time ever.

*

Kate dressed carefully. She had found some of her old clothes from years ago and was surprised they still fit after she'd

161

had two children. But she still had a decent figure, she had just been too busy to notice, covering it up in whatever was closest to hand, usually leggings and warm jumpers. High heels had also become alien to her but the heeled boots she had paired with her jeans made her legs look long and lean. The girls had been in bed since 7 p.m. and she'd had a little time to get ready. Her husband was already immersed in the TV, which she could hear from her bedroom. Some car programme, by the sound of it. As Kate said goodbye, picked up her bag and left the house, she felt a pang of sadness that he had barely even noticed that she was dressed up. But this was immediately superseded by stirrings of excitement, her previous resolution completely forgotten now that her children were safely tucked up in bed.

The North-East weather was harsh, especially in January, and Kate braced herself for the cold. But nothing could chill that slightly giddy feeling her newfound freedom had brought her. Mr Barnes had offered to meet on Elvet Bridge so they could walk to the book club together. She had had every intention of telling him she couldn't make it, but when she rang to cancel, he sounded so excited that she was going that she didn't have the heart to disappoint him.

He had explained that it was held at a different member's house each month. This month it was at Cara's. Cara worked at the main library. 'Bohemian and eccentric' was how he had described her, and Kate had imagined an older lady who wore mismatched clothes and her hair in a long plait. However, the curvaceous but petite brunette who greeted them at the door was in her early twenties and had the dewy skin of someone who got a full eight hours' sleep each night. While her long hair was indeed plaited, it fell to the side with escaped loose waves framing her undeniably pretty face. Rolled up jeans exposed her slender ankles and painted toenails, while the woollen crop top gave a hint of firm, tanned skin. Isn't she cold? Kate thought, and then mentally chastised herself for slipping into the mother role so easily.

'Welcome!' greeted Cara, kissing Mr Barnes on each cheek. 'Hello! You must be Kate – come on in!' Kate idly wondered how the two of them had met.

The house was warm and inviting. Hues of pastel peach covered the walls, while two Venetian masks hung over the fireplace. A sensual line-up of black-and-white Athena posters framed the back wall, while the bookcase was stuffed full of books. It was the type of place Kate might have chosen, should she have lived on her own, she thought wistfully: a feminine retreat where there was nothing to do but relax and enjoy your own company.

Seated on the sofa were two young men, one of whom was playing with a Rubik's Cube and didn't bother to look up when Cara introduced Kate. The other, a student called Ronald, stood up to greet her. Along with his good manners, Kate noticed his clothes looked expensive. Despite political and cultural boundaries being pushed to their limits in Thatcher's Britain, university was still much more accessible to the rich.

Cara inserted herself between Ronald and the Rubik-playing guy on the sofa, while indicating to Kate to take a seat on the cane Cesca chair. Playfully pushing 'Rubik' from the couch onto the floor, Cara indicated that Mr Barnes should take his place, embracing him again warmly before animatedly involving him in conversation. That left Kate to talk to Ronald.

'So, have you been to a book club before, Kate?' asked Ronald.

'Actually, no,' replied Kate, slightly distracted as Mr Barnes leant his head in to hear Cara speak.

'Well, we actually don't talk about the book much,' continued Ronald. 'We have a few drinks, listen to some music, talk about politics and chill out. Are you a student as well, then?'

'No, well, not really. I have been attending Mr Barnes's writing class.'

'Ah, that explains it,' Ronald said, so ominously that Kate wondered what he was referring to.

'He's never brought someone before,' explained Ronald as he caught Kate's quizzical look. 'And Cara knows all his usual students. She was curious.'

Kate glanced over at Cara and Mr Barnes. Fully engrossed, Rubik had his head bent over the cube, furiously trying to match the colours, while Cara absent-mindedly stroked Rubik's hair, much like stroking a dog. Well, he had got the eccentric part right. Cara was speaking passionately but quietly to Mr Barnes, who was listening intently. Glancing up, he smiled at Kate as if to say, *See? I told you she was slightly strange!* Mollified, Kate turned her attention back to Ronald, who was asking her what she thought of the book.

'Yes, the book,' said Mr Barnes, catching wind of their conversation. 'Cara, what do you think? Shall we try and spend at least half an hour discussing the book this time? We are a book club, after all,' he teased. Joining in, Cara pretended to sulk, her bottom lip slightly protruding into a pout. The men laughed and Kate wondered what was so funny.

'OK, but let's get drinks first,' said Cara. 'Long Island Iced Tea, everyone?'

Without waiting for anyone to answer, Cara stood up and

walked to the open-plan kitchen. As the men started chatting, Kate was unsure what to do. Eventually, she stood up, and asked Cara if she could do anything to help. Thatcher's Britain it might be, but ingrained habits were hard to break.

'Thanks – that's good of you. That lot never lift a finger. If you could get the lemons from the fridge and the ice from the freezer—'

Her words were interrupted as music blared out from the speaker in the living room. Kate recognised the voluminous pump of 'Rhythm of the Night' and as she pulled out the lemons from the fridge, she heard Cara say to her, 'So you're the latest new student?' More of a statement than a question, her words sounded false to Kate's ears. She wondered if Cara was implying something else.

'Yes, I've been attending his writing classes at the local college.'

'Really,' said Cara, her perfectly groomed eyebrows lifting a fraction. 'Well, I hope you're enjoying your studying?' Did she imagine it, or was there a slight emphasis on the word 'studying'.

'Yes, it's great to be back in a classroom again. I had a place at university but I didn't take it up when I had my daughter.'

'Such a shame,' responded Cara, and this time there was no doubt that Kate could hear the pity in her voice. Cara was starting to make the cocktails when the doorbell rang. It was amazing they could hear it over the music.

'Kate, could you get that?'

'No problem,' replied Kate, happy to escape further conversation. She opened the door to reveal several students standing on the doorstep, their cigarette smoke piercing the cold air.

'Hello,' said Kate. 'Cara's inside.'

With a quick nod, they trooped in without speaking, four boys and two girls. Two of the boys were dressed as punks while the girls looked like they were heading for a night on the town rather than to a book club. For a brief moment, Kate had a harrowing insight into what her future may look like with her daughters as young teenagers.

'Everything all right?' asked Mr Barnes when she joined him in the living room. Kate could hardly hear him. The music was blasting and she wondered what the next-door neighbours would think. Someone handed her a Long Island Iced Tea and as she looked around the room, she felt a decade older than the group instead of just a few years. Many of them were now dancing, their limbs matching the thump of the music.

'Yes, I'm fine, thanks, although when you said the words "book club" I had imagined something slightly different,' she shouted.

'Yes, sorry about that,' replied Mr Barnes, equally loudly. 'Cara has failed one of her papers so she's gone into party mode.'

Sipping her Long Island Iced Tea, Kate felt herself relax as the concoction of spirits began to infiltrate her blood stream. As the music continued, she began to sway to the music and Mr Barnes led her onto the space cleared as a dance floor. Drink still in hand, she sipped it through a straw and didn't protest when someone handed her another one. Mr Barnes danced with her and as the person's face in front of her changed and became Rubik, and then one of the punks, Kate realised she was having a good time. When was the last time she had danced? She could see Mr Barnes in the corner talking to one of the students. She lifted her arms above her head and winked at him. Smiling, he winked in return before she turned back to the group, who were now dancing to Wham's 'Wake Me Up Before You Go-Go'. All of sudden, the music stopped and the sultry sounds of 'Careless Whisper' changed the mood. A chorus of boos went up, but Cara insisted, grabbing Mr Barnes by the hand and slow dancing with him. Before Kate could do anything, Rubik grabbed her arm and tried to dance with her, though his glazed eyes told her he would have no recollection of her tomorrow. She saw Cara lay her head on Mr Barnes's shoulder. Just how close were they, Kate wondered. The realisation that she knew nothing about her writing teacher sobered her up. Excusing herself from Rubik's grip, she grabbed her boots, which she had flung off during the evening, pulled them on and headed for the door, collecting her coat on the way. She opened the front door and slipped out into the night. The cold air was piercing, and she drew a sharp intake of breath, the sharpness sobering her senses. Turning to walk home, she thought how lucky she was to have got a glimpse of the real Mr Barnes before it was too late. It had been fun but she had children and a husband at home. Hearing footsteps behind her, Kate panicked. But the familiar call of her name made her turn round. Mr Barnes was jogging towards her.

'Kate, where are you going?'

'Home,' she replied.

'I'm so sorry,' he said. 'I know that wasn't the best introduction to the group – it's usually a little more civilised than that.'

'Not at all,' replied Kate, coolly. 'I had a good evening – it was just time for me to leave.' She tried to take the ice out of her voice. What was her problem? She was a married woman and Mr Barnes could slow dance with whomever he chose.

'I'm sorry about Cara,' he said. 'She was rude. She gets like that when things aren't going well with her work.'

'I thought she worked in the library,' said Kate.

'She does, but she's also a Ph.D. student.'

'Are you one of her lecturers?' asked Kate.

'Not officially, but she often comes to me when she needs help.' Kate stayed silent, not really sure what he meant. 'Hey,' he said, gently. 'Are you OK?'

As he turned her to face him, Kate saw the concern in his eyes. In the distance, the lights of the bars and restaurants glimmered, a perfect backdrop to Elvet Bridge. Neither of them spoke. She felt his hand gently on her cheek, their breaths showing up as clouds intermingling in the cold.

'Are you happy, Kate?' he whispered. Kate's thoughts battled with each other, her head spinning. She wasn't sure if it was from the cocktails or the closeness of him. 'She means nothing to me,' he went on. 'You, on the other hand...' His words trailed off. 'From the minute I met you, I thought you were the most beautiful woman I had ever seen. Then I discovered you could write.'

Kate stopped thinking. As his lips came down on hers, she felt her own passion rise to meet his. Her hands ran up the bulk of his chest, while he cradled her face, his tongue probing deeper and deeper. After what seemed like a lifetime, they pulled apart. Breathless, Kate felt her hand in his as he walked her part of the way home.

'Better not come any further,' he said, when they had reached the end of her street. 'I'll call you.' With a brief kiss, he was gone.

25

Catherine

7 February 2011

Dear Catherine,

How are you? I'm glad to hear you had a great New Year. Normally, I would be happy just to tick another year off the calendar but I'm hoping this year I will be up for parole. I suspect I will have to meet with the parole board and plead a case. I don't have an exact date yet, but possibly in June or July. I will keep you posted if I hear any news.

Your last letter really struck a chord with me and I thought about what you said for a long time: 'Our unconscious mind will always bring the truth to the surface.' Now at night, instead of being irritated with all the noise, I imagine a series of truth clouds floating around the prison as the inmates release their darkest, most hidden secrets through their shouts and screams. But the truth clouds have nowhere to escape and simply return to their owners, reminding them of their crimes.

I have been wondering if I contribute to the noise – if my crime causes me to release my own truth cloud. I'm sure it did at one point. Over the years, I have woken up on many an occasion with a pounding heart and also went through several periods of insomnia. Whether I was too frightened to sleep or kept awake by my imagination, it was torture. It got so bad, I ended up hallucinating and became so paranoid, the prison sent me to the psychiatric ward. Needless to say, that was a low period, which went on for months. I'm still prone to it now, but am able to manage it better and I think over the years, as the privileges increase, it becomes easier. But eleven hours a day in isolation, which is typically what most high-risk inmates do, certainly in the first few years, can incite a form of madness. Afterwards, I did some reading on the topic of isolation. It's designed to make prisoners think and reflect on their crime. And I have to agree, it's a very effective method.

I suppose the point I'm trying to make (in a very long-winded way) is that for some reason, I feel compelled to reassure you that I have spent time thinking. There's not a day that goes by when I don't remember what I did – all I can say is that I wasn't in my right mind at the time. That's not an excuse, just fact. Over the years, I have had so much time to try to make sense of it all and learn to live with it, as I'm forced to do every day. Some days are harder than others but that is my battle now and I choose to fight it.

The weekly visit of the priest helps. It's twenty minutes of the week where I am not being judged, simply listened to. When you're considered the scum of society with no understanding as to the reasons that led you to commit the crime in the first place, those precious minutes of confession, compassion and tolerance become a lifeline – much like your letters. I have to say you must be a very special person to reach out and volunteer. And if I haven't said it before, I'd like to thank you for being one of the very few who is able to see me as a human being.

Michael

*

15 February 2011

Dear Michael,

That's good news about your potential parole date and it will certainly give you something to look forward to and work towards.

Thank you for your last letter. I have to admit it took me some time to digest your words and I wanted to think as carefully as you have about some of the topics you raised.

While it must be difficult to go through such isolation, it's good to hear that you feel it's effective. So often we read in the newspapers that prisons are a waste of taxpayers' money and that a whole new world of crime exists in such places. It's even common to read about all the comforts an inmate receives, with some of the more sensational papers comparing them to a hotel!

I cannot pretend to empathise with your experience

but your descriptions have given me a little more understanding about life on the inside. I'm just happy to hear that my letters are helping in some way and providing another touch point with the outside world. My reasons for volunteering – and I do a lot of it! – are purely for self-interest I'm afraid. It keeps me busy and gives me some sort of purpose in life. As I understand it, the letters are a way of preparing inmates for life after they're released and it gives me pleasure to be able to help in some way. After all, as the rehabilitation centre told me, the more support a released prisoner has, the less likely they are to offend again, which can only be a good thing for everyone.

Catherine

Slipping into bed that night, Catherine thought about Michael's last letter. His talk of thinking about his crime had surprised her, although he hadn't actually mentioned repenting. And what did he mean when he wrote: '... with no understanding of the reasons that led him to commit the crime in the first place...'?

She had read somewhere that prison staff checked most letters sent and received by prisoners. Perhaps this was a technique he had used to prepare for his parole board? They had to be convinced that he wasn't a danger to society any more, and what better way than to gain empathy and make them believe the prison system worked? While a part of Catherine knew Michael would never really have a normal life, even after his release, he would still be a walking, living human being, unlike his victim. And there would never be a concrete guarantee that he wouldn't do it again to someone else. The rehabilitation centre had warned her that writing to a prisoner – especially to one committed for such a serious offence – wouldn't necessarily be straightforward. Catherine recalled the volunteer manager's words over the phone:

'Throughout the process of letter exchange, you will have negative thoughts, doubts, questions, fear and judgement. At the other end of the spectrum, you may also start to develop positive feelings towards the prisoner. We had one volunteer who even fell in love with the inmate, despite never meeting him. As well as being volunteers, we are human, after all, but it's important to maintain a sense of self and not become too involved in their lives. You are there purely for support purposes.'

The statement hadn't meant very much to Catherine at the time – she was just keen to get her application approved to write to Michael – but now it was vividly brought to her mind.

Michael's open, honest accounts and descriptive prose about life on the inside were so much more than she had expected. They had been writing for over half a year now and if his parole date did come in June or July, that was just five or six months away. She was glad she had managed to create some kind of connection with him and she had no doubt that letter writing, rather than email, made for a deeper, more personal relationship. While she had embraced the digital era – her tendency towards efficiency demanded it – she had secretly mourned the decreasing use of the more traditional pen and paper. Despite receiving an e-reader as a gift from Helen, she still preferred the solid comfort of a proper book and all her notes and lists were done by hand. She didn't keep a diary any more – she had given that up years ago, telling herself she didn't have the time or the luxury to write a diary. She suspected, though, that she just wanted to do a different type of writing – something that was more meaningful and had a result, as opposed to the rather pointless chronicling of her own thoughts.

Writing to Michael was the perfect way to do that, and if she could impact someone's life in the process, even better.

26

Alison

Alison was lying in bed in her dorm room when the call from The Professor came through. He rarely called her, preferring to communicate via SMS. Alison let it ring before reluctantly picking up her phone.

'Hello,' she whispered. Her voice sounded hoarse to her own ears.

'Alison, are you OK? I woke up this morning and have absolutely no recollection of getting home. Then I discovered you weren't here and I panicked, wondering what I had done to scare you off!' He laughed down the phone, as if he had entertained her with his drunkenness.

'Oh God, Alison, tell me,' when her silence became impossible to ignore. 'What did I do? Did I get a bit handsey? I'm so sorry! You poor thing! What a nightmare having an octopus like me all over you. You're just too irresistible, that's the problem!'

Alison stared at the phone in disbelief. Was he serious?

'Listen, let me make it up to you. How about dinner tonight?

And if you agree, I promise to be a complete gentleman.'

Alison wavered. She had invaded his privacy. Had she overreacted? Was he just being 'handsey'? Doubt flickered across her mind. She had been so tired and stressed. Perhaps she hadn't been thinking properly.

'I'll think about it,' she said to him.

The Professor laughed. 'Still playing hard to get, eh? OK, let me know when you're ready.'

As she hung up the phone, Alison's head was pounding. The lack of sleep from the night before had compounded the pain in her neck. Closing her eyes, she breathed deeply, trying to relax. The arrival of a text message interrupted her thoughts:

Dinner. Lumley Castle. I'll pick you up at 7 pm. x

Lumley Castle? He really was trying to make an effort. Putting her phone down, she decided to make him sweat a little longer.

*

The dinner was lovely and The Professor had spared no expense. Gently lit, the restaurant had a romantic feel and the food was delicious. Two glasses of champagne were brought out as if they were celebrating. Gradually, over the three courses, The Professor had reduced the incident to nothing more than a drunken fumble and Alison felt silly for making such a mountain out of a molehill. He listened to her intently as she conveyed her worries of being too young for him and not as experienced as his previous girlfriends. She confessed her doubts and he, in turn, reassured her that he only had eyes for her. As they walked home after the meal, he took her hand and kissed it.

'Don't worry about anything, Alison. I will take care of you. The only thing you have to focus on is your studies. Can you do that for me?'

As he leaned in to kiss her, she felt relieved they had managed to sort out their argument. She shouldn't have been so suspicious and he shouldn't have got so drunk. She certainly wouldn't go prying again. She had been stupid to question his loyalty. Walking back to her own room as she had an early lecture the next day, she vowed to do better. With her heart and stomach full, she finally slept.

*

It happened so gradually, she didn't even notice. But another three weeks went by, and Alison suddenly realised the only people she had seen were her classmates, The Professor, and the barista at her favourite coffee shop. She hadn't even seen Laura. But somehow, The Professor always managed to convince her to be with him. Not that she needed much persuading. She wanted to be with him all the time but she was also aware on some level that it perhaps wasn't the healthiest for either of them.

She was also feeling guilty. She hadn't apologised to Laura yet for missing her birthday and Laura hadn't knocked on her door to ask where she had been. Was Laura slowly giving up on her? Alison vowed to make it up to her. She would take her out for lunch, she decided. But for the most part, Alison stopped making arrangements with people because she couldn't bear to have to keep cancelling.

*

Laura was unusually quiet when they finally saw each other again. Alison had eventually decided on Laura's favourite café in town, a traditional, rustic place that charged a fortune for home-made baked treats. Alison didn't see what all the fuss was about, but she wanted the lunch to go well. She had even called them in advance to book Laura's favourite table – a hard-to-get-unless-you-were-super-lucky intimate corner by the window.

Each of them had a double free period so there was plenty of time to talk and eat. While Alison was worried she was sacrificing precious study time, she was determined to try to make amends and repair the friendship. She knew she was in the wrong and if there was one thing her parents had taught her, it was that the sooner you owned up and apologised, the better you would feel. And she had been feeling bad. She missed Laura. Her bright optimism and energy were infectious and Alison always felt good around her. She missed the comforting reassurance of having a good friend along the hall to whom she could turn at any time. She missed the music coming from her room, the messy spread of make-up across the sink, her clamorous requests that Alison do her hair, because she was 'really good at it'. One of the reasons she had decided to live in college was that she wanted the camaraderie of living with people her own age: the jokes, the late nights, the gossip. And here she was sacrificing it all.

After they had ordered – Laura a beetroot and feta salad and Alison a bowl of soup, the cheapest thing on the menu – Alison handed over her gift. She had chosen a bright, colourful scarf that Laura mentioned she had liked once when they were window-shopping. It was from one of Durham's upscale boutiques and it had cost Alison a week's worth of groceries. Laura opened it and smiled her thanks. Alison started to get worried; she had never known her friend to be so quiet.

'So, how you've been?' Alison said brightly, trying to break the awkward silence.

She sipped her coffee and waited for Laura's answer. But in the long silence that followed, Alison realised this wasn't going to be a friendly catch-up.

Without any preamble, and looking her directly in the eye, Laura didn't waste words.

'Alison,' she said firmly. 'Where have you been? I've been really worried about you. You didn't turn up for my birthday, you don't return my calls or my texts, and you haven't been in halls for weeks.'

Surprised at the extent of Laura's concern for her whereabouts, Alison considered lying, saying she had had to go home for a family emergency. It sounded better than the reality, which was that she had basically dumped her for a man. But Alison, so uncomfortable with the lies she had told already, couldn't seem to summon up deceit of that degree now. Little did she know how good she would become at lying.

'I'm so sorry, Laura, I've just been so busy with studyi—'

Laura cut her off before she even finished the sentence.

'Oh, come on – don't give me that crap.'

Shocked at Laura's aggressive tone, Alison's cheeks burnt as she realised her friend wasn't buying any more half-truth excuses.

'Well, that's p-p-part of it,' Alison stammered.

'Look,' Laura said forcefully. 'I'm not sure whether to tell you this or not but there's a rumour going around that you're seeing one of the law faculty members.'

Alison recoiled, feeling the flood of horror that she was being talked about.

'What do you mean?'

'What do I mean? I mean just that – it's all over the college. Is it true?'

Alison's silence told her everything.

'Wow,' said Laura.

Alison wondered if she detected a sliver of admiration in her tone.

'Why didn't you tell me?' she continued. 'You didn't need to lie. I would have understood. Why did you make up all that rubbish about seeing a student from another college?'

'I know – I'm sorry. It just all happened so quickly and I…' Alison trailed off. Why hadn't she said anything? Because she was ashamed. Ashamed of being such a cliché, ashamed of the need to hide it.

'Look', said Laura again, 'apart from the fact that you've just bullshitted me – and I don't bullshit easily – just be careful, OK?' Her tone became more confidential. 'According to the rumour mill, this isn't the first time he's been into a student.'

Alison looked up in surprise. 'What have you heard?'

'Oh, Alison.' And Alison definitely didn't hear admiration then – she heard pity and it made her angry. Why would she say such a thing?

'It's not true. You're just jealous. You don't know him like I do,' she retorted crossly. Although a flicker of doubt crossed her mind as she remembered the pretty, flirty, graduate student in his office. 'I know he's had previous girlfriends – of course he has. But another student? He would have told me.'

'Would he?' questioned Laura, ignoring her irrational accusation, raising Alison's doubts even further.

'Of course, he would!'

Heart pounding, Alison started to gather her things.

'Alison, come on, don't leave. I'm sorry, I don't want to upset you but I don't want you to get hurt either.'

'It's fine, don't worry about it,' Alison replied, trying to smile and act like everything was normal. 'I have to get to my next lecture anyway.' She felt the tension in her shoulders increase. She shouldn't be surprised that people had found out about her and The Professor. It was going to happen sooner or later, and at least she had heard it from a friend. Maybe it was a good thing. No more secrets. Sighing, Alison remembered why she had arranged the lunch. She didn't have many friends and she knew she needed to work on keeping the ones she had. Alison stopped packing up her things and looked at Laura.

Sitting back down, she said, 'I'm really sorry about everything. I know I've been a crap friend lately.'

Laura sighed. 'It's OK, I understand. I just miss you, that's all, and I worry about you as well.'

'I know,' replied Alison gratefully, 'but there really is no need.' Unexpectedly, she felt tears start to form. Reaching out to Laura, she hugged her, trying discreetly to wipe her tears at the same time. 'I miss you too,' she mumbled, trying to compose herself. What was wrong with her? It must be coming up to that time of the month.

Laura smiled and hugged her back, and a part of Alison was relieved that her friend knew and she didn't have to keep any more secrets from her.

'Hey, hey, no need for tears. I'm sorry – I really didn't mean to upset you.'

'You didn't,' responded Alison. 'I'm just relieved we've sorted it out.'

'Me, too! Let's catch up next week for a coffee, OK?' enthused Laura, trying to get back on safer territory. 'Oh, and on Thursday night, we're all going to Newcastle again – are you up for it?'

'Of course! What's the theme this time?'

'We're going to the school disco so it's schoolgirl costumes!' Laura practically squealed.

Alison knew that if she wanted to keep Laura as her friend, there was no way she could miss this night out.

As Alison was leaving, Laura leant over and grabbed her in another hug.

'Promise we'll see each other soon?'

'Absolutely – and, Laura, I'm sorry again about your birthday.'

'That's OK. We were all plastered by the end of the night anyway,' she grinned.

*

Satisfied that she and Laura were back on a firmer footing, Alison felt her worry dissipate, only to be immediately replaced by doubts about The Professor. What had Laura meant by 'This isn't the first time he's been into a student'? Was she just one of many? Pushing the thought aside, Alison told herself that they were just stupid rumours and Laura was probably just jealous, although she wasn't really the jealous type. The Professor was youngish and good-looking – of course, there would always be tales and whispers among students. Heading to the library, Alison mentally added it to her list of things to talk to him about tonight. They would have a good laugh about it, she decided. She would also have to let him know that she wouldn't be coming round on Thursday evening.

That night, as Alison was cooking some pasta and The Professor was finishing marking some papers, she tried to think how she could bring up the conversation she had had with Laura earlier that day in a jokey way.

'I met Laura today for lunch,' she started. 'It was nice. It's been so long since I've seen her. I took her to her favourite café – you know, the really expensive one.'

Barely glancing up, he murmured an acknowledgement before going back to his papers.

'It seems like there's a few rumours going around about us,' she said, aiming for a light-hearted tone.

The Professor looked up. 'What rumours?' he asked, his full attention now on her.

'Well, the fact that we're seeing each other. In fact, she even warned me off you, saying that it wasn't the first time you had been into a student. Of course, I didn't believe any of it.' Alison laughed, trying to show that she had brushed it all off and was just making conversation.

The Professor, on the other hand, didn't say a word.

Alison nervously continued. 'She's wrong, isn't she? About you being into other students?'

The Professor's eyes narrowed and Alison wondered what he was thinking. His face looked almost contorted as if he were trying to suppress some emotion. She noticed his fist tighten around his pen. It would have been imperceptible to anyone else, but she noticed everything about him. The way his knee tapped when he was concentrating, the angle of his head when he was reading a recipe while trying to cook at the same time, the small scar on the side of his right hand, where he had caught it with a penknife when he was younger. And the tightness of his face when he was angry. The image of him pinning her down, her arms unable to move, burst across her brain, and for a moment, she struggled to breathe.

But then he smiled. 'Of course, they're just daft rumours! What a load of rubbish! Honestly, this city sometimes – you students have far too much time on your hands!'

Alison laughed just a little too loudly. 'That's exactly what I told her! OK,' she said, quickly changing the subject. 'Dinner's ready – do you want wine?'

She felt relief flood through her, but as she ladled out the pasta she was surprised to find her hands were shaking.

*

Alison was running – running hard. Her lungs burnt with the effort but still she ran on, impervious to the fact that she had no idea where she was going, and there were no streetlamps to guide her. All she knew was that she had to get away. For one split second, she faltered – the enormity of it all taking her breath away and making her wonder how she would survive. Maybe she wouldn't. But for now, she is being hunted and she knows she must somehow escape.

Alison woke from the dream covered in a film of sweat. She blinked as it slowly dawned on her that she was actually in her room and not down a dark alley. She turned on her bedside light and looked at the clock. It was just after 4 a.m. The dream had been so vivid, and while the fragments gradually fell away like shattered glass, a feeling of unease stayed with her. She threw back the covers to get some water and looked around her room, reassured by the sight of her own things, and was surprised by how much she had missed the familiar comfort of her own place.

She tried to recall the events of the previous day to see what could have triggered such a nightmare. Her thoughts turned to earlier that morning. It had been an innocent enough request. Over breakfast, she had mentioned to The Professor that she would be staying in halls for a couple of nights as she wanted to collect some more things, and as she was waking up at odd times during the night to study, she didn't want to disturb him. At the time, he had simply nodded at her, lost in his papers. It was only after she had left his house that she breathed a sigh of relief. She didn't want to admit it to herself, but she had been nervous about telling him she would be staying in her college room for a few nights and had deliberately chosen to mention it when she knew he would be preoccupied with his work. But on some level, she knew they each needed a bit of space. Subconsciously, Alison was becoming hyperaware of her actions and words around him.

That evening, after having a good gossip with Laura in her room, she climbed into bed with a hot chocolate and a good book. Her mum had sent her a parcel with a few of her favourite foods and supplies, and Alison was using the letter as a bookmark. As she reread the letter, she smiled at the relevance of her mother's words.

I hope you're still enjoying living in college – you know you're welcome to move back home any time. I will even do some of your washing! But I know you want to have the full 'uni' experience and I think it's wonderful that you're being so independent.

Slipping the letter back into the book, Alison decided to switch off her light. Enjoying her own company and happy to be in her own bed, Alison was just drifting off, when her phone beeped.

Hope you sleep well tonight. I'll be watching you x

Dozily, Alison thought, maybe he meant dreaming of you. Dismissing it, she quickly wrote back before snuggling back down under the covers. She fell asleep quickly, not having any idea that such a message would lie in her unconscious mind, dormant, until the early hours of the morning.

*

Over the next two days and nights, Alison enjoyed the simplicity and daily rhythms of university life made up of lectures, friends, course mates and tea and toast in her own bed. She felt a sense of freedom that she hadn't enjoyed in a while. She had expected to miss The Professor more but she felt the tension gradually release from her shoulders as she laughed with Laura and caught up on all the news. How much I have missed by never being here, she thought.

The break away from The Professor did her good, and as she gathered her things together, she realised she was looking forward to seeing him. She had arranged to go to his for dinner that night – he was cooking and she imagined relaxing over a nice bottle of wine and a bowl of pasta. She was envisaging an extra special evening.

She arrived just after seven. They embraced like they had been apart for a few months rather than just a few days.

'I've missed you,' he said simply.

'I've missed you, too,' she replied.

'Sorry about the mess,' he said as he led her into the living room, hurriedly clearing up. Alison tried to hide her shock at the state of the room. Papers lay on the floor surrounding the dining table as if they had been brushed aside while empty cups and plates littered the coffee table, and several bottles of wine stood empty, along with wine glasses.

'Had a party?' Alison asked.

'Not quite – just a few colleagues over for dinner,' he replied.

As Alison looked around the room, she felt something was wrong. She tried to work out what it was but was distracted by his furious cleaning. She pitched in to help and within half an hour, the place looked somewhat back to normal.

Eventually, it was Alison who ended up cooking as The Professor said he had a bit of a headache. They sat in front of the television, eating their food. There was no more wine left, as apparently it had all been drunk the previous evening, and Alison couldn't help feeling slightly disappointed that the dinner party had taken such a toll on him, especially when he dozed off on the sofa. Covering him with a blanket, she headed upstairs to bed by herself and it was only as she was brushing her teeth, that she realised what was bothering her about the scene in the living room. There had only been two of everything – two wine glasses, two plates, two cups and two bowls.

*

Alison hadn't forgotten her promise to Laura for their next night out. She had even had a quick run through Topshop to buy a white shirt and had asked her mum to send her old school tie and the slouchy white socks that she used to wear.

She already had a black skirt, which Laura had convinced her to roll up a couple of inches, so at six o'clock, she was ready. She had decided to pass by The Professor's house before she met the girls at the train station. She felt sure he would appreciate her outfit.

She rang the bell with her coat wrapped round her, and he welcomed her in his usual way, with a hug and a long kiss.

'I missed you,' he whispered into her hair, closing the door behind her.

'I saw you only this morning,' she laughed, delighted that he seemed to be in such a good mood.

Kissing him back, she took off her coat, and watched in glee as his eyes took in her fancy dress costume.

'Is that for me?' he winked. 'You really shouldn't have!'

Heading up the stairs, Alison took The Professor by the hand, feeling unusually powerful.

Afterwards, lying there on the bed, Alison looked at the time. She knew she would have to leave in a few minutes in order to meet the girls and get the train.

Getting up, The Professor grabbed her round the waist.

'Hey, where are you going?'

Giggling, she responded: 'I need to get ready and go. I told you, I'm meeting Laura and the girls at the train station at eight o'clock to go to Newcastle.'

Bending down to slip her shoes on – a black, towering pair of platforms that made her legs look even longer, she didn't see him coming up behind her.

He grabbed her by the arm. Sure he was still playing, Alison pushed back. But as she began to feel the pressure of his fingertips increasing, she winced.

'Ow, you're hurting me,' she cried, not sure if this was still part of the game.

'Why are you going to Newcastle?' he demanded. 'Especially in that get-up.' Trying to stay calm, Alison tried to reassure him, making light of the situation. 'Remember? I told you about it. I promised Laura I would go with her to Newcastle. I'd much rather stay here with you but I've cancelled on her so many times.'

The Professor, finally letting go of her arm, pushed her backwards and her head smacked against the edge of the wardrobe.

'Only sluts go out dressed like that,' he said, before flinging her shirt at her, storming into the bathroom, and slamming the door.

Clutching the back of her head, knowing now that it clearly wasn't a game, Alison was stunned into silence, too afraid to say anything else. His temper was as unpredictable as a volcano. Head hung low, her right hand gently probed where her head had struck the corner of the furniture, while her left hand held her steady against the offending wardrobe. Not feeling any blood, she took a moment to look at her arm, the red fingerprints beginning to emerge. Buttoning her shirt all the way to the top, she finished getting ready, wondering how long he would stay in the bathroom. She was still shaking at the outburst when a few moments later, as she was packing her bag, he came out of the bathroom, apologising.

'Alison, I'm so sorry, will you forgive me? I didn't mean to shout. I'm just under huge amounts of stress lately with this research project and I was looking forward to spending an evening with you.'

Alison looked up at him, the wheels in her brain trying to keep up with the fast-switching two sides of his personality.

Still in shock, she didn't move when he came up to her

and wrapped his arms around her. 'You're the only one who seems to be able to calm me these days,' he added sheepishly.

What about my head? Alison wanted to scream. *You didn't just shout at me, you physically hurt me.* But she seemed unable to get the words out. They lodged in her throat and she swallowed several times.

'I'm so sorry, Alison. Will you forgive me?'

Not wanting to risk another outburst, Alison simply nodded. At the door, The Professor took Alison's face in his hands, gave her a last kiss and said goodbye.

'Is your head all right? I'm so sorry, it was an accident. If you need anything, just call me and I'll be there.'

As the front door closed between them, Alison felt out of control, and confusion coursed through her veins. Love, desperation, hate and anger stifled her, the mix settling like a thick layer of glue in her mind. Unsure as to what to do next, she began walking to the train station. The last thing she felt like doing was going out to Newcastle but she knew she couldn't cancel now. How would she explain it to Laura? As she walked, she pulled the coat around her even more tightly, suddenly feeling ashamed of her outfit. What had seemed like a fun night out had degenerated into an evening spent feeling self-conscious. Was she slutty? But everyone was dressed up the same, she thought resolutely. Still, the thought lingered longer than it should have done, and as she walked the streets of Newcastle, bar-hopping before finally arriving at the nightclub to the blast of the Spice Girls, Alison promised herself never to wear anything so ridiculous again.

*

Without wanting to admit it to herself, Alison knew his temper would erupt again at some point, she just didn't know when. And that was perhaps the worst part. Like the oppressive calm before the storm, her nerves were strung so tightly her muscles ached. She knew on some level, she and The Professor had to sort this out. She also knew that she had to take control somehow. She couldn't live like this anymore – the fear, the unpredictability. She decided to meet him and see if she could talk to him about it. If she approached it sensitively, he might respond better. She sent him a message asking him to meet her at the pub. It would be better to choose a public place.

As she entered their usual meeting spot, her heart hammered in her chest. She knew this meeting was make or break and she could only hope he would understand the pain he was causing her. It took a while for Alison to see him. Unshaven, and wearing an old T-shirt and shorts, he looked like he had been at the pub for a while. He was sitting at the bar with a few other drinkers and was chatting to the barman.

'Hey! Here's my girl! Come here, Alison, and say hello to the lads.'

Alison sat down, trying her best to act normal.

'How are you?' she asked.

'Great, never been better!'

'Lads, this is my woman – isn't she a looker?'

Alison cringed under the gaze of the men as they looked openly.

'Come on,' he said. 'Let's get out of here and get some coffee. See ya, lads.'

Happy to be out in the fresh air, Alison gratefully took up his suggestion, leading him to a coffee shop and buying the largest coffee available. As they walked, the fresh air and caffeine seemed to help, and The Professor, impervious to her seriousness, was in a playful mood as he persuaded her to play 'Poohsticks' from the bridge into the river. He knew she had a fondness for the Winnie-the-Pooh stories, and she couldn't help but eventually laugh at his enthusiasm as he ran from one side of the bridge to the other, gauging whose stick had won. When, finally, he determined she was the winner, he took her hand and began walking along the towpath. He didn't say anything for a long time. Alison kept quiet, waiting for him to speak. Without looking at her, he started.

'I know I haven't mentioned much about my family. To be honest, I don't really like to talk about them. I was fairly close to my mum growing up, but my father was a bully. He made life quite difficult at times.'

The Professor paused, looking over the view of the water. He seemed to be thinking, trying to determine how much to tell her. It was obviously something quite painful.

'I wanted to go to boarding school but my parents – well, my dad – wasn't having any of it. And whatever my dad said, my mum usually went along with. But for some reason, my mum decided to back me up on this. It wasn't something she usually did as we all wanted a quiet life and sometimes it was easier just to let him get his way. I was only fourteen but I could hear them arguing downstairs. I was in my bedroom and after a bit it all went quiet. I heard my father's footsteps on the stairs and knew he was coming for me. I'd had thrashings before but I knew this was going to be different. He was angry with me that I had managed to get Mum on my side.'

Alison could barely breathe.

Sighing heavily as if trying to release the memories,

The Professor continued, 'Needless to say I never went to boarding school. My father wanted me to study law and what he wanted, he got, of course,' he said bitterly. 'I studied law but I hated it. I managed to take a few literature classes, though, to keep me sane, which I enjoyed. I graduated and worked in a law firm but I was never good enough to progress very far. After a while, I left and went travelling. I kept in touch with my mum but things with Dad were always strained. Eventually, it became easier just to keep in touch from afar.'

The Professor glanced over at Alison. 'You must be wondering why I'm telling you all this now.'

Alison looked into his eyes. Behind the drunken haze, she could see his pain. 'I'm sorry I hurt you. I will get counselling, you know,' he told her. 'I promise.'

'I know you will,' Alison responded, her heart reaching out to the little boy who had faced such violence growing up. As they wrapped their arms around each other, Alison felt something inside her shift. Compassion replaced anger, understanding replaced fear. It was difficult to imagine growing up in such a household, especially as her upbringing had been so safe and full of love. Her parents doted on her and her sister, showing only love and kindness. There and then she made a promise to herself to do the same for him.

27

Kate

He called her every day now. Normally, just after lunch when her youngest was taking her nap and her eldest still in school. They talked for almost an hour every time. He had asked to come over to her flat on several occasions, but so far Kate had refused him. What if her daughter woke up and found a strange man in the house? It made her feel sick to her stomach just thinking about it. She was responsible for the welfare of two children and she knew she was playing a risky game. So why was she still seeing him? Why was she loitering near the phone waiting for it to ring like a love-struck teenager? She felt ridiculous but at the same time unable to stop. His calls gave a sense of meaning to her days, something to look forward to, a break from the predictability.

She attended the writing classes and the book club but they had now become a pretence – a veil masking her secret life. She told no one, not even Jan, although Jan still teased her about being the teacher's pet. She went along with it to avoid arousing suspicion, but she didn't like lying to her friend. At the end of the class, she walked home with Jan but then slipped back again to meet him. Sometimes it was eleven thirty before she got home at night. Her husband was normally fast asleep but on the rare occasion that he asked, she told him she'd gone out for a drink with the rest of the students. If he ever noticed that she was distracted, he never mentioned anything. If she thought about it, their relationship had undergone a subtle change; she no longer asked him to help out with the kids. She no longer complained if he was late, or missed the train or didn't talk to her. She just got on with it and left him to his own devices. He normally took the girls out on Saturday mornings, to the park if it was good weather, and into town if it wasn't. She used to spend the time relaxing but these days she took the opportunity to write. The words poured out of her and she hoped to write enough for a book rather than a novella. A dam had broken in her mind and her thoughts were flooded with ideas, plotlines and characters. Endless discussions with Mr Barnes about structure, syntax, phraseology and different genres kept them connected, and Kate felt like a sponge soaking it all up. He wasn't long out of graduate school and was a little younger than she was, yet he seemed much more mature to her, due to his extensive knowledge. Every question she asked, he had an answer, or if he didn't, he knew where to find it.

One Saturday morning, when the family had gone into town, Kate had spent her precious few hours of free time at Durham Main Library. From the outside, it was a 1970s monstrosity, but inside it was a haven of information. Everywhere she turned, books beckoned and the topics of psychology, mathematics and art made a welcome change from *James and the Giant Peach* and other Roald Dahl books. The choice was almost overwhelming, but as she browsed the shelves she became oblivious to everything but the array of titles. Her mind turned them over, deliberating, debating. She put no boundaries on herself. If a title appealed to her, she would gently slip it from its place and sit herself at one of the many tables, ensconced in the silence. It was the first of many weekend visits, and occasionally Mr Barnes would join her, so it was perhaps inevitable that he would eventually ask her to his place. The first few times she declined. She knew that if she accepted it would take their relationship to a different level, something she wasn't sure she was ready for. There was a part of her that encouraged her to go, whispering that she deserved it and that no one would ever know. But there was also a part of her that was frightened. Frightened at how deep she had got herself into this situation and now wasn't sure how to get out. Whatever problems there were at home, she knew that infidelity was not the answer. But Mr Barnes was persistent and the dangerous mix of flattery and vulnerability adulterated her soul. While their meetings were regular, their alone time was intermittent because of her family commitments, but as in so many affairs, it made their secret liaisons all the more intense.

'If you don't want to come to my house, why don't we book a hotel for the afternoon?' he asked one rainy Wednesday afternoon on the phone.

Kate laughed at the absolute implausibility of his suggestion. 'Yep, I'll just leave the kids at home and tell my husband I'm popping to the shops,' she joked.

'I'm being serious,' he responded. 'If we plan it, we could easily make it happen.' He paused. 'I need you, Kate, I need to be alone with you,' he whispered into the phone. 'Have you any idea how frustrating it is to see you every week and not be able to touch you?'

Kate's breath quickened at the sudden intimacy.

'Imagine spending an entire afternoon in a beautiful hotel, talking and relaxing in each other's arms.'

Despite the sordidness of the suggestion, he had managed to make it sound glamorous.

'It would be amazing,' she said, quick to reassure him.

'Surely, you can get away for a few hours?' he asked. 'Any day, just let me know and I will be there. I will arrange everything.'

Beneath the urgent tone, Kate sensed a slight impatience to his voice. It had been several weeks since that first kiss on the bridge, and since then they had had just a few snatched moments here and there. Eager to placate him, Kate promised she would give it some thought. 'Let me have a think and see what I can do,' she promised.

'You do want to be with me, don't you?'

'Yes, of course! It's just not easy with the girls.'

'I know, but I'm sure you can find a way. I'll call you in a few days.'

He hung up the phone, and Kate was left staring at the receiver, a slight panicky feeling rising in her chest. She didn't want to lose him but how could she manage to arrange it?

As it happened, it was easier than she had hoped. Ironically, the opportunity came through her husband.

Arriving home one evening, he told her about the family day trip his company had arranged. It was to take place on a Saturday, in three weeks' time. The company was paying for the whole department and their families to take the train to Edinburgh for a family day out. The girls were beyond excited. They had never been to the Scottish city and their father had enticed them with stories of castles and beautiful gardens, princesses, palaces and dungeons. It was a full day trip and Kate knew that this was her opportunity. Somehow, she would have to get out of going and her husband would have to take the girls alone. He would be reluctant to cancel and disappoint them. Kate had never been deceitful, but she was amazed at how easily it came to her once she had made the decision. Over the next couple of weeks, she built up the trip to massive proportions. She read everything she could get her hands on about Edinburgh and promised the girls the day out of a lifetime. Her husband was amused by their enthusiasm and by the time the Saturday in question dawned bright and clear, Kate was actually sorry not to be going. But the night before, she went to bed early, telling her husband that she didn't feel well. During the night, she went to the bathroom several times, making loud retching noises.

'Are you OK?' her husband asked her as she loudly groaned her way back into bed.

'Food poisoning,' she whispered. 'I'm sure I'll be fine in the morning.'

The train was leaving early the next day and as she made her excuses, promising to stay in bed until the bout of sickness had passed, Kate wished them an enjoyable trip.

*

They were on the early train but Kate still waited two hours before getting up in case they came back. As she swung her legs out of bed and onto the floor, she felt removed from herself, as if it was another woman who was lying to her family and going to a hotel to meet her lover. She had surprised herself by falling back to sleep. What kind of person can sleep when they're doing something so deceitful?

Kate thought. Heading to her wardrobe, she tried to choose what to wear, but, still undecided, she took a long shower, washing her hair and shaving her legs before applying layers of lotion. She couldn't remember the last time she had spent so much time on herself and it felt like luxury. Slowly towel-drying her hair, Kate looked in the mirror. Her eyes were bright and her skin was glowing. She dropped her dressing gown and looked at herself from every angle. What would he see? Would he see the scars from childbirth or a tall, slim figure with endless legs? In the early days, her husband had constantly referred to her legs – said they were the best he had ever seen. Kate pushed the uncomfortable thought aside. Things had moved on since then, though, and she was now both a mother who had brought two children into the world, yet still a young woman who needed to be desired. Putting on her only set of matching underwear – years old now but hardly worn so they were in fairly good condition – Kate eventually chose a casual outfit of jeans and a warm top. She didn't want to make it look like she had made too much effort and, besides, would he really care what she was wearing on the outside?

*

She had agreed to meet him at lunchtime and as the time grew closer for her to leave, Kate was becoming more and more apprehensive. What the hell was she doing? Having got her bag and jacket, she tried to block out the image of her family in her mind by shutting the front door firmly behind her.

*

As Kate made her way to a hotel she had never heard of on the outskirts of the city, whatever guilty second thoughts she was having were brushed away as soon as she saw him. Dressed all in black, in jeans, T-shirt and a leather jacket, with the ever-present current book he was reading in his hand, he represented everything she had lost: her youth, her freedom, her education. In that moment, she forgot about everything she had gained. She saw and felt only her need for him. She needed this, she told herself, and she deserved it. He didn't embrace her in public. Just led her to the lifts and up to their room. Neither of them spoke. But as soon as they were locked in the privacy of the room, her passion rose to meet his own, the shame of being such a cliché melting under his touch.

*

Afterwards, alone while he took a shower, she lay on the bed in the hotel room, her eyes focused on the ugly ceiling lamp. She had expected to feel guilty but all she could feel was regret that their lovemaking was over. She would never forget the afternoon, locked in a room with him, putting everything aside as she revelled in the pleasure of his attention, his hands, his words. She had surprised herself by just how confident she was in bed with him, her own demands matching his. As the bathroom door opened, she brazenly stood up, the sheet slipping to reveal her nakedness. With her eyes she conveyed exactly what she wanted and in three steps, he was upon her, their lovemaking starting again in earnest.

*

'So, Mrs Robinson, how was your afternoon?' he joked, as he made her a cup of coffee from the hotel room's amenities.

She punched him playfully on the arm. 'Enough with the Mrs Robinson! I'm only a little older than you. Besides,' she said flirtatiously, 'is it not adding to your street cred to be with an older woman?'

'My older woman – I like it! Sugar?' he asked.

'Just one, please.'

Coming over to join her back in bed, he put the coffee on the side table and started to nuzzle her neck. 'As much as I would like to stay here for the rest of the afternoon, I have to get back,' he said.

Disappointment washed over her like a pail of cold water. Hadn't he said the whole afternoon? She had envisioned them ordering room service and lounging together in bed for a few more hours yet.

'Yes, me too,' she replied, pretending that she had other things to do.

He bounded out of bed, pulling his clothes on, and she followed suit. 'Don't worry about anything; I will sort the bill out downstairs,' he said with a brief kiss. 'You go on ahead and I'll give you a call tomorrow.'

It was an abrupt ending to the afternoon, and Kate felt her emotions fall fast and hard from the crest they had been on. Taking the stairs two at time and into the lobby, Kate stepped through the main doors. She kept her eyes down, avoiding eye contact with the hotel staff, wondering if they guessed what she had been up to. Shame – so blissfully absent earlier – came over her in waves.

28

Catherine

2 April 2011

Dear Catherine,

Thank you for your letter – I really don't know what I would do without them anymore. The newspaper you sent was also very much appreciated. I hope you're enjoying some of the warmer weather. At last! It's been a long winter this year. This morning, I could see bunches of daffodils growing, a welcome sign of spring.

Another month has finally passed – some seem slower than others but, as I approach my parole, the time really seems to be dragging. As you can imagine I'm hoping for a good outcome so trying to keep as low a profile as possible. Even just one misdemeanour can affect the decision, so I have been spending a lot of time reading and researching. Preparing for a parole interview is quite intensive. I have decided not to use a lawyer in the actual interview – no one knows my situation better than me so I will represent myself. There's a lot of paperwork to gather and everyone needs copies in advance so they can read through it. In a way, though, it's good for me to have something to focus on and keep me occupied. It's beneficial to have a project to work towards rather than just ticking the days and the nights off, one by one.

As I have been preparing, a lot of memories have been coming back to me. I remember my disbelief that I, a respected and educated member of the community, could end up in a place like this. It seemed so unfair. I was in shock, I suppose, and couldn't really associate myself with being a convict. The people in here are seriously evil – the complete scum of society. For the few first years, it was a long hard struggle to accept that I was inside with such people. I went through the emotions of anger, denial, rage, blame and depression and, after a very long time, finally acceptance. As humans, we are all capable of killing – all it takes is provocation and the loss of control for just one second and your life is never the same again.

There are people in here for all types of crimes but, as Category B status, they are mainly the worst of the worst – rape, murder, robbery with firearms... I'm sure you get the idea. And we all have an opinion of the person, depending on the crime. For example, anything to do with children is severely looked down upon and that prisoner is pretty much an outcast with little protection. It's almost like we have built our own judgement system within our imposed system. I suppose it's a way for us to take back a little control.

Or perhaps it's just human nature to be able to categorise people into boxes. I also think it's a way of making us feel better about ourselves – sort of like, 'well, yes I did a bad thing but it's not as bad as the raping and killing of a child'. I promise you I'm not trying to be flippant, just trying to explain how it works. Either way, the irony is not lost on me, but we do what we can to survive in here – both mentally and physically – and we do need each other, whether for cigarettes, protection or company. When being isolated, there's a strange sort of comfort in knowing that just on the other side of the wall there's another person.

The other people we regularly interact with, of course, are the guards. We give them nicknames, depending on the way they treat us. Some are better than others. 'Thefty', for example, loves nothing more than confiscating things. We dread him being on postal duty because he's been known to pocket a few things from the inmates' letters. But he's not the worst. 'Suit' (rhymes with Brute) likes to get unnecessarily physical, especially if a fight breaks out. Sometimes, I think he almost encourages it, taunting us. I suspect he just likes the action. It wouldn't surprise me, though, if one day he ends up in here as well. Some of the guards are all right, however, and you can have a bit of banter with them if you catch them in a good mood. The morning shift seems best but those doing the night shift tend to be harsher. I guess the time must pass slowly for them with little to do except patrol. Not half as slowly as it does for us, though. I'm sure the guards will be happy to get rid of one extra prisoner. It can get really crowded in here at times. I often wonder what made the prison guards decide that this career was for them. I mean, did they just wake up one day and decide they wanted to work in a prison? I wonder how much they get paid. Anyway, I seem to have digressed so I best leave it here.

Michael

*

7 April 2011

Dear Michael,

I'm glad you enjoyed the paper and, hopefully, it wasn't too out of date by the time you received it. They are easy for me to save so I will try to send you one each time. There should be one included in this letter as well. Check out the article on page five – I really found it quite amusing!

You're right, the warmer weather is more than welcome, and in the Lake District it also feels like it has been a long time coming. But with the celebration of Easter approaching and the arrival of flowers (we also have lots of daffodils), it's starting to feel a little more like spring. At this time of year in the Lake District, I always like to think of William Wordsworth's poem. Do you know it?

I wandered lonely as a cloud
That floats on high o'er vales and hills,
When all at once I saw a crowd,
A host, of golden daffodils;

Beside the lake, beneath the trees,
Fluttering and dancing in the breeze.

Visiting the Wordsworth House and Garden was one of the first things I did when I arrived in the area. Set in Cockermouth, it's the birthplace of the poet and is still kept as it would have been in the 1770s. It was truly magical. Do you like poetry? I'm not an avid reader but I do like the odd piece.

This season also means spring-cleaning. Although I dread it, once I get into it I get quite a lot of satisfaction from a good clear-out. I literally do the house from top to bottom over a couple of weeks. Nothing goes untouched and even my husband gets involved by doing the garden, the gutters and the drains. What an exciting life we lead! Saying that, we have perhaps had more than enough excitement and I find a general contentment in the routines of daily life. Spring-cleaning is my chance for a new start and every year, I have the same thought: perhaps this year will be different? Cleaner, fresher, better. Isn't that what we're all looking for?

I remember when Helen used to start back at school after the Easter holidays, there was always such promise in the air, although some stress as well, as exams were usually held during that term! I don't know who used to get more anxious, Helen or myself! Looking back, I realise all that anxiety was a complete waste of time. She loves studying – did I mention she has a Ph.D.? It was a very proud moment for my husband and me.

I'm also planning our summer holiday at the

moment. We're going abroad this year and very much looking forward to it. Even Helen has decided to tag along with 'the olds', as she calls us! It's been a very long time since we have gone abroad for a holiday, or even taken a local holiday, for that matter, so the trip will do us all good. While the Lake District is beautiful, I'm ready for a change of scene and some stable weather! We're planning to go for a fortnight and I'm in the middle of researching where to go. It has to be mixture of relaxation for Helen and me, and things to do for my husband. I was thinking of a cruise, as you can visit many destinations in one holiday, but I'm not sure Helen would be too keen. My other idea was to visit the Caribbean. Personally, I have always wanted to go to Asia but it's such a long flight, and I'd rather spend the time on the holiday and not on a plane, if that makes sense. Still, I dream of tasting sushi in Japan or exploring the Ganges in India. There's still so much to see in the world!

Your last letter really gave me a true picture of your life there. If only for some company, the other inmates must provide some distraction to the daily grind of incarceration. I can imagine there are some really dangerous people and you are on your guard at all times.

I think it sounds like a good idea to lay low in the lead up to your parole. It's only a couple of months now and I really hope it works out in your favour. It will be good to have something to look forward to.

Catherine

Catherine placed her pen down. She headed to the kitchen

to put the kettle on for a coffee and absent-mindedly watched the water boil. The simple routine brought her back to her own domestic reality as opposed to the darker themes of her letter writing.

Sitting back down at her desk, she reread the letter. She feared she had written too much about the holiday. She was not convinced that a prisoner would want to hear about someone else's holiday plans, especially after being locked up for so long. But she was starting to run out of things to talk about and it was true, she was really looking forward to the break. She had convinced Richard to go all out – business-class flights, a five-star hotel, and she was planning to book some spa treatments. She had even managed to get Helen to agree to a shopping trip to Manchester to get some new summer clothes and swimwear. Catherine wanted to make it as special and as memorable as possible as she suspected it may be the last one they took together as a family.

29

Alison

Out of habit, Alison had started sitting in the same seat for each of her lectures. She noticed that another student was sitting next to her but it was only when he finally turned to introduce himself that she realised he had been sitting next to her for the last few days. His name was Mark and he was from Dublin. He was quick to laugh and had an easy-going nature that relaxed Alison immediately. It became the norm for them to have a few minutes of catch up before and after the class. After a year sitting by herself, it was nice to have a friend whom she could chat to and talk with about the course. They often bumped into each other in the library or study hall and started having a sandwich together for lunch. His sense of humour and easy take on life made her laugh and she enjoyed his company.

'You know,' he said one morning as they walked to the law library, 'I had a bet with a friend on how long it would take you to notice me.'

Alison laughed apologetically. 'I'm sorry, I get so engrossed in taking notes, I rarely notice what's going on around me!'

'No kidding! I even tried borrowing your pen to get you to realise a handsome chap was sat next to you!'

Smiling, Alison remembered. 'Yes, and you didn't realise that you had a pen right in front of you, which sort of gave it away.'

'Ah, so you did notice something?'

'Of course! Go on then, how much money did you lose?'

'Twenty quid,' Mark replied, deadpan.

'What? Seriously! Why would you bet so much money?'

'Because I was certain you wouldn't be able to ignore my Irish charm! Little did I know how much of a bookworm you were,' he teased.

Still unable to believe that he had lost so much money, Alison said, 'I'm really sorry it took so long to formally meet you but it's your own fault for betting on me!'

'That's OK. How about you make it up to me, by writing up my notes for a week?' he winked.

Alison laughed. 'I have enough of my own work to do, without doing yours as well! Come on, let's get going before the library gets too full.'

'Aw, Alison, you're such a tough task-master, and there's me feeling sorry for myself, and you just throwing salt into the wound now,' he complained, his Irish accent sounding like music to Alison's ears.

'How about this?' Alison countered. 'I'll buy you a meat pie on the way and we can each write up half the notes, photocopy them and swap – will that make it up to you?'

Mollified, Mark replied, 'That's more like it!'

*

Of course, he never let her buy the pie, but instead cheerfully chatted with the shop girl, who was so charmed by him she gave it to him on the house.

'See!' he said gleefully to Alison, as they stepped out of the pie shop into the sunshine. 'Not everyone is impervious to my charms. Just you!'

'Unbelievable! If only that poor girl knew what I have to put up with!'

'Come on now, Alison, why do you want to bring a man down?'

'I don't – I just want this man to move a bit faster so we can get to the library!'

'OK,' he replied. 'I'll race you!'

And with that he was off, running ahead until Alison, a great runner in her school days, could no longer resist the challenge and raced to catch up with him before gleefully pipping him at the post.

*

They were twenty minutes into their study session before he could no longer resist talking again. 'You cheated!' he announced. Alison smiled to herself, winning her own little bet that Mark wouldn't be able to last a full hour without getting the last word in.

'What? No, I didn't! It's not my fault you're out of shape! Too many pies?' she asked cheekily.

'I have the physique of a gazelle,' he retorted, making her laugh as he flexed his arms and legs. 'And besides, who was carrying all the books, then? I was at a disadvantage.'

Fair point, Alison thought. He was an old-fashioned gentleman in that respect and always offered to carry the books.

'I thought you said you were the utmost of upstanding citizens and your father would stop your allowance if he caught you letting a woman carry the bags.'

'True, true,' replied Mark, 'but he also said, "To let a woman win, you will reap the rewards," so I, Mark Gallagher – which means lover of foreigners, by the way – challenge you, Alison O'Studious One, to a rematch!'

'Ssh!' A girl with large round glasses looked over at them impatiently.

Stifling their giggles behind their textbooks, Alison struggled to compose herself. How did he come up with this stuff, she thought, suppressing the urge to laugh uncontrollably as Mark continued to dramatise their rematch with his eyebrows.

Taking her pen, Alison wrote 'Stop before you get us kicked out!' on a piece of paper and slid it under his nose before determinedly focusing on the chapter she was meant to be reading.

Things were quiet for a good ten minutes before a note came back surrounded by doodles. 'Rematch! Tonight, along the towpath, winner gets their notes done for a week.'

As she looked up at him, he winked at her and whispered to her to get back to work before she got them kicked out of the library.

*

Alison breathed in deeply. She had always loved the river and, as the nights got lighter, the view of the water lifted her spirits. It was good to be outside and as she gently stretched her muscles in preparation for the run she felt her body respond in protest at the amount of weight she had put on.

Mark jogged up to her, exclaiming in mock surprise, 'Hey, you made it! I made a bet with my friend that you wouldn't show, but here you are, and I'm twenty quid down again!' he joked.

'You have to stop betting, but most of all you have to stop betting on me!'

'Never!' he said, winking.

'OK, so let's get down to business,' said Mark. 'A 100-metre sprint is approximately from here to the third bench – can you see it?'

'Yes.'

'Whoever reaches the bench first is the winner. You ready?'

'Yep, bring it on, Gallagher.'

As both of them adopted the starting position, Alison could feel the blood surging through her body.

'Ready, steady, go!' shouted Mark.

Feeling the adrenalin, Alison focused only on the finish line. She didn't notice the team of rowers as they pulled their way up the water. She didn't notice the birds as they called to each other, or the way the leaves of the trees whispered as the gentle breeze stroked them. For the first time in a long time, her mind and body were working as one, moving together to achieve a goal. It didn't matter that it was just a stupid race. Alison felt alive and connected, so it was with a sense of surprise that she noticed Mark had overtaken her and was just crossing the finishing line.

'Come on, slow coach!' As he cheered her on, Alison pretended she was running a marathon, breaking the ribbon with her body.

'Whoop! You did it!'

'I did, didn't I?' said Alison, breathing heavily. 'Shame

you beat me, though. I'm so out of practice!'

'Don't worry, if you like I'll let you practise with me,' he joked. 'No, seriously – you're fast – where did you learn to run like that?'

Alison felt her breath return to normal. 'I did a lot of running at school. I loved it but I have let the student lifestyle get the better of me, unfortunately!'

'It's a way of life for me,' said Mark in a rare moment of seriousness. 'It helps get rid of stress, and keeps me fit.'

'You? Stressed? I don't believe it!'

'Ha-ha, no, you're right. It doesn't happen often. Maybe because of the running. Right, shall we go and recover with a pint?'

'Why not?' responded Alison. 'I'll quiz you on the chapter over a beer.'

Mark groaned. 'You always have to spoil everything!'

Swatting him on the head, Alison laughed. 'OK, how about I invite my friend Laura to join us. You'll love her!'

'Now that sounds more like it!'

'Come on, I'll race you to the pub!'

*

Laura had arrived just as they had found a table and were sitting down. She looked gorgeous, thought Alison, even with no make-up on, and her hair scraped back in a ponytail.

'Nice to meet you at long last, Mark! Alison's talked a lot about you,' said Laura, winking at Alison.

'Let me guess, she says I'm tall, handsome, funny and charming?'

Alison laughed. 'More like distracting! Do you know

what he did today?' turning to Laura. 'We nearly got asked to leave the library!'

'Anyone who is able to get Alison kicked out of the library is a genius, in my book!' joked Laura. 'Alison works far too hard!'

'You see,' Mark pleaded to Alison. 'Genius. Now that's what I'm talking about.'

'Was she about to quiz you when I walked in?' Laura asked Mark.

'What? How did you know that?'

'Because she has done it to me sooooo many times!'

'Er, hello! I'm right here!' Alison wasn't sure how she felt about being the topic of conversation.

'Right, ladies, shall I get the drinks?' asked Mark, standing up. 'What are we having?'

Over a few beers, Mark kept them both entertained with stories of his childhood and his extensive family. With four sisters, and being the only boy, Mark grew up being the centre of their affection.

'Well, he's nice!' said Laura as the girls walked back up to their rooms together.

'He is, isn't he?' responded Alison, missing the subtle inflection in Laura's voice.

'He seems very fond of you,' continued Laura.

'Really? No, I think he sees me as an easy target for all his jokes!' laughed Alison.

'But you have a good time together?'

'Always,' replied Alison thoughtfully. 'He's so easy to be with.'

'And how's things going with... you know who...?'

'Fine, fine,' responded Alison quickly. 'He's good. Busy, actually.'

'Well, better for me, then,' said Laura. 'Thanks for inviting me today. I really enjoyed it.'

Alison beamed at the unexpected thanks. 'You're welcome – I enjoyed it, too.'

'You go on ahead to your room,' said Laura. 'I'll bring the tea and the biscuits.'

'Sounds good!'

While she was waiting, Alison straightened up her room and prepared her bag for the next day. Just as she had finished packing, her phone beeped. Opening the message, she saw a message from The Professor.

What are you up to? x

Quickly writing back, she typed:

Thinking about you and revising x

It wasn't strictly a lie. She was planning to do some work shortly, but it had been good to have a break and The Professor had told her he couldn't meet up tonight as he had work to do.

Her phone beeped again, just as Laura walked in with the tea. Glancing down, she read:

Will be away for work for a couple of days. Call you soon x

The race forgotten, Alison's heart beat a little faster. Where had that come from? Remembering her vow to trust him, Alison stifled the urge to call him and ask him what was going on. Surely he would have known he was going away in advance? They had just seen each other yesterday and he had made no mention of it.

'Everything all right?' asked Laura, placing the tea next to her. 'You look a little tense.'

'No, everything's fine.'

'That damn phone – it owns you.'

Alison looked up, her thoughts still on The Professor. 'Sorry?'

'See what I mean? It distracts you. You're always checking it.'

Alison sipped her tea. It was true, she did seem to be continually checking her phone and she got nervous if she forgot it in her room. In fact, she had been known to run back for it, making her late for her class. Not many students had a mobile phone and she had told Laura her parents had bought it for her as a way of keeping in touch. She tried to keep her bills down, but having looked at her bill last month, Alison could see she had already gone way beyond her budget.

'Here, give it to me,' said Laura, and before she could stop her she had taken the phone and put it in a drawer.

'But—'

'No buts,' replied Laura, determinedly. 'Here, have a scone.'

Helping herself absent-mindedly, Alison tried not to panic about not having access to her phone. What if he called tonight? She hadn't responded to his last text and she needed time to think about how to word it.

'… and then I said, well, I need to check with Alison to see what she's doing. Shall we go shopping for new outfits? I'm so bored of everything in my wardrobe.'

Alison slowly realised Laura was talking about the

up-coming social. It was going to be a grand affair and every student looked forward to it.

'Sorry, check with me about what?'

'About who we're having on our table. Shall we invite Mark? I think he would scrub up rather well in a tuxedo!'

'Sure, sounds good. I'm happy to shop with you but I don't think I'll buy anything.'

'Do you want to have a look in my wardrobe? Perhaps we can swap?'

'Sure, that sounds good but I don't think you'll find anything in mine that you like.'

'Why don't we take a look in mine now?'

As Alison started to try different outfits on, encouraged by Laura, she realised what a good friend she had. There weren't many people who would open up their designer wardrobe and let someone help themselves. As she looked at herself in the mirror, a chiffon creation swathing her body, Alison didn't see her beauty. Instead all she could think about was where The Professor was going and for how long.

*

'He's coming!' announced Laura over breakfast.

'Who's coming?' replied Alison, still half asleep.

'Mark.'

'Coming where?'

'Duh! You're really not with it today, are you? To the social! He's on our table. I definitely think you should wear the red dress – it looked amazing on you. He'll love it.'

'I don't think Mark will really care one way or the other what I'm wearing,' said Alison tiredly.

After Laura had left the night before, Alison had called

The Professor but he didn't pick up the phone. Instead she sent him a text.

She had stayed awake most of the night waiting for the phone to ring and finally, at 2 a.m., she accepted that it wasn't going to – certainly not that night, anyway. Having fallen into a fitful sleep around three thirty, she had woken up late and stumbled to breakfast. Laura, in contrast, was looking fresh and rested.

'So that's you sorted, but what about me? Shall we go to Newcastle on Saturday and try to find something?'

'Sure, sounds good.' Picking up a piece of toast, Alison decided to eat on her way. 'OK, I'm off – I have a ton of work to do.'

'Maybe you should go back to bed,' said Laura. 'You look wrecked.'

'Thanks – I feel it. I would love to but I have so much to do today. I'll see you later.'

Relieved to be with her own thoughts and not to have to make conversation, Alison walked slowly along the towpath towards the library, the energy she felt from the night before nowhere to be found.

*

Alison and Mark were sitting in a quiet coffee shop, near the window. They were supposed to be reading and planning for their next course-work assignment but instead they had found themselves talking about the much-anticipated social. She hadn't admitted it to Laura at the time, but she was looking forward to it even more now that Mark was on their table. The events were always a lot of fun and much-needed respite from all the hard work.

As Alison looked out of the window, she could see the cobbled streets leading up to the cathedral, and while the temperatures were freezing, the sky was clear and blue. She felt a moment of contentment as she wrapped her hands around the mug of coffee and enjoyed the warmth of the café, the smells of freshly baked bread and cakes, and the easy-going company of Mark. They had become firm friends and she felt she could talk to him about anything. Well, except The Professor. If Mark had heard the rumours, he never mentioned anything. She hadn't really had a male friend before, and she enjoyed the subtle differences between him and a female friend. He was slightly traditional in his manners, holding doors open for her, carrying her book bag and walking her back from lectures if it was dark at night. But it was his easy take on life that really appealed to Alison. He never seemed to worry about anything (he didn't see the point, apparently), and would always see the funny side of a situation. As a result, he was well liked and Alison couldn't help feeling just that little bit special that he chose to spend so much time with her. As they sat there, talking and laughing, Alison felt a chill ripple across her body. She looked around, thinking a gust of cold had blown in, but was surprised to see that the door of the coffee shop was closed. Her unease increased and she was suddenly aware of being watched. Out of the corner of her eye, she caught the scarlet hue of a scarf through the window as a man abruptly turned and walked away. Noticing her distraction, Mark said, 'Are you OK? You look like you've seen a ghost.'

Bringing herself back to the present moment, Alison replied, 'Yes, of course – just thought I saw someone I knew, but it couldn't have been. It must have been someone else.'

Quickly changing the subject so Mark couldn't see how

shaken she was, Alison said, 'Right, we really need to get on with this reading! How about you do chapters one to four, and I'll do five to eight and then we can swap notes and discuss.'

'Aye, aye, Captain!' He was always joking with her about her dedication to study and he'd told her that if he passed the course it would be because of her pushing him to work.

Settling into the textbook, she could still feel the gaze of the man she'd seen through the window. It couldn't have been The Professor – he was away on a conference... wasn't he?

Chiding herself, she realised how paranoid she was being. There were lots of people with red scarves in the city. It could have been anyone. She tried to read. When she lost her train of thought for the third time, she took out her phone and texted him.

Hi, how are you? How's the conference? Miss you x

He never replied.

*

It was three days before she heard from him again, and by that time Alison felt like she was going mad. Despite numerous texts to check where he was, there had been no response and no calls. Her anxiety had increased into full-scale paranoia and she was constantly checking her phone. She found it difficult to eat, study and even sleep. In fact, when she did manage to sleep, her mind was haunted with darkness – strange, undefined images that couldn't be described.

Finally, he got in touch, and Alison could've sobbed with relief at the thought of the mind games finally coming to an end.

'Where have you been?' she asked, trying to calm the hysteria in her voice.

She had expected him to call full of apologies, explaining that his phone had broken or the battery had died and he'd forgotten the charger. Instead, his tone was cool.

'I told you I was going to a conference.'

'Yes, but why didn't you respond to my messages? I was worried sick!'

'Really? It seems to me like you've been too busy to spend much time thinking about me.'

'What do you mean?'

'How's Mark?' he asked before promptly hanging up.

Alison stared at the phone in disbelief. What was he playing at? Doubts chased each other around in her mind and as she struggled to work out what was happening, the stress of the last three days took its toll. Frustrated, she grabbed the nearest object, which happened to be a hand-held mirror, and threw it as hard as she could at the wall. As she stared at the broken pieces, she felt she didn't know who she was any more. Certainly she didn't recognise this violent, paranoid person. As she felt herself falling deeper and deeper into an abyss of confusion, the last of her self-confidence was washed away by doubt and fear.

30

Kate

While waiting for her family to come back from Edinburgh, Kate spent the remainder of the afternoon and early evening in bed trying to concentrate on reading her book. But what should have been a rare few hours of bliss turned into a horror movie as her mind started to explore the various potential scenarios. What if the train had crashed and her last interaction with her family was based on lies? What if someone had seen her leaving the hotel? What if someone had seen her and Mr Barnes together? As the thoughts tumbled around in her mind, Kate became more and more agitated. The guilt came over her wave after wave, each one more powerful than the last, until she couldn't bear to lie still any longer. Pacing the small flat and not knowing what else to do, she made a bargain with God, a ritual she used to do when she was a little girl, although of course the stakes were much higher now.

'Dear God,' she whispered, 'if you bring my family home safely today, I promise I will never break my marriage vows again.'

She rarely went to church these days but her childhood had been punctuated with visits from the local priest to their school and she had developed her own sense of faith over the years. Saying the short prayer over and over again, it was only when she heard the key in the lock that she got up and ran to take the girls in her arms as if they had been away for a lifetime rather than just a day.

'You seem better,' her husband commented, as he closed the front door behind them.

'I feel better,' she replied. 'It must have just been a twenty-four-hour thing.' Quickly avoiding his gaze, Kate turned her attention back to her daughters.

31

Catherine

Catherine was lying in bed half asleep but she knew someone was there watching her. The king-sized bed was on the same wall as the bedroom door, and as she turned her head to the left, she could see through the hazy darkness the slow movement of the door opening just inch by inch. She placed her hand protectively over her belly, feeling the kicks of life that often woke her in the early hours of the morning. Strangely, her husband wasn't next to her and she had expected to feel scared. Instead she felt outraged. Like a volcano, adrenalin surged through her body like an energy force at the audacity of the intruder. With no warning, the door suddenly flung open, and the shadow of a figure took three jumps across the bedroom and sat in the armchair in the corner of the room. His arrogance was reflected in his position as he placed one ankle on his knee, his fingers interlinked behind his head, looking as relaxed as if he was sunbathing by a pool. The volcano erupted and Catherine jumped out of bed, screaming at him, while throwing every object within arm's reach at him. Laughing, the shadow slowly dissolved, leaving nothing but a burning inferno in Catherine's heart.

As she abruptly woke up, her hand on her flat stomach, Catherine turned over, trying to get rid of the imprint of anger stamped on her mind.

32

Alison

Alison arrived home for the summer holidays fifteen pounds heavier. She felt her body was a representation of what was going on in the inside, and she knew her inner self was in turmoil. She rocketed from incredible highs, when she felt she could take on anything, to soul-destroying lows that saw her spend endless hours in bed, trying to block out the world. The last few weeks had been very stressful with exams and coursework, and towards the end of term she had rarely gone out. She had never managed to find out if The Professor had been at the conference or somewhere else. He had told her it was a last-minute arrangement covering for someone who was ill. There seemed to be no way to know for certain. Besides, she wasn't even sure of herself any more. The lack of sleep didn't help. With a huge amount of effort, she had managed to reassure him that she and Mark were just friends and, while The Professor seemed placated for now, she felt as if they had gone one step forward but two steps backwards.

When the exam results had come out at the end of term,

she was disappointed to see that her marks hadn't improved very much at all – certainly not as much as she would have liked, and it sent her into another spiral of worry and anxiety.

She decided to go and see The Professor in his office. She normally went after lunch, around two o'clock, but feeling the urge to talk through her disappointment regarding the exam results, she decided she would pick up some sandwiches and head over an hour earlier than usual. It had started to rain as she was leaving the sandwich shop and she hurried to the law building, cursing herself for forgetting her umbrella. Having finally arrived, Alison was soaked through. She hurriedly wiped under her eyes, certain that her mascara was streaming down her face. No matter, she would sort herself out in his office.

Without knocking, she entered, expecting him to be pouring over one of his papers. Instead, the blonde post-grad student was sitting on his desk, while he was leaning over her, showing her something in a book. They were so close, they were touching and Alison could only stare as the two of them looked up in surprise at the drenched figure who had burst in, holding a soggy paper bag of sandwiches.

He recovered quickly. Standing abruptly, he closed the book, and said: 'Alison! Of course! I'm so sorry – I forgot we had an appointment today to discuss your coursework.'

Alison, finally catching on that he was making a point of her being a student, responded, 'No problem. I can come back another time if you like.'

'It's fine – can you just give us another few minutes while we finish up here?' he asked.

'Of course.'

Alison backed out of the room, distractedly heading to the toilets so she could dry off, her unease growing as she battled to remove the image of their heads touching as they poured over the book. She remembered what Laura had said about him being into students. Was it true? Surely she would know if he was seeing someone else? Alison thought back to the odd missed arrangement, the last-minute conference, the phone number, the unanswered texts. Was she being completely blind or just paranoid?

Despite his confession of his violent childhood, the various incidents she had experienced with him had frightened her, and while he seemed to play them down, she was uncomfortably aware that they were more than just arguments. It seemed to get worse when he drank. He was a big man and he could easily put away a couple of bottles of wine in a night. But sometimes, even when he hadn't had a drop, he was a little rough, especially in bed. So much so that Alison had become nervous about sleeping with him, which of course made her tense up even more. After one particularly difficult evening, he had said to her, 'You know, I love it when you resist me – it just makes me want you even more.' Alison hadn't known what to say. She wasn't deliberately resisting, she just felt a sense of unease. Maybe this is how sex is supposed to be, she thought miserably. But she missed his gentle touch and when she asked him about it, he had laughed.

'Come on, Alison, you're not a quivering teenager! Besides, I know you like it!' he added with a conspiratorial wink.

And sometimes she did. But sometimes, it seemed to go too far, and she really didn't like it. His temper still flared and she never knew what would set him off. And while she wasn't being beaten black or blue on a regular basis; the indent of fingerprints, the slight bruising around the neck and the shoves and pushes all inevitably left their mark, both physically and emotionally.

Mark had noticed a bruise once. It was on the inside of her wrist, revealed when she had taken off her coat, her sleeve rucking up. She had quickly pulled it down again, but not before Mark had caught sight of it.

'Hey, how did you manage that? It looks nasty,' he asked.

Caught off guard, Alison wasn't sure what to say. She tried to keep it vague. 'I banged it between the door and doorframe. You know that quick-shutting door in the library? That's the one. I was trying to hold on to a load of books, get through the door, while answering my mobile. Needless to say, the door won that round!' Alison laughed, aware that she was talking too much and laughing too loudly. That was several weeks ago now. How long had she been covering them up for?

She tried not to annoy The Professor. She rarely brought up Laura's name and she certainly didn't mention Mark. Her workload and the pressure of the exams had provided an excuse that she didn't have time to go out with her friends, so it wasn't an issue. Instead, when Alison had cautiously broached the subject of summer plans and the fact that her friends were going on a girls' holiday, The Professor had suggested that the two of them go on holiday instead.

Alison was taken aback by his suggestion. She had never been on holiday with a boyfriend before. She was partly excited and partly petrified, but maybe it was exactly what they both needed.

'We would have to keep it a secret,' he said. 'But it would be fun, wouldn't it?'

'It would be,' responded Alison, trying to keep the uncertainty out of her voice and wondering what on earth her parents would think.

As if reading her mind, he said, 'You could tell your mum and dad that you're going on holiday with the girls.'

'Yes, that's an idea,' responded Alison, although she wasn't keen on such levels of deceit, especially to her parents, whom she knew would prefer to know the truth, even if they didn't agree with her decision.

Without telling her, he made all the arrangements that very same week and it was booked for the first week of August – a trip to Santorini. He showed her the brochure and it looked absolutely beautiful – and expensive.

'Don't worry, I know what it's like living as student. I've taken care of everything. Just bring a little spending money and your bikini,' he said, smiling. Pushing away her annoyance that he had booked something without checking with her, Alison kissed him, trying to feel lucky that she was with someone so generous.

Now, lying on her bed at home, she imagined the two of them, hand in hand, strolling along the beach, tanned and relaxed, able to enjoy each other's company without worrying about being the subject of gossip. As she sat up, she felt the extra tummy rolls over her waistband and realised she also needed to lose those extra pounds before she would be seen dead in a bikini.

*

As Alison relaxed into the comfort of her childhood home, she could feel the tension of the term fall away and she took comfort in the daily routines of family life. Away from everything, it gave her chance to think, and she was surprised to find that she was sorry she was missing the girls' holiday in July. When she spoke to Laura on the phone, it was all Laura could talk about. Perhaps she could do both, thought Alison. But there was no way she could afford it. Despite

Laura begging her to change her mind, she hadn't told her friend her holiday plans – she just mentioned that she might be going away with her family for a bit. Another lie. Lying was all she seemed to do lately. And she was about to tell another one.

Sitting down to breakfast with her parents one morning, she explained that she would like to go on holiday with some of the girls from her course in August and while she had some savings for the actual holiday, would they mind giving her a little spending money? Her parents, eager to make their daughter happy, were pleased that she was taking a break with friends and, after getting all the details of the hotel and the flights, agreed. Her mum even took her shopping, generously splashing out on some new summer outfits, a beach bag, new sandals and a beautiful sundress. It would have been the perfect day if it hadn't been punctuated by deceit, and the fact that her mum was so excited about spending a day shopping with her daughter only made Alison feel worse. She had never lied to them before – she'd never had the need to – and it tainted the experience of what should have been an enjoyable trip.

Alison tried to ignore the growing feeling that something about the upcoming holiday felt wrong. But as August drew close, she found she could push the doubt away and she got excited at the thought of a week with The Professor. It would be different when they were on holiday. Their lives in Durham were so stressful with all the studying and research, it was bound to have an impact eventually. But in the Santorini sun, surrounded by glorious views, she knew they would be able to relax. She had only seen him a handful of times in July as he was busy working, but unlike at the start of their relationship where his communication had been sporadic, he was now regularly messaging and calling. Alison started to feel something like happiness again and her mum commented on it. She was pleased Alison had settled into university and had made some good friends. If only she knew.

*

The night before she was due to leave, Alison and her friends from school had arranged to meet up in town for a few drinks. They were planning to go to a new restaurant and bar. It had a large outdoor terrace and Alison was looking forward to an evening outdoors to enjoy the long summer night. Saying goodbye to her parents, she left the house at seven o'clock and while en route quickly messaged The Professor to tell him her evening plans and that she couldn't wait to see him tomorrow. She was meeting him at Newcastle Airport at lunchtime to catch their afternoon flight.

Arriving at the restaurant, the girls quickly settled in to an evening of conversation over drinks and food, and Alison got so caught up with her friends' news that it was a good three hours before she thought to check her phone. Picking it up, she was shocked to discover ten missed calls. Thinking an emergency had happened, she quickly checked her phone. They were all from one number – The Professor. Slipping away from the table, she called him back immediately, wondering what could have happened. Perhaps his mum was ill again and he was unable to go on holiday? He answered on the first ring and before she could even say hello, he was shouting down the phone.

'Where the hell have you been?' he roared. 'I've been calling you for hours.'

'I'm sorry,' Alison sputtered, her mind conjuring up all sorts of emergencies. 'My phone was in my bag, and I didn't hear it above the noise. What's happened? Are you OK? Is your mum OK?'

Alison barely deciphered the following outburst; it was so full of rage and accusations that it was some time before she managed to work out that there was no crisis; no one had died or had an accident, he had simply wanted to get hold of her. He started accusing her of lying and being with another man, she could feel his hatred emanating down the phone, and her hands started to shake. She became frantic, and it took over twenty minutes, and a lot of reassurance that she was simply with her school friends and would be heading home in less than an hour, to calm him down. Finally, she hung up but not before he extracted a promise that she would message him when she reached home. Her heart was hammering in her chest, and she wondered how a nice evening could have gone so wrong in just a few minutes.

Agitated, Alison felt the happiness drain out of her and, as she headed back to the terrace, she called a cab to take her home.

*

Alison rooted around for some change for a coffee. She hadn't slept well at all, and her eyes were puffy from the mix of crying and lack of sleep. Her parents, thankfully, had put it down to too much indulgence the night before, and had cheerfully waved her off in the taxi, none the wiser. Alison was dreading seeing The Professor; what would he say to her? What would she say to him? But if she was expecting an apology, none came. Instead he had acted like nothing had happened, gave her a kiss, hugged her warmly and seemed genuinely happy to be with her. Alison wondered if perhaps he had been drinking the night before and simply couldn't remember. Or was this just simply normality now? Either way, she wasn't going to tempt another argument by bringing it up. Confused, she excused herself to the ladies' and spent a few minutes making herself breathe normally. It's all going to be OK, she told herself. After a few minutes, she splashed her face with cold water, applied some mascara and lip-gloss and plastered a smile on her face. Heading out to join him, she tried her best to match his good mood about their holiday.

*

Looking back a few weeks later, she thought their trip had turned out better than she'd expected. He was the perfect gentleman while they were away, making her coffee every morning, preparing her sun lounger, pulling her chair out for dinner as they enjoyed juicy fruit and vegetables, crumbly feta cheese and ice-cold glasses of crisp white wine. He was also the perfect tour guide, explaining all the different landmarks and their history. Santorini was made for lovers and they saw several weddings during their holiday. As a series of volcanic islands, the rugged cliffs made for beautiful vantage points for watching the sunset. The Professor was an excellent storyteller and the legends he told made the island come alive for her. Even their lovemaking – and Alison could now call it that – had taken on a less aggressive rhythm and he spent time caressing her, gently pulling her into a world of pleasure. Gradually, Alison relaxed into him, enjoying the romance of her first love. Their life in Durham seemed a lifetime away and as the lazy, sunny afternoons gave way to carefree, romantic evenings, Alison's apprehension gradually receded as quietly as the tides of the Aegean Sea.

33

Kate

'You're complaining that there isn't enough money for food shopping, yet you just spent a fortune on a dress. When the hell do you wear a dress anyway?'

It was a Sunday, the day after the Edinburgh trip, and neither she nor her husband had slept well the night before. Both girls had come into their bedroom, complaining of monsters under the bed. Having taken them back to their own room twice, sheer exhaustion had made Kate let them slip into bed between them. It was the only way anyone was going to get any sleep. Despite sleeping through most of the girls' midnight antics, her husband still looked tired and his mood was sour. It wasn't helped by the fact that he had found a receipt in the desk drawer for a dress she had bought. She had meant to put the receipt somewhere else but she must have forgotten. She hadn't planned to buy anything for herself. The girls needed new shoes and they had gone into town to see if she could find any in the sales. It was the bold, black and white polka-dot pattern that attracted her attention, along with the eye-catching, red 'SALE' tag, in the window. The dress was fitted with a wide black belt that emphasised her tiny waist, made to look even smaller by the shoulder pads. Going into the shop, Kate slipped it from the hanger. The girls were agog at their mother wearing something so different from her usual leggings. As soon as it slipped down over her frame and she heard the girls' cries of approval, she knew she wanted it. The sales assistant had zipped her up at the back.

'You look lovely, pet,' she had said, her blonde bouffant bobbing up and down with her nods of approval. 'Is it for a special occasion? An anniversary, perhaps?'

'Sort of,' replied Kate. 'Well, not really. I just wanted to treat myself to something nice.'

'That's as good a reason as any,' laughed the assistant. 'I would say that dress is a keeper!'

Making a snap decision, Kate had bought it. Even at half price, it still wasn't cheap but it was hardly the fortune that her husband was making it out to be.

'Please don't exaggerate. It's been months since I bought myself anything and I have worn dresses, if you'd only just bother to notice,' she retorted. His annoyance antagonised her. She was fed up of being criticised. She made do on so little and got no thanks for it. Recklessly, she continued, 'I don't hear you complaining about the money spent on new shirts I bought for you.'

'They're for work!' her husband blustered. 'I need to look somewhat professional.'

'Oh, and I don't – is that it? Just because I stay home and look after the children, I shouldn't feel good about myself? I work just as hard as you do, the only difference is, you get paid for what you do, I don't.'

Slamming the kettle on to boil, Kate started warming to

her theme, her tiredness, frustration and guilt combining into one flammable outburst. 'And while you're at it, you may also want to consider the fact that I'm on call 24/7. When do you get up with the girls at night? Never. When do you give them their breakfast? Never. You only have to consider yourself and your needs. Well, I'm fed up of your selfishness. I'm fed up of always being the last person to be considered, while everyone else always gets what they want. I'm always the one in this family to make sacrifices.'

'What, you mean like your writing classes and your book club?' he responded. 'I would hardly say that's putting yourself last. You've been going out more and more lately. What ideas have they been putting in your head?'

'Nothing. Or rather, nothing new, anyway. I have ideas of my own, believe it or not, and it's about time you started appreciating that I'm more than just a housewife who's here to cook and clean after you.'

'Please, Kate, give me a break and stop acting like the down-trodden wife you are so clearly not. I really don't have to stay and listen to this!'

'That's right, you don't. Storm out like you usually do and leave me to do everything. Nothing new there.'

From the girls' bedroom, she could hear crying. 'Great,' she said sarcastically. 'The girls are crying now – just one more thing that I have to deal with. Well, while you're out, enjoy yourself at the pub. You're quite happy to spend money on a beer, aren't you, but when it comes to something for me, that's a different matter.'

'What the hell is wrong with you, Kate?' he stormed, as he put his jacket on.

'You and your treatment of me – that's what's wrong. I deserve more,' she said with a certainty that surprised both of them. 'Maybe you want to think about that when you're out at the pub with your mates.'

The door slammed and Kate simmered, slightly frightened at the depth of the feelings she had just unleashed. Her guilt was making her act in ways she hadn't anticipated. Out of the two of them, she was usually the peacemaker, or at least the one who left the arena first. This time she had kept going. Why, she asked herself, as she went to console the girls. What was the point? It made no difference. Nothing changed but she didn't know how much longer she could keep going. He was the father of her children and the breadwinner, but as a husband, she needed more from him. Time, attention, appreciation – was she really being so demanding? She understood that they were both tired but surely a civil conversation between them shouldn't be too much to ask for?

*

It was surprisingly early when her husband came home. Kate had been reading and only had the light out a few minutes before she felt him join her in bed.

'I'm sorry,' he whispered. 'I know I can be a right idiot sometimes, taking you for granted.' The absence of beer fumes was unexpected. Turning to him, she could only just see the outline of his face in the darkness. He gently touched her cheek, and Kate closed her eyes under the gesture, wishing everything could be different. She let the apology settle like a snowflake, before it evaporated into the night, lost in the void between them.

34

Catherine

20 June 2011

Dear Catherine,

Finally! The date of the parole board has been set for 10 July. I got the news from the warden this morning and wrote immediately to let you know. For some reason, I feel that you have brought me good luck and I hope it will continue. Thank goodness I have been preparing – you have given me the encouragement not to lose faith and, of course, you were right all along.

I'm hoping for full release. It's happened before in certain situations when an inmate has done a minimum of ten years with minimal disruption during their time. But anything could happen so I'm not going to be too optimistic. I have tried to be patient by focusing on preparing for my interview with the aim of a full release. Many inmates often end up back here because they simply can't cope with the outside world, or the only world they know is crime so they inevitably end up back in the system. The prison provides access to mentors and workshops to help make the transition from prison and I know that I need to somehow be able to build a stable life once I'm out, as well as a strong network. I may be a changed man from the one who came in but I know I will face difficulties from the people I once knew in Durham.

I have dreamt many times of the day I will be released. How it will feel, what I will do, how the world will have changed, how I will have changed. I think one of the first things I will do is head to the sea and look out across the horizon. I think only the vastness of the water could get me to comprehend just how big the world is out there after the confines of a prison cell. I would also enjoy the simple things – a hot cup of coffee, a comfy chair, a bookshop, an art gallery. But even if I get released, I will always be on parole and there are a lot of rules to follow. They can take me back inside at any time and I won't be able to travel further than a fifty-mile radius without permission. Ironically, there's a security factor when being in prison. You don't need to think: you get told when to get up, when to eat, when to shower, when to exercise. On the outside, there's so much choice I suspect it might be overwhelming. I have tried to keep up with everything that's been happening in the world during the last eleven years through books and newspapers, but things will still have changed a lot, especially technology. I haven't actually used one myself but they say the smart phone has changed everything.

Writing to Friends of Inmate Rehabilitation is also

a way to prepare prisoners for release and I think over the last few months you have really helped me.

This is a short letter as I now have kitchen duty, but I wanted to get this off to you as quickly as possible to let you know about the parole date and to thank you for your support so far. I will write again very soon.

Michael

P.S I hope you had a great holiday – you must tell me all about it in your next letter.

*

4 July 2011

Dear Michael,

I am so happy for you that your date of parole has been confirmed. That's a huge step forward and I feel sure that the outcome will be in your favour. Your dedication to good behaviour, repentance and commitment to reforming will pay off, I'm sure. I have also enclosed a letter of recommendation of your character following our months of correspondence. I'm not sure how much it will influence the parole board's decision but every little helps. It sounds like you're in with a good chance. I'm sure you have so many thoughts running through your head about it all, it must be quite mind-boggling, to say the least. The world has definitely changed in the last eleven years – the smart phone has pretty much taken over. Social media – although I don't use a lot of it – is also huge. My daughter, on the other hand, never seems to be off it.

I'm sure, though, that the city of Durham hasn't changed that much – maybe some new shops and park benches but the river still flows and the cathedral is still standing, so that will be a comfort for you.

Thank you, yes, we had a really good holiday. It was very relaxing and the Caribbean was simply beautiful. It was good to get a change of scene and spend some quality time with family, especially in a destination such as St Lucia! While Richard had imagined himself doing all sorts of activities and exploration, when he got to the resort, he found himself so relaxed, he ended up with Helen and me by the pool most of the time. I think it was good for him, though. He clearly needed it and we all slept a lot, lulled to sleep by the sound of the ocean. The resort was all-inclusive so we didn't have to worry about where to go for meals or drinks, as it was all provided for us. And the food was incredible. We ate grilled fish caught that very same day, followed by tropical fruit as well as papaya salad, coconuts, aromatic chicken and rice, all washed down with a thimbleful of rum, of course! In the last week, we hired a car and explored the island. We took some amazing photos and there's a particular one of the three of us looking so happy. The ocean and the blue sky are in the background and we have our arms around each other. Helen and Richard are giggling about something, and when I saw it I knew I had to get it printed and framed. It now sits pride of place on my desk, and I look at it often as a reminder of the happiness we shared. For now, though, it's back to the daily routine. Richard has gone off to work and I am returning to my volunteer

*work. Sadly, I doubt we will be taking another holiday
like that again for a while.*

*The other news is that Helen recently received a
job offer of a teaching post in Lancaster, so we're all
thrilled about that. She has been job-hunting for so
long, it's great to see her so excited about this new
stage in her life. Over the next couple of weeks, I will
help her move to her new home. Once she's settled, I
will feel a huge sense of relief, as well as sadness. My
job as a mother to Helen is almost done.*

*Do keep me posted on how your parole hearing
goes and I shall keep everything crossed for you. Who
knows, perhaps once you're released, we can meet up?
It would be good to meet you in person.*

Best of luck,
Catherine

Catherine sat back in her chair looking at the photo of her
family on holiday. It really had been an idyllic time and she
would treasure those memories for ever. And with Helen now
getting a job and moving to Lancaster, everything seemed to
be falling into place. Catherine had been worried about her
daughter and had said so to Richard on several occasions.

'Do you think she's all right, Richard?' she'd asked one
evening when Helen was out. 'I do worry about this economic
climate. The papers think that 2011 is going to see the highest
levels of unemployment since the nineties,' she added.

'I know,' replied Richard. 'This year is not looking good
for anyone, and youth unemployment is especially high. But
she has so much going for her. She's qualified up to the hilt
and she's persistent. She must have been for a least twenty-

five interviews. Plus, you have to remember, she's not in London or any other major city – she's in Cumbria so of course it's going to take a little longer than normal.'

'I know you're right,' said Catherine, slightly buoyed by her husband's words. 'But still...'

Knowing what his wife was waiting for him to propose, he saved her the time by offering. 'Would you like me to have a quick word with her and just check in to see how's she doing?'

'Would you?' Catherine's relief that Richard would sort it was visible. 'Yes, if you could, that would be a load off my mind.'

'You know, you could always just ask her yourself,' suggested Richard.

'I know,' Catherine responded. 'But she'll take it so much better coming from you. She might just think I'm interfering.'

'Of course, she won't,' said her husband. 'But if you prefer it, I'll have a chat with her this weekend.'

And that had been the end of it. Richard had checked in and reported back that Helen was fine, and even hopeful about her latest interview. But still Catherine had worried. So, when Helen gave them the news that she had been offered a position and was moving to Lancaster, Catherine had been thrilled. She was also feeling emotional that her daughter was leaving the nest. To overcome it, she went into full organisational mode, vowing to put all her energies into helping Helen find a flat of her own and move her things. An Excel spreadsheet was drawn up and checklists were prepared. Helen laughed when she saw them.

'Mum, I really don't think we need a project management tool on this one. It's just a case of packing my clothes and my duvet and off I go. It's only down the road.'

'But what about flat hunting? Won't you want your own place?'

'Oh, no. For the first few months I'm going to flat share until I get a feel for the city. In fact, I'm planning to look at a few places this weekend. Do you want to come with me?'

'Yes, of course! I would love to.'

It had been an enjoyable day out for Catherine, although she was slightly horrified at some of the flats they saw. Some were no better than student digs, with the sink overflowing with dishes and beer cans littering the living room. But the last flat was something special and Helen loved it on first sight. The large bedroom was flooded with natural light and had an en-suite bathroom, which gave a little more privacy. The kitchen was brand new and even the small garden was well maintained. The owner, Sarah, was a young woman in her mid-twenties who had recently qualified as a dentist and was looking for someone to help pay the bills. Catherine liked her immediately and Helen paid the deposit on the spot.

'Well, I'm so glad you got sorted, love,' Catherine said as they drove back from Lancaster. 'I have to admit I was getting a bit worried after seeing the first couple!'

'I know – me, too! I didn't think it would bother me, to be honest, but I've obviously got too used to you looking after me so well!'

It was rare that Helen gave compliments and Catherine squeezed her daughter's hand in recognition. She knew that Helen was more than ready for this new chapter in her life, but she was going to miss her daughter immeasurably.

*

The day of Helen's departure arrived quickly, and as she

said her goodbyes on the doorstep, Catherine hugged her daughter close, hiding her tears in the embrace.

Embarrassed, Helen jokingly protested. 'Mum! I'm only going down the road – it's just forty minutes away!'

'Be careful there, won't you, love?' Catherine almost pleaded.

'I promise I will, Mum. Please don't worry.'

'I know, I know... I just want you to know, though...' Catherine paused. It was now or never. She wasn't one for sentimental platitudes but she needed to say this to her daughter now otherwise she would regret it for the rest of her life.

Holding her daughter's face in her hands, Catherine spoke. 'I just want you to know that I love you very much, OK? Always remember that, and no matter what happens, never forget it.'

'I love you too, Mum,' replied Helen, surprised at her mother's outpouring of love. 'Take care, and I'll call you when I get there,' she shouted as she jumped into the car with her father, the car so full there was only room for the two of them.

Catherine watched the car disappear, and, with tears streaming down her face, went back inside.

35

Alison

As she lay on the floor, Alison felt a ringing in her ears. She wondered if her eardrum had burst. Curling into a ball, she instinctively wrapped her arms around her head. Although she was expecting blows to rain down on her, one after the other, they didn't come and the suspense was almost as agonising as the pain. The blow had come out of nowhere and, as she fell backwards, shock and disbelief fought for her attention, swiftly overtaken by pain, as her head collided with the coffee table. Wedged between the sofa and the iron legs of the table, Alison tried to crawl forward, but the ringing in her ears was getting louder and it seemed easier to lay her head back down and wait for the maelstrom to pass.

*

Alison looked at herself in the mirror. How could she go to her lectures, or anywhere else for that matter, looking like this? The bruise was making itself comfortable on her cheek, a vivid flash of colour that would eventually turn an ugly mix of purple and green. Gingerly, she examined the rest of her body. Her head didn't seem to be bleeding, but there was a large bump that was pulsating under her fingers, which she tried to ease by holding an icepack against it. She would have to use make-up to cover her face. Her head pounded in protest at being upright, and a headache had started to form. She wasn't sure if it was caused by fear or the coffee table. Either way, she had to go to her lectures. He may be controlling every other part of her life, but she was determined not to give up on her studies. The icepack still held to her head, Alison walked slowly to the bedroom, checking for signs of dizziness. As she sat at the dressing table, ready to do her make-up, her eye caught sight of a postcard from Santorini. They had picked it up during one of their evening walks of the island and never sent it. Alison had brought it home as a souvenir. Her fingers traced the outline of the startling blue and white domes against the endless view of the sea, trying to hold on to a happier time. It was only the presence of the postcard that confirmed their holiday hadn't been a dream.

The term hadn't started off like this, thought Alison. In fact, it had started off great. She was full of energy, feeling relaxed after her break and ready to start a new academic year afresh. Her skin was lightly tanned, her hair struck through with golden highlights from the Greek sun.

'Wow, you look like you had a great summer,' said Laura when they met on the first day of term.

'I did, thanks! Very relaxing,' responded Alison, smiling.

'I wish I was that happy when on holiday with my parents,' said Laura, a tinge of envy underlying the statement. 'They used to do my head in, always wanting to know where I was going and who I was with!' She paused. 'They're good eggs really, though, and I couldn't do without them!'

She waited and then, when Alison wasn't forthcoming, she asked, 'So where did you go?'

'What?'

'With your parents – where did you go?'

'Santorini,' Alison said, relieved at being able to tell the partial truth.

'Very nice,' responded Laura. 'Did your dad change his mind or something, then?' she asked.

'Sorry?'

'You said your parents had decided against going abroad this year,' reminded Laura.

'Er, oh, yes, well, in the end he decided to treat us,' said Alison. Eager to get off the topic of holidays and her parents, she went to put the kettle on. Alison was too engrossed in her happiness to see Laura watching her back, quizzically.

The first few weeks of the new term passed by in a flurry of activity. They were second-year students now, no longer the newbies, and the arrival of a new batch of freshers gave Alison a renewed feeling of confidence. She knew what to expect, she knew where she was going, and most importantly, she was in love. Their holiday had cemented their relationship. One evening on Santorini, he had turned to her and told her he was in love with her. It had been the perfect moment with the sun setting, and the gentle bubbly effect of the champagne. Alison had never felt so happy. Any previous doubts were washed away as she gazed into his eyes and leant in to kiss him.

It was a few weeks into the following term when it happened. Alison was at The Professor's flat, her books spread out on the dining table before her. He was sitting on the sofa, flicking through the TV channels. He seemed agitated, unable to watch one show for too long. Out of the corner of her eye, Alison saw him get up and go into the kitchen. She heard the bottle uncork and he returned with it along with a full wine glass. He hadn't brought one for her, which was unusual, but she tried not to read too much into it, focusing on her books instead. The class was in the middle of family law and she was quite enjoying it. In fact it was her favourite part of the course so far. It was an hour later when she realised that the television had been switched off and he was sitting there looking at an empty screen. The wine bottle was half empty. He wasn't moving and his face was unreadable. Alison felt a knot of fear and quickly suppressed it.

'Everything OK?' she asked, cautiously.

He didn't respond. Alison got up and went over to sit next to him.

'Hey,' she said gently.

He slowly turned his head towards her, their eyes meeting – his of steel and hers of apprehension. She went to hold his hand but he placed a firm grip on her forearm.

'Why do you have a love bite on your neck?' he asked.

'Wha-what?' Alison responded. She was confused – where was this coming from? Her mind raced, trying to work out what he was seeing.

'There's a love bite on your neck.'

'Well, that's from you,' she said logically.

'No,' he responded firmly. 'It's covered in make-up. Why would you cover it in make-up if it was from me?'

'I had classes today and I couldn't go in like that,' responded Alison. She knew very well what it was. It wasn't a love bite – it was a bruise from their lovemaking the night before, when his hands had been around her neck. It was quite large and difficult to cover so she had added a layer of concealer along with the scarf bought especially for the purpose.

The grip on her forearm started to get stronger. Alison tried to ignore it.

'I spent all that money on you for our holiday and this is how you repay me?' said The Professor, his voice rising. 'Who the hell is it? Is it that guy you always sit next to in class? Eh? What's his name?' He already knew his name so she didn't know why he was asking. When she didn't respond, he shouted. 'Answer me!'

'Mark,' she said quietly.

'Mark,' he confirmed menacingly. 'Exactly. Is that who you've been carrying on with behind my back?

Alison instinctively knew she had to do something quickly. She began to protest, declaring her love for him, now and for ever, and how she wouldn't be able to live without him. She wondered if it sounded to him like she was begging as much as it did to her. And then something snapped inside and she became angry. She couldn't live like this anymore.

'It was you, you idiot!' she screamed at him, tears of frustration threatening to fall. 'You were the one who did this to me. Nobody else, and certainly not Mark. He would never do something like this. And, by the way, it's not a love bite!'

It was the wrong thing to say. But it was too late. As the back of his hand collided with the side of her face, she felt herself thrown against the coffee table by the sheer force of him. Bending down, he grabbed her by the hair, yanking her head back. As he leaned over her, she could smell his sour breath and she thought she was going to be sick.

'If you so much as even look at that guy Mark, never mind

have cosy cups of coffee with him, it's over between us. And what's more, your law career will never even get started because I'll make sure the whole faculty knows exactly what you're like – a slut.'

As he let go of her hair, her face fell on the carpet. Unable to move, she heard the front door bang shut, and as she lay there, the shock of such an assault flooded her entire being. Absorbing the pain, its throbbing undulations peaking and falling, she felt a familiarity that she was coming to dread.

36

Kate

It was a couple of days after their meeting in the hotel that Kate had received a call from Mr Barnes. 'Hey, Mrs Robinson,' he said warmly. 'How are you?'

Her body responding before her mind, Kate felt herself flush with warmth at the sound of his voice.

'I'm fine, thanks. How are you?'

'Good, good. Sorry I had to rush off like that. Afterwards, I thought it may have come across a bit rude.'

'No, not at all. You have things to do, I understand,' replied Kate, not really understanding at all.

'I do – in fact, I'm trying really hard to get my thesis finished but I'm finding it harder than I thought I would,' he said ruefully.

'I'm sure writing a thesis can't be easy,' said Kate. 'How many words do you have left to do?'

'Pretty much all of it!' he laughed. 'No, just kidding. I would say I'm around halfway there but I seem to have lost all motivation to work since I met you! How about you make it up to me and we meet tonight after the class so I can get my inspiration back?'

Unable to resist, Kate found herself agreeing. One drink wouldn't hurt, she decided. She would be out at the writing class anyway.

'OK, but just for an hour as I have to get back.'

'That's better than nothing. Let's meet in our usual spot after class. See you later.'

Kate slowly replaced the handset in the cradle. Her heart had already begun thumping at the thought of seeing him again. What was wrong with her?

'Was that Daddy on the phone, Mummy?'

'No, darling, it wasn't.'

'Who was it then?'

'No one important.'

'Can I watch TV, Mummy?'

'Yes, just for a few minutes.'

Surprised at her mother's consent, her younger daughter jumped onto the sofa before Kate could change her mind while Kate made herself a cup of coffee.

'Mummy,' her daughter said, her eyes still glued to the screen.

'Yes?'

'What's a thesis?'

And in that moment, Kate knew if she was going to continue down this path, she would have to be more careful.

*

Kate was cold, the watery sunshine of the day long gone. Slipping her cardigan out of her bag, she waited for Mr Barnes to arrive. It had been several weeks since their illicit afternoon, and these walks along the riverbank had become something of a regular thing. At night it was quiet, apart from a few students walking into town, too lost in their own groups to pay much attention to them. The walk ran alongside St Hild and St Bede College, with the flow of the river guiding them through the scenic surroundings, contrasting with the grey stone of HM Prison Durham, which stood solitarily in the distance. While loving her hometown, since meeting Mr Barnes Kate had a new-found appreciation for how lucky she was to live in such a beautiful city. With its iconic cathedral and historical buildings, the familiar landmarks had taken on a new meaning with him: Elvet Bridge where they shared their first kiss under the stars; the grounds of the cathedral as they strolled amongst the tourists, their hands no more than brushing against each other in an attempt to be discreet. But Durham was a small city and she knew that she was being reckless by meeting in public during the day. As a result, they met in the evenings, the darkness hiding what had now become a full-blown illicit affair.

Kate checked her watch. He was already fifteen minutes late. She paced impatiently. She couldn't be held up too long. She had told her husband she was just popping round to see Jan to discuss a homework assignment.

Where was he, she wondered. Usually, he was early, often impatiently waiting for her, claiming that he was too eager to see her to wait at home. They had made the arrangement a few days ago and normally he called her on the day to reconfirm he could still make it. Today, he hadn't called and Kate wondered if she was being stood up. Glancing up, she heard him before she saw him, quick footsteps almost running towards her.

'So sorry,' he said, catching his breath. 'I was doing some research and lost track of time.'

Surprised, yet understanding, Kate replied, 'No problem, you're here now. I missed you.'

'And I missed you,' he said, his arms around her, but when she looked into his eyes, she sensed distraction.

'Shall we walk?' he asked.

Kate let the silence settle around them as they strolled down the towpath, the gentle hum of nature providing a therapeutic backdrop. Tentatively, Kate spoke. 'Is everything OK?'

'Yes, sorry,' he reassured her. 'I've just got a lot on my mind at the moment with work. How was your week? You did great in class this week, by the way. Your book is really coming along.' Pleased that he had noticed, Kate jumped on the conversation, explaining a new idea for a character she wanted to include. As they walked back towards the city, Kate was reluctant to leave; yet she had to get back. Saying her goodbye with a kiss, she tried not to mind that he had not made another arrangement to see her. Usually, he wouldn't let her go home without making her commit to a date, a shared joke that had become their parting conversation. Hurrying back, Kate tried to put it out of her mind.

*

He didn't call the next day. Or the next. By the third day, Kate thought she might go slightly insane with his game-playing. She had done everything possible to distract herself, including baking, which had ended in disaster. She hadn't left the house in three days apart from dropping and picking up her daughter from school and her younger child was getting fed up. Kate had checked the phone several times to make sure there was a ring tone and it hadn't been disconnected. Finally, on the fourth day, he had rung. He sounded normal but busy.

'Hi, how are you?' he had asked.

'I'm fine, thanks,' the slight chill in her voice conveying her displeasure. She would let him do the talking, she decided.

'What have you been up to? Sorry, I haven't rung for a few days, it's been really busy.'

'That's fine, I've been busy too.' Kate could hear a lot of noise in the background, as if there was music being played.

'Good, good... Listen, I have to go. Can I call you later?'

'Yes, if you manage to find the time,' Kate retorted, before slamming down the phone. Furious, she paced the living room. What was the point in him calling if he was only going to speak for a few minutes, she asked herself, forgetting that she had stayed by the phone for three days.

'Mummy!' her little girl called out from her bedroom.

'What?' she snapped.

'Are we going out now?'

Kate sighed. She couldn't let him get to her like this, to the point where she was taking it out on her daughter.

Composing herself, Kate walked slowly to her daughters' room before taking the girl in a big hug. 'Of course we are! Where would you like to go?'

Her daughter looked at her in astonishment, before quickly announcing, 'To see Emma!'

'Then to see Emma, we shall,' said Kate in a singsong voice. 'Would you like to wear your princess outfit? It's a nice day.' Unable to believe her luck, the child ran to her wardrobe to put on the dress, then placing the tiara firmly on her head. Taking her sister's tiara, she put it firmly in her mother's hands, informing her that she could be her lady-in-waiting. 'You have to do everything I say,' she instructed.

'Yes, Your Royal Highness,' Kate replied with mock seriousness. She took a moment to enjoy the innocence of childhood. If only everything was as easy as make-believe princesses.

'Are you ready to go, Your Royal Highness?'

'Yes, Mummy. And Emma can be my second lady-in-waiting.'

'I'm sure she would love to be,' said Kate, keeping the doubt from her voice. Emma could be a bit of handful. 'Let's go then and see if they're at home.'

*

They had spent an enjoyable afternoon at Emma's house. Her mother, Susan, was easy to get along with. They had met at the baby clinic just after the girls were born and had bonded almost immediately. Their daughters were just a month apart in age, but both had suffered from colic as babies and both girls had older siblings. Susan was also a housewife and Kate felt they had a lot in common.

'Hi, Kate, so nice to see you! It's been a while,' said Susan, when they had arrived.

'I hope you don't mind us dropping by?'

'No, not at all! I was just wondering how to keep Emma entertained, so perfect timing! Come in, come in, I have the kettle on. Coffee?'

'Yes, please!'

'So, how is everything? I haven't seen you for ages! All OK?'

Kate felt guilty that she hadn't been in touch with her

friend for a few weeks. Something else Mr Barnes was responsible for, she thought angrily.

'Yes, sorry about that. The family has been keeping me busy!'

'Yes, I know what that feels like,' sympathised Susan. 'Emma has decided that she no longer wants to sleep through the night and would like to have a tea-party at 2 a.m.'

Susan was making light of it, but Kate could see she looked tired. 'Oh dear,' she said. 'It isn't easy, is it? People say it gets easier but I'm beginning to think that's only going to happen when they leave home!'

'And we've still got a long way to go before then!' chuckled Susan. 'Anyway, in the meantime, there's always cake. Here, try some of this carrot cake. You look like you've lost a few pounds, Kate.'

'Yes, I think I have – probably from running around after the children.'

'I wish I could lose a few – I can't call it baby weight anymore.'

As Emma and her daughter played together, Kate relaxed in Susan's warm and good-natured company, regretting not having been in touch sooner.

At three thirty, they went to collect their elder children from school before heading to the school library for story time. After two hours, Kate hugged Susan goodbye. 'We'd better be getting back home for tea and bath time.'

'Ah yes,' said Susan, 'my favourite part of the day.' She winked. 'It was great seeing you and the girls – take care of yourself.'

Hurrying her daughters out, Kate started walking back home. The weather was still fine, and the girls skipped ahead of her as she pushed the empty buggy. After five minutes, her younger daughter got tired and wanted to ride home in the buggy. Kate strapped her in and was just straightening up when something caught her eye. The coffee shop on the corner was always busy. She never went there herself as it was one of the more expensive ones, but as the door opened Mr Barnes stepped out. He was smiling and talking to someone behind him: a woman with blonde hair and a slick of red lipstick, which made her stand out. Inexplicably, Kate wanted to call out to him, but before she could do so he had turned towards the woman and reached for her hand. As she stepped out of the coffee shop, both turned to walk down the street, but not before Kate saw them lean into each other. She watched as she saw him kiss the woman full on the mouth, her red lips crushed under his.

*

Inserting her key into the lock, Kate noticed her hands were shaking. Her thoughts were whirring around her head as she tried to understand what she had seen. Maybe it was just a friend? But deep down she knew that the woman with the red lips was more than that. Going on to autopilot, she got the girls fed and into the bath before putting them to bed. Having kissed each one good night, she closed the door quietly. Only when she was in her bedroom did she let out a shuddering sob of disappointment. How could she have been so foolish? What did she expect? He was a single, educated, good-looking man with a fantastic career ahead of him, surrounded by beautiful, young students. She was a bored and frustrated housewife who could only reference high school and sixth form on her CV. Had it all been one big lie? Was his praise of her writing just a way to get what he wanted? The thrill of the chase? As she lay down on her bed, she saw her papers covered in her scrawl on her desk. She thought of how he had flattered her, telling her how talented she was, how much he had enjoyed her writing. Yet, it was all a scam. His praise meant nothing and he probably said it to every woman who took his fancy. In one quick movement, she had grabbed the papers and was ripping them into shreds, her anger propelling her to destroy any reminder of him. Exhausted, she lay back down, the pieces scattered around her like confetti. While she had known their relationship wouldn't last for ever and eventually he would move on, she hadn't expected it to end so abruptly. And while it hurt to see him with another woman, what hurt more was the doubt that now plagued her about her work. Perhaps he hadn't thought she had promise after all and had only said all those things in order to get what he wanted?

37

Catherine

13 July 2011

Dear Catherine,

I still can't quite believe it. But the parole hearing went well and I am to be released next month. As I'm writing this, I feel like I'm living a dream. I'm sorry I didn't have time to write in the lead-up – I spent even more time preparing and there was a lot to do, especially as I didn't have any legal representation and decided to represent myself but I honestly believed that I could do a better job and I did! Saying that, it wasn't easy. As you can imagine, I didn't sleep that well the night before, but at 9 a.m. the next day, I felt ready to answer all their questions. I had a lot of material to present to convince them that my risk of harming again was negligible. I had to source all the reports of good behaviour, written reports from the warden, testimonials from my inmates, all the courses I had taken and achieved, and so on. I even presented my diary. There were three of them on the panel, and the discussion went on for longer than I expected – in fact, I was in the room for most of the morning. My main message was that this was my first and only crime, and during my time in prison, I had done as much as possible to learn from it. I feel sure that your letter of recommendation influenced their decision, so from the bottom of my heart, thank you very much. I didn't have any others to share apart from the testimonials so it was so beneficial to have such a positive recommendation from someone on the outside.

You have been a wonderful support over the last year and I have felt your trust and encouragement in every letter. Not many people would take such a risk so I think you must be a very special person to be so giving. Your suggestion of meeting is very welcome – I would very much like to meet you, if you're comfortable doing that? It would be a pleasure to meet your family as well. It would be nice to thank you personally for all the support you have provided.

My release date is confirmed for the beginning of August so perhaps we can meet a couple of weeks after then? The rehabilitation centre will spend the first week with me, helping me sort my accommodation and assisting with the transition to normal life. I will be based in Durham and I am not able to leave the city – are you able to come here? I'm sorry to drag you all this way and completely understand if it's too far.

With warm and thankful regards,
Michael

As Catherine read Michael's last letter, her heart hammered in her chest and, feeling slightly sick, she sank down thankfully into her armchair. While she had hoped and prayed for his release, she couldn't actually believe it had been confirmed. Who could possibly agree that eleven years was sufficient to atone for the life of another? But the decision had been made and now they were arranging to meet in person. Fear rose up in her throat in the form of bile, swiftly swallowed and replaced by an intensity so powerful, it surged through her blood stream, her body shaking in shock.

After a few minutes and a several deep breaths, she cautiously stood up, testing her legs. The now-framed holiday photo of herself, Richard and Helen in St Lucia caught her eye. Sitting down at her desk, she picked it up and studied it closely. Everyone looked so happy and relaxed. The holiday had been a huge success, and Catherine's only regret was that they hadn't done it sooner. But it was too late for that now. She had wanted to create some incredible memories for her husband and daughter, and she had achieved that – that was the main thing. A change of scenery and a good rest had been more beneficial than she had anticipated.

She would go and see Michael in Durham, and she would go alone. It was her job to help him on his journey and she would do whatever it took to complete the commitment she had made to him. Besides, she couldn't tell Richard about it all now after a year of hiding the correspondence. And he definitely wouldn't approve of her going to visit him. He would think it madness. But she would have to tell him sometime, and she knew when she did that he would, if not support her actions, then at least understand them. Before she could change her mind, she wrote back to Michael immediately, asking for his new address and promising to go to see him on 15 August.

38

Alison

Alison woke up, the side of her face throbbing. But she couldn't face reality just yet. She took a slug of water along with two more painkillers, and succumbed, gratefully, to sleep and its blissful gift of oblivion.

*

Through the haze of her slumber, Alison heard voices in the corridor, outside her room. People laughing and joking, high on pints of cider and black, doors slamming as they all congregated in the kitchen to make themselves the traditional tea and toast before heading back to someone's room. The normality of it made Alison want to cry. Instead, she drank more water, nibbled on some crackers by her bed, and sank back into her stupor.

*

Alison tried to open her eyes. She had no idea how long she

had been in bed, but judging by the state of her, it must have been several days. Her mouth felt as dry as the desert and she was aware that she hadn't brushed her teeth in a while. She could also smell her own body odour and felt somewhat repulsed. But was she disgusted enough to get out of bed, she asked herself. Her limbs felt weak and she tentatively tested her strength by placing her feet on the carpet. It was a strange sensation to be upright. As she walked to the sink she discovered her head no longer hurt. In fact, even when she looked in the mirror and barely recognised herself, she felt very little. She took comfort in the absence of feeling. She had spent too long worrying, too long wondering. This is who she had become and she felt the acceptance wash over her. So, she wasn't the star student she had hoped to be – in fact she was a long way from that – but she was so exhausted from trying to keep up, trying to keep him happy, trying to live a dual life. She had no control, so why fight it? Alison brushed her teeth but decided a shower was too much effort. She simply didn't care enough and crawled back under the duvet.

*

Eventually, Alison's stomach forced her to get out of bed and go in search of some food. She was weak and her diet of water and some crackers she had found in her bedside table was making her feel dizzy. Scavenging the kitchen, she found some bread and cheese, which most likely belonged to another student. She hesitated before taking it but she was so hungry, she helped herself. Making herself a cup of tea, she headed back to her room. It was ten in the morning and most of the other students from her corridor were at lectures. Alison idly wondered how many lectures she had missed and relished the feeling of not caring. It was an alien response and once again, she felt a sense of relief that she had finally accepted that her journey to becoming a lawyer had failed. She got back into bed, turned on her small TV, and lost herself in mindless morning television.

*

It was several hours later when Alison thought to check her phone. She was surprised to see a slew of missed calls and messages. Mark, Laura. And to her surprise, him. Why was he calling her? Seeing that some of the messages indicated panic that she hadn't been in touch, she quickly texted Mark and Laura, saying that she had flu and had spent the last few days sleeping. In a few days, she told them, she should be well enough to call. She didn't bother to call The Professor back – she simply didn't feel up to it. Sinking back under the covers, she took refuge in her duvet and pillows and the comforting hum of voices from the talk shows.

*

A week had passed and Alison still hadn't made the effort to be in touch with anyone, although she was rather pleased with herself that she had finally taken a shower and changed the bed sheets. As she lay there, she had a lot of time to think. Why had she been so averse to a life at home in the first place? Why was university and a career so important anyway? Sleeping, eating, watching TV, reading novels – it was the most relaxed she'd felt in months. No need to worry about lectures, no heavy law books to memorise, no exams to prepare for, no papers to write, no waiting for mobile phones to ring and, most importantly, no surprises to deal with. With herself, she knew exactly where she stood. Was she about to give all that up for the stress of being a student? Absolutely not.

*

She was in the middle of discovering why an eighteen-year-old boy had cheated on his girlfriend with a stripper, when she heard the knock above the noise of the TV. Ignoring it, Alison carried on watching. There had been numerous knocks over the last few days, she had ignored them and eventually they had gone away, but it came again, this time with a voice, and it was insistent and demanding.

'Alison! Open the door, please!'

Recognising Laura's voice, Alison waited.

'Alison, open this door now, or I'm calling security.'

Reluctantly she dragged herself out of bed, quickly combed her hair, and opened the door. She was surprised to see Mark with Laura.

As she expected, Laura didn't mince her words.

'Alison, I don't know what's going on with you but as far as I'm aware you've been locked in here for over a week. What the hell is going on?'

Mark took a more subtle approach, giving her a hug, and gently asking how she was.

'I'm fine,' Alison replied. 'Never been better. What's new with you?'

Laura stared at her in disbelief.

'Alison, you haven't been to any of your lectures, you haven't been answering your phone, you've not left your room in days, and you look like hell. For the second time, can you please tell me exactly what is going on?'

'Nothing's going on – I've just not been feeling very well, that's all. But I feel better now.'

'Good, then you can come to breakfast with me tomorrow morning at eight, and Mark will accompany you to your lectures. Don't be late. I'll be waiting for you.'

And with that, she walked away, clearly frustrated at Alison's insistence that everything was fine.

'What is this?' Alison tried to make a joke. 'An intervention?'

As Mark turned to leave, he paused, as if trying to decide whether to say something or not.

'She's just worried about you, Alison. We both are. If you ever need someone to talk to, I'm here for you, OK?'

His voice was so soft and gentle, Alison wanted nothing more at that moment than to throw herself into his arms and hide. She wanted him to make everything go away. But it wasn't going to go away and there was nothing Mark could do to make it better.

As the door clicked softly behind him, Alison locked it and sat down on the bed. She put her head in her hands and wondered how an earth she had got to the point where she was too frightened to leave her room.

*

That same afternoon, there was another knock at the door. Thinking it was Laura and Mark coming to check on her again, she opened the door without thinking and there, standing in front of her, was The Professor with a large bouquet of flowers.

As Alison lay in bed that night, the smell of roses and lilies wafting across the room, a part of her was so relieved that they had sorted everything out. He had apologised over and over, explained that he was jealous and a fool and that he would do everything possible to make it up to her. After a long talk and a few tears, he had finally left. He had promised he would do anything for her, and she had asked for a little time. He understood that she could no longer be in a relationship with him at the moment, but he was hopeful, with time, that she would decide to trust him again.

'Can we see each other, though?' he had pleaded. 'Just for a coffee, at least?'

She had agreed as he seemed so desperate to please her. She knew he had taken a huge risk coming to a student's room. He had even brought the work from the last week's lectures so she could catch up.

'Anything you need, just call me,' he said as he was leaving.

Alison finally started to feel in control, but as she lay there she wondered if she was kidding herself. She looked over at the papers he had brought, then started to skim through the questions. She knew most of the answers. It was the final term of the academic year and it seemed a pity to waste all her efforts of earlier in the year now the exams were so close. Might as well finish off the term properly, she thought, and, taking them over to her desk, she began writing, barely even noticing the setting sun casting a surreal light over the prison in the distance.

39

Kate

Kate moved through the days like she was walking through treacle. She saw no one and spoke to no one except her children and her husband. Jan called her to see why she wasn't attending the writing class anymore and she told her she was too busy to attend now. She knew Jan didn't believe her, but she didn't press it any further. The daily grind had returned and, with it, Kate's sense of despair. It wasn't so much the physical side of the relationship she missed but the shared conversations and interests. The praise he had heaped on her for her writing, the encouragement she had received on reading, and just the general acknowledgement that she had so much more to offer than just being a mum. With him, she had felt interesting, worthy and talented.

When the phone rang after lunch, she didn't pick up. It rang for a few days after that but then it didn't ring again. The lack of closure only added to her frustration. She felt used and stupid, and horribly old before her time. As the days turned into weeks, Kate began to feel closed in. There was nothing to look forward to, nothing to break up the long days of monotony. She turned down invitations for play dates, and instead asked if she could drop her daughter off and pick her up later so she didn't have to interact with the mothers who had become her friends. She lost even more weight and her sleep was fitful. Her life had become grey. The absence of an emotional connection, interesting conversation and engaging human interaction gnawed at her. He had made her feel important and special, someone with her own dreams and ambitions. But she realised now that it was all just a ploy, that it was just a game for him. Well, she had played and lost. She had lost him to someone younger, prettier and probably more intelligent. Someone without ties who didn't need to sneak away, who was as free as he was, who led an interesting life of travel and adventure. How could she possibly compete? She lived in a council flat, had never even left the country, and took the girls camping in the Lake District for their holidays because that's all they could afford. Kate thought of the lady with red lips. Even from a distance, you could tell she wouldn't be the type of woman to wear old leggings just because they were warm and comfortable. She wouldn't just throw her hair back into a ponytail and make do. No, hers looked blow-dried to perfection. But then again, she probably didn't have two children, who, while they were Kate's life, took up all her time and attention, leaving little room for anything else. All these thoughts churned around in Kate's mind like a washing machine on a spin cycle, teasing her about what her life could have been if she had made different choices. If she had listened to her mother's subtle advice. But she had chosen, and as her great-grandma used to say, you've made your bed, and now you need to lie in it. Kate balked at the cliché. Yet, it was true, as so many clichés were.

Kate lay back on the sofa. She had just an hour to go before she had to pick her daughter up from school. She put on the TV for her younger daughter and closed her eyes, letting the sound of *Postman Pat* wash over her as she dozed into her depression.

*

Several weeks had passed since Kate had last seen Mr Barnes. She was surprised, and grateful, that she hadn't bumped into him before now. While the shock of seeing him with someone else had worn off, the disappointment and anger at his deceit still shook her to her core. He had been fully aware that she was married, and she knew that she was in the wrong as well. But she had been honest with him, she told herself, and he should have been the same with her.

In such a small city, it was inevitable that she would come face to face with him at some point. She had been shopping one Saturday morning, leaving the girls at home with her husband. She had been out since nine o'clock and was desperate for a cup of tea and a toasted teacake. It was freezing cold and her hands and feet felt like icicles. Stepping into the warmth of Vennel's coffee shop, Kate struggled with her shopping bags as she made her way to the glass counter to order her food. The café was intimate and cosy, and she was looking forward to a hot drink.

Claiming a table, she was about to place her bags on the chair opposite when a familiar voice said, 'Can I help you with those?' Before she even looked up, she knew who it was. He was smiling at her, with his arms outstretched, reaching for her bags. Kate's heart pounded. How could he act so normal when they hadn't spoken for months?

'No, thank you.' And turning on her heel, she fled, her tea forgotten, bumping her bags against the other customers in her hurry. Turning right outside the café, she walked quickly, with no idea where she was headed, only that she needed to get out of there and away from him. Breaking into an awkward run, she heard footsteps behind her and with dismay realised he was following her.

'Kate!' he shouted. 'Wait!'

Head down, Kate ignored him and tried to get lost amongst the shoppers. Instead they slowed her down, and Kate felt a firm hand on her arm. 'Get off me!' she said through gritted teeth, not caring that she was drawing attention to herself. 'What do you think you're doing?'

'Kate, what's wrong? What happened? Why didn't you pick up my calls? I was worried about you.'

'Well, you couldn't have worried that much because you didn't try very hard to contact me. Probably too busy with one of your other girlfriends.'

'Kate, now come on. We never agreed to be exclusive. In fact, you yourself are married – what did you expect?' Her fury was fuelled even further by the fact that he was right.

'Perhaps some sort of conversation to let me know that you were seeing other people would have been nice,' she retorted.

'I'm sorry, really I am. I thought you understood it was just a bit of fun,' he countered.

'Well, I'm not someone you can just have a bit of fun with and then drop like a hot potato.'

'Come on, Kate,' he cajoled. 'Where's that girl I used to love meeting up with? Don't be cross. Here, let me make it up to you. How about a drink tonight on me?'

Kate looked at him in disbelief. 'I don't think so.'

He shrugged, his mind already elsewhere. Kate realised it was neither here nor there to him if she had a drink with him or not. There were plenty of other women who would be happy to take her place.

Turning to leave, she said to him, 'I really hope I don't see you again, Mr Barnes. You have taken advantage of your position and one day it's going to come back and bite you.'

He laughed but there was a sinister grin on his face. 'I doubt it, Kate. I'm not the one who's married and carrying on like I was single! Better hope your husband doesn't find out.'

Shaking, Kate knew she didn't have a leg to stand on. He knew where she lived, where her family lived. How could she have been so stupid? Hopefully, he wouldn't want the drama of causing any trouble, but for now, he had her over a barrel and he knew it.

Whistling, he sauntered off with a quick throwaway remark over his shoulder. 'Cheerio for now!'

Kate could have slapped him, his nonchalance a perfect expression of the casual way he had treated their relationship, and the power he now held to destroy her marriage with one word to her husband.

*

It was 3:26 a.m. and Kate was lying awake listening to the sound of her husband sleeping. He was not noisy but she was irritated that he slept so easily when she had been struggling for hours. It had been a week since she had encountered Mr Barnes in the coffee shop, and she hadn't been able to think about anything else since. She was living in constant fear that he would tell her husband about their affair, the consequences of which would fall on her, and fall heavily.

She had broken her marriage vows, broken the sacred bond of trust, and she didn't know how to fix it. She couldn't concentrate and the fear seeped into her bones making her feel ill with worry. The irony was that her relationship with her husband was improving. Having become so preoccupied with Mr Barnes, she had inadvertently given her husband the space he so desperately craved from her. He had been promoted at work in the last month and while he was still commuting long hours, the extra salary had taken the pressure off their finances, allowing a few extra treats for the girls. Coming home one night, he had presented her with a bunch of flowers along with the news of his raise. Taken aback, Kate hid her surprise by burying her face into the lilies, smelling their scent.

'I'm sorry I have been so difficult to live with these past few months,' he said. 'The job loss really took its toll and I felt useless and ashamed that I couldn't provide for you. I know I haven't made much of an effort lately but things will change from now on.'

It was one of the very few times her husband had apologised to her in the last two years and she could have wept at hearing those words. If only he had said them a few months ago, perhaps everything would have been different. Holding him close, she whispered her thanks, trying to hold back the tears.

'Hey,' he whispered to her. 'I know it was bad, but I hate seeing you cry. I promise I'll make it up to you.'

Sinking in to him, Kate hoped she hadn't lost everything with her reckless behaviour. No matter how bad things had become she should have been stronger.

'I'm sorry, too.' Her words conveyed a deeper meaning than he understood. 'I'll try harder as well.'

'You do more than enough, Kate. It's me who's been the idiot. I've just been so incredibly stressed and tired. It all started to get to me.'

'I know. Me, too. From now on, I'll try and be more supportive.'

Hiding her relief, Kate went to put the flowers in some water, hoping that the lilies weren't a prophecy of the death of her marriage.

40

Alison

It was with mixed feelings that Alison went back to her lectures. Her self-imposed isolation had changed her in some way, but how, or in what way, she was unsure. She was grateful for the company of Laura and Mark as they accompanied her throughout the day. Although neither of them said anything, Alison could feel herself being observed closely, as if she was a doll that might break. She couldn't make up her mind if their treatment annoyed her or comforted her, but either way, it was good to have the support. She hadn't told them about the state of her relationship, although she suspected they both knew something wasn't quite right. Perhaps it was the way Laura had started talking about feminism, the rights of women, how women didn't need men and how they were just a distraction. Or it could have been the constant blaring of the Spice Girls from her room. Mark was subtler and showed his support by being with her as much as possible. He kept her distracted with his jokes and funny stories and accompanied her to all her lectures.

Day by day, she felt herself become stronger and more

confident. She met The Professor in a coffee shop in town once a week and so far, he seemed to be respecting her wishes to take everything slowly. He had briefly mentioned another holiday but Alison didn't want to commit to anything yet, never mind a holiday, and he seemed to respect that. As the end of term drew to a close, the stress of exams kept everyone busy. Alison did the best she could and hoped it was enough, but these days she was sleeping at night rather than studying and felt more rested and laid-back as a result. Mark's presence helped a lot as they studied together, and she found his rhythm of concentrated work with regular breaks and walks a lot more enjoyable than her previous frantic pace. Each evening she saw Laura and they chatted over a cup of tea. The ritual soothed her and once in her own bed, she fell asleep quickly. Neither Laura nor Mark pushed her for answers about her relationship and she was grateful for that.

*

After so much work for the exams, results day eventually came.

'Oh my God, I didn't sleep a wink last night, I was so nervous!' said Laura over breakfast.

'Why?' replied Alison. It was the first time she had seen Laura looking less than perky.

'The papers were sooooo hard,' complained Laura.

'But you're set for a first,' Alison reassured her friend. 'You'll be fine.'

'I hope so. My parents will kill me if I fail.'

'I'm pretty sure you're a long way from failing.'

'I know but still...'

'Come on,' interrupted Alison. 'Let's walk down together. We can each go and get our results and then meet for lunch. How does that sound?'

'OK, I suppose I could always make myself feel better with some chocolate cake.'

As the girls walked along the towpath, Alison remembered her race against Mark. She would like to start running again. It had made her feel invigorated and healthy, and gave her brain a break.

'What are you thinking about?' asked Laura.

'I was just thinking about starting running again over summer.'

'That's a good idea. Then you can join the running club here at the college in September.'

'Well, I won't be here in September most likely.'

'What? What on earth are you on about? Of course you will! Why would you say that?'

'Well, after a week off, I'm guessing my results aren't going to be great today.'

'A week off is not going to affect your grades. Besides, you were ill. There's not a lot you could have done about it.'

'Well, let's see what the results say. See you at twelve?'

'Yep – good luck!'

'You, too!'

As they parted ways on Elvet Bridge, Alison took in the beauty of the city. She was so happy to call Durham her home but, at the same time, she also wondered what else was out there for her. Heading to the law faculty, she braced herself. Let's get this over with then, she said to herself. There was a crowd of people around the notice board and as she waited her turn, she heard the shouts of happiness, the cries of dismay and her classmates supporting or celebrating each other. When her turn came, Alison ran her finger down the list of names and traced it to the right to the corresponding result. That can't be right, Alison thought to herself. Checking again, Alison came up against the same result. 2:1.

'Hey, Alison! Congrats!' Someone grabbed her in a hug before she was moved aside by the rest of the waiting students clamouring to get their results.

There must be some mistake, Alison thought to herself, there's no way I achieved a 2:1. She would have to go and check. Approaching the head of department's office door, she tentatively knocked.

'Ah, Alison, how nice to see you. I know we've only briefly met before so thanks for coming at such short notice. I was a bit worried you wouldn't get my email to be honest.' Reaching out to shake her hand, Alison noticed the large desk name plate. Dr Taylor.

'Email?' Alison asked. She normally checked her emails in the afternoon.

'Yes,' replied Dr Taylor. 'I sent it this morning, just wondering if you could come and see me after you picked up your results. Did you not see it? Either way, you're here now. Have a seat, please.'

So, it was a mistake, Alison thought to herself. She wondered how much of a mistake had been made and what her actual mark was. As Dr Taylor sorted through her papers, Alison took in her surroundings. Even seated behind an expansive desk, Dr Taylor was an impressive figure. Tall, slim and elegantly dressed, she looked in great shape for what Alison guessed to be the age of fifty. But what was most striking was her confidence. It wasn't brash but more of an inner calm that resonated from her. She conveyed the appearance of being completely in control. I want to be like that, thought Alison suddenly.

'Right, here we are. Yes, your papers. Alison, I brought you in here because I wanted to congratulate you on your results today. You are one of the few students who has really shown steady and continual improvement throughout the two years. We see all types of students here. Some start off strong and then crash and burn, some struggle in the beginning and eventually give up, but you, Alison, from what I hear, have worked consistently hard, and it shows in your results today.'

Alison stared, open-mouthed.

Dr Taylor smiled. 'Well, don't look so surprised!'

'I'm sorry, yes, th-thank you.' Alison felt flustered. As Dr Taylor stood up, Alison started to gather her things. Seeing her out the door, Dr Taylor said, 'We're expecting great things from you, Alison. It just goes to show how hard work really does pay off.'

'Thank you.'

With a final handshake, Alison left the room and walked to the entrance. Standing stock still on the steps of the law building, she absorbed Dr Taylor's words again.

Smiling, she broke into run to meet Laura.

*

It was only when her parents arrived at the university to collect her for the summer that she realised one of her friends – she was guessing Laura – must have called them. How worried she must have been to go to the trouble of getting in touch with them, Alison thought as she took in her mother's drawn and anxious looks, while her father's face was set with worry. As she fell into the familiar comfort of her father's embrace, ripples of relief rolled over her and she knew that her nightmare would soon come to an end.

*

They let her settle back in at home for a few days before they brought up the topic of her relationship, and while Alison knew it would come up at some point, she was content to relax in the familiar rituals of daily life with her parents. She barely even looked at her phone anymore and she could feel the anxiety dim each day.

However, one morning she came down to breakfast to discover her father in his casual clothes sitting at the breakfast table with her mother. This was odd, as he had usually left for the office by the time she came down.

'Sit down, Alison,' he said gently, as her mother placed some coffee before her. 'Do you want to tell us what's been happening at university?'

And slowly but surely, the whole story came out. The Professor, the holiday, her struggle with the course, her fear of failure... she left nothing out, except the violence she had endured. At certain points, Alison bowed her head in shame as she recounted the lies she had told. Her parents said nothing, just listened to her, and while she knew she had disappointed them, she also felt their support, simply by their lack of judgement. As she finished, tears rolling down her face, she told them how sorry she was, and as her father gripped her in a strong embrace, reassuring her and promising her on his life that he and her mother would sort this, she finally broke down as the huge racking sobs took over her body.

*

Over the next few weeks Alison slept a lot, but it was a peaceful, deep sleep that recharged her body. She had a plan and she was feeling good about it. By talking everything through, she could see that she couldn't resurrect her relationship with The Professor, but the thought of not being with him any longer petrified her. In fact, she knew it would be a relief to have it sorted once and for all and to be able to concentrate on her work, her friends, and all the fun that came with university life. For two years, she had been consumed by The Professor but it felt like a lifetime. Unbelievably, she only had one more year of university to go and she wanted to make the most of it. The final year was also the most important one in terms of her final mark, of course.

She had agreed with her parents that she should use the summer to recharge and relax. She would need to speak to The Professor to tell him her decision and her parents had also suggested she go on holiday with Laura for a week in August for a change of scene. Her parents kept a close eye on her but gradually, with the warmth of the long summer days, she felt like she was returning to her old self. Alison also realised that she had a lot to look forward to and she had an opportunity to make a real difference in her chosen field of law. She had met Dr Taylor again and talked through some of her worries with regard to the work load for the final year. Dr Taylor had given her some suggestions as well as some reassurances about her progress. She accepted she was not going to be the best student in the graduating class of 2000 but she knew she was a long way from being the worst. Dr Taylor had also helped her set up a short law internship in Newcastle for a few weeks over the summer. It was the perfect antidote to the dryness of the lectures. The lawyers were young, passionate, dynamic and eager to prove themselves. They believed in fighting for causes, justice and using the law to make a better world. During her few weeks there, Alison remembered why she had chosen law as a profession. Each intern was given a mentor and Alison's was a partner in the firm, called Amanda. Her reputation as one of the best solicitors in the city preceded her and Alison soaked up everything she could. Amanda was highly sought after as a mentor and there was a lot of envy from the other interns.

'You're so lucky,' said Kelly, a law student studying at Newcastle. 'She's amazing!'

'Yes, she is rather, isn't she? Today, she let me attend one of her client meetings and tomorrow I'm going to court!'

Alison couldn't believe her luck. Every day, she sprang out of bed, eager to see what Amanda had in store for her. She felt she had learnt more in those few weeks than she would in a lifetime of studying books. When the internship came to an end, Alison was crushed. But on her last day, Amanda had called her into her office.

'Alison, I just want to thank you for all your hard work over these past few weeks.'

'Thank you so much! I've really enjoyed it!'

'So, Durham, huh? I went there, too. It's tough, but keep persevering because I know you can make it. And who knows? I may meet you in the courtroom one day soon.' And with that, she swept out of her office, leaving Alison her business card and asking her to get in touch if she wanted to intern again next year.

On the train back, Alison turned the business card over and over in her hand. Under Amanda, Alison had flourished and for the first time in a long while she felt excited about her future. All she had to do was get through the final year and then she could get on with her career. In the meantime, she had her girls' holiday to look forward to.

Alison hugged herself, urging the train to go faster so she could tell her parents about her day.

41

Kate

The doorbell rang and Kate's heart started pounding. It was 7.15 a.m. and her husband still hadn't left for work. They both looked at each in surprise, wondering who could be at the door so early. Kate had been living in fear ever since Mr Barnes had made his parting veiled threat to her. Her secret had started to burn her brain, making her paranoid, and the thought of being found out preoccupied her mind, both day and night. Her husband went to the door, bringing back a parcel that was too big to go through the letterbox and had come by special delivery.

'Addressed to you, Kate. I wonder what it could be.' His smile, however, gave away the fact that he knew exactly what it was. It was February, Valentine's Day, she realised now, looking at the calendar hanging in the kitchen. The date had utterly escaped her. They hadn't bought presents for each other in the last few years and she had an awful feeling she was going to be upstaged. She opened the parcel to find the contents much smaller than the packaging. A ring box rested amongst a cloud of tissue paper. As she lifted the lid, she took an intake of breath as a small diamond gleamed back at her.

'I never did get you an engagement ring,' he said to her, giving her a long kiss. 'Happy Valentine's Day.'

Overcome, Kate heard the girls shriek in delight as her husband slipped the ring on her finger. It fitted exactly. The moment would have been perfect had it not been for the piercing terror inside her that had escalated to epic proportions when she'd heard the doorbell ring.

'It's beautiful,' she said, tears sliding down her face. Mistaking them for happiness, he kissed them away while their daughters danced around them.

*

Kate sank into the sofa gratefully. After presenting her with his gift, her husband had left for work, and she had dropped off her elder daughter at school and her younger at a play date before coming home. The ring sparkled on her left finger, its single diamond stunning in its beauty. Kate had never been one for jewellery but she had to admit her husband had good taste. It was exactly what she would have chosen for herself. How could she have forgotten that he knew her so well? On her way in and having gathered up the post, which had been delivered by the regular postman, Kate began to idly sort through it. Most of it was bills, but then she came to one envelope that was handwritten and addressed to her. She felt her heart go cold. Don't be silly, she admonished herself. It's probably just a letter from her mother. Yet, Kate knew her mother's handwriting and it wasn't this. Opening the envelope, Kate slowly pulled out a Valentine's card, which contained just one single sentence on the inside.

'*Happy Valentine's Day Mrs Robinson.*'

Kate cried out and dropped the card, disbelief and hysteria welling up in her that he would do something so visibly threatening to her marriage. As she stood up, she knocked the cup of tea from the arm of the sofa, but her only thought was to get the card out of her home as soon as she could. Grabbing her keys and purse, Kate ran out of the flat to the large rubbish bins and started ripping the cards into shreds, letting the pieces fall where they belonged.

*

'And how long have you been feeling like this?' asked the doctor, busy sorting out the papers on her desk.

'A few months,' replied Kate vaguely. 'It's just the sleep, really. If you could give me something to help with that, I'll be on my way. I can see you're busy...' She trailed off. The din in the waiting room hadn't receded. If anything, it had become worse. There must have been at least twenty people in there and the cries of children as they got fed up of waiting started to claw at Kate's nerves. After a delay of two hours, she had finally been called into the doctor's office. All she wanted was to sleep but at night she tossed and turned, only drifting off in the early hours of the morning. It had become a lot worse since she received the Valentine's card and Kate wasn't sure how much longer she could carry on.

'How's your eating? Have you noticed any increase or decrease in your appetite?'

'No, not really,' replied Kate, wanting to get back to the issue of sleep. In fact, she had lost weight. She'd had to use a belt on her jeans just that morning.

'Is there a particular event or incident that may have led to you feeling like this?'

'No. As I mentioned, it's just the sleep really. If I could just get into bed and fall asleep and stay asleep, I'm sure I'd feel much better. Is there anything you can give me for that?'

For the first time during the whole conversation, the doctor looked up at her. 'It doesn't work like that, I'm afraid. We always like to run some tests to see what might be causing the sleep issues.'

Moving on, the doctor glanced through her papers again. 'It says here you have two young children.'

'I do,' replied Kate, wondering what that had to do with anything.

'Could they be the reason you're not sleeping well?'

'Well, sometimes they're up at night, yes, but—'

'In that case, I suggest you try to get some help with them so you can rest. Are your parents or other family members able to help out?'

'I understand what you're saying, but my children have never been the best sleepers. This is a different problem.'

'OK,' said the doctor. 'Let's run some tests first to make sure there's no underlying cause for your insomnia and we can go from there.'

'So, can you write me a prescription for some sleeping pills?'

'Once I'm satisfied that there's no medical reason, then we can look at possible remedies. Here, take this form to the nurse and she'll do a blood test. You should get the results in a day or two. Make an appointment to come back in five days.' It was clear this appointment was over.

Kate stood up, taking the form. How on earth was she going to survive another five days? The nights were becoming unbearable and the days were not much better, but at least she could keep herself busy and distracted. Muttering her thanks, she fought the fear that had lodged its way into her life and was refusing to let go. Leaving the clinic, she checked her watch. She had about thirty minutes before picking up her younger daughter from Jan's house. Despite Kate not attending the classes any more, Jan had remained a good friend.

They sometimes had a drink together and she had gone over to their house for lunch. Both Jan and Trevor had full lives with their family and grandchildren, and they were happy to welcome Kate into their home. Jan had offered to look after her younger daughter if she ever needed a break and, up until today, Kate had not needed to take her up on the offer. But as the nights became more and more troublesome, she had decided to make an appointment with the doctor and leave her youngest with Jan for a couple of hours. Knowing that she hadn't prepared anything for dinner, Kate decided to stop off at the supermarket before going to pick up her daughter.

*

As she browsed the shelves, Kate tried to find an-over-the counter solution that might help her insomnia. She had tried everything, though: hot milk, a relaxing bath, music, but nothing seemed to work and she knew nothing was likely to work as long as she still had the threat of Mr Barnes hanging over her. How could she have been so utterly stupid and reckless, she asked herself a thousand times. At any moment, she prepared for her husband to come home with the news that he had discovered what she'd done. She imagined him telling her their marriage was over and that he was taking the girls. She imagined him packing up their things – their toys, their clothes – and leaving her in the small flat with nothing but her shame to keep her company. And she knew that he had every right to do that. It didn't matter what the reasons for the affair were. What mattered was that she had broken his trust and it could never be repaired. Kate tried to gulp down the panic that was rising within her. If she lost her girls, she wouldn't be able to live with herself. It was that simple; her life would be over. But in a way her life already felt over as she was living with the constant threat of being found out. Kate had seriously considered telling her husband everything herself. But what would it do? Yes, it would make her feel better but it wouldn't make it right, and who knew what her husband would do?

Walking to the checkout with her shopping, Kate hoped she would be able to last five more days. Otherwise, she may have no choice but to tell her husband her sordid secret and she knew that would destroy everything.

42

Alison

Alison closed her suitcase with a satisfying snap. In twenty-four hours she would be lying on a sun lounger with nothing more to do than read her favourite book and enjoy a long cool drink. She was meeting Laura at the airport the next morning and they had talked about nothing else for the last few weeks. They had planned their outfits down to the smallest detail and researched all the best beaches and bars. It was going to be a week of sheer bliss and for Alison it signified so much more than a holiday, it signified a fresh start, a new beginning. There was only one thing left to do before she could move on and she planned to tell him tonight.

*

They had been in touch only sporadically via text since Alison went home from university and she was grateful The Professor was keeping his promise to give her space. Yet when it came to Mark, she missed him more than she thought she would. They had been messaging most days, and while he was still his same jokey self, their messages had taken a more intimate tone lately. Alison didn't think too much about what it meant – she was more focused on herself these days – but she was glad of the friendship and she was looking forward to seeing him in September. In fact, he would be the first person she called. He was in Ireland at the moment with his family, before heading to London to do an internship. He had mentioned maybe visiting her for the weekend while he was in England and she had messaged him back immediately saying she would love to see him.

*

Alison didn't tell anyone that she was planning to visit The Professor that evening. She wanted to speak to him face to face – she felt she owed him that much after he had been so patient with her. And she also felt that the fact he hadn't been in touch with her, as much as she had expected, demonstrated that he had also moved on. It was now simply a case of making it official. She dropped him a message to let him know she would visit him around seven that evening. He responded telling her he was looking forward to seeing her and she ignored the flash of warning that went through her at the speed of his response.

43

Kate

'She needs to visit a doctor,' she heard Jan say with authority.

Slowly coming to, Kate looked around her. She realised she was in her own room. But why was Jan at her house? Wasn't Kate supposed to be at Jan's house? She turned her head to try to hear the voices that were drifting towards her from the living room. 'But what's wrong with her?' asked her husband, the worry evident in his voice. 'You've been with her at these writing classes and book club – has she said anything to you?'

'I haven't—' Jan stopped abruptly, suddenly realising there may be more to the story.

'I'm so worried about her, Jan,' said Kate's husband, his voice small in his confusion. 'She's lost so much weight and she seems to be in a different world half the time and then incredibly sad the rest of it. Do you think it's depression? Or women's troubles?' He lowered his voice further on the last few words, almost afraid to hear the answer, his traditional working-class background making him reluctant to pry further.

The questions hung in the air and Kate could imagine Jan rapidly thinking. 'Now, don't you worry, I'm sure she's just fine – probably she's just got herself a bit overtired. It's easily done when you have two kids to look after. My grandkids take their toll on their mother, that's for sure. Just the other day, I was saying to my Trevor, "I don't remember it being this much hard work when we had kids," but it's a different world today, isn't it? The young people have so much more to worry about than we had in our day.'

Kate tried to sit up but discovered she felt dizzy if she moved. Lying back down again, she called for her husband. He came at once, with Jan close behind him.

'Kate! Thank God you're awake – are you OK? I was this close to calling an ambulance,' exclaimed her husband.

'What happened?' Kate asked weakly.

'You fainted and bumped your head,' said her husband. 'Luckily, you were at Jan's and she and Trevor brought you home in their car. How are you feeling?'

'A bit dizzy,' Kate admitted. 'Where are the girls?'

'They're fine, love. Don't worry about them, they're both here watching TV.'

'Perhaps Kate would like a cup of tea,' said Jan pointedly. 'I would also add a spoonful of sugar for the shock as well as maybe pop round to the shop for some biscuits to go with it.'

Keen to have something to do, Kate's husband left her with Jan in the hope that she could help with whatever was bothering her.

'You have about fifteen minutes to tell me everything,' said Jan firmly, after closing the bedroom door.

And so Kate did. In hushed tones, everything that had happened over the last year poured out from her – the highs, the lows, the guilt, the feelings of despair, the money worries, the affair, the Valentine card. She left nothing out and by the time she'd told the whole sorry story, Kate felt empty. Jan didn't interrupt her once and when she'd finished, Jan sat back, closed her eyes, and didn't speak. After a few minutes, she opened her eyes, and looked at Kate very directly.

'OK, Kate, here's what we're going to do,' she said, 'and then we're going to forget this ever happened and never talk about it again.'

*

Jan arranged everything. She booked Kate an appointment with a doctor – a different one to the one she had seen before – as well as booked an appointment with a counsellor to talk through some of her feelings. Jan also gave her a pill – 'something to help you relax, pet,' she said vaguely when Kate asked what it was – so whether it was that, the bump on the head, or the fact that she had revealed her anguish to Jan, for the first time in a long time, Kate slept for twelve solid hours. She woke up to her husband bringing her a cup of coffee.

'How are you feeling?' he'd asked her gently.

'Better, thank you,' she replied, taking the coffee gratefully. 'Hmm, real coffee,' she said, smelling the aroma.

'Well, I thought you needed a treat.'

'Thank you.'

'Listen,' her husband said to her hesitantly. 'I know I haven't been the best husband for a while, and I'm sure I'm a part of your unhappiness, but I want you to know...' He stalled, emotion welling up, preventing him from speaking. Taking a deep breath, he tried again. 'I want you to know,' he continued, 'that I love you deeply and I will always love you, and whatever it is that is bothering you, I am here for you. I hope you can forgive me and we can start to let go of the past and move forward. Whatever I've done, whatever you've done, it's over and I hope we can start afresh.'

Kate gulped, fighting down the tears. She wondered if her husband had an idea of her betrayal.

'Can you do that for me?' he asked.

Kate nodded, not trusting herself to speak.

Sitting on the edge of the bed, he held her face in his hands.

'We're turning a corner, Kate,' he whispered to her. 'I can feel it. I know things have been hard but we can rebuild our marriage to what it used to be. Do you remember?'

Kate did, and the memories finally made her tears spill over.

Kissing them away, her husband brought her close. 'I love you, Kate. You're the only woman for me.'

'I love you, too,' she whispered, and as she wrapped her arms around him, she knew they would survive this.

*

Kate never did find out how Jan had dealt with Mr Barnes's veiled threat. When she had asked, Jan had told her it was all sorted and she didn't need to worry about Mr Barnes any longer. She had a suspicion that Trevor must have had something to do with it because when Kate saw Mr Barnes in town one afternoon, he immediately turned and walked the other way, almost running. Kate was too afraid to ask Jan what that meant but, either way, she was happy he wasn't bothering her and she did as she was told. It was good to have someone else take charge. Kate felt bruised and vulnerable, and Jan, with her brisk, can-do attitude, was just what Kate needed. Later, she heard from Jan that Mr Barnes had decided to take up a post at the University of Bath and the news reassured her. Gradually, over time, she started to sleep better and the paranoia began to recede.

44

Alison

Getting off the bus, Alison was surprised to find she was nervous. She could feel a small knot developing in her stomach. Pushing the feeling aside, she reassured herself that in less than an hour this would all be over and she could get on with her life. Smiling, she thought about her holiday: she couldn't wait to get on the plane with Laura – they were going to have so much fun. But first, I have to do this, she thought, and then I will be free.

As she approached his front door, the late summer sun slipped behind a cloud and with that first knock, Alison realised there was no turning back. Perhaps she should have told someone what she was doing? But it was too late now, and as the front door swung open, The Professor welcomed her with an embrace and a long lingering kiss. Gingerly extracting herself, Alison caught sight of the living room behind him. The table was set for two, with a bottle of wine already uncorked. The room was gently lit by two flickering candles and she could smell the slow-cooked flavours of a beef bourguignon – her favourite meal.

'Hi,' he whispered into her hair. 'I've missed you so much! I'm so glad you decided to come over. Come, have a look what I've been cooking for you.'

He was clearly in the middle of finishing cooking the meal. A half-full glass of red wine sat on the counter and as he talked he went back to chopping the fresh thyme, the final ingredient for the stew.

'I can't tell you how happy I am to see you. I'm so sorry about everything I put you through. I've started the counselling now and it's really making a difference. I've also cut back on the drink, although I have made an exception for tonight,' he smiled. 'I thought we would celebrate.'

'Actually,' began Alison, 'I came to see you because—'

'I'm just so happy you're back,' interrupted The Professor. 'It's been torture not being able to see you. But from now on, everything's going to be different – a fresh start – that's exactly what we need. And I think we should celebrate by going on holiday. What do you think about Malta? I also hear Cyprus is lovely. Perhaps we can go to the travel agent this weekend and see if anything takes our fancy. I was also thinking one of those all-inclusive holidays might be quite a nice option?'

He turned around to look at her, his face full of expectation, the knife in one hand, his glass of wine in the other.

'I'm so sorry,' stammered Alison. 'But I'm not actually here to get back together with you.'

The Professor lowered his wine glass, slowly placing it on the kitchen counter.

Taking note of his shock, Alison tried to lessen the blow.

'I'm really sorry; I just feel that at the moment, this isn't the right time for me to be in a relationship. I need to focus on my studies and graduation. You can understand that, can't you?'

'But I can help you with that,' he said. 'Didn't I help you before? Haven't I spent hours with you going over all the course material?'

'Yes, but—'

'Why are you doing this?' he asked quietly.

'I'm really sorry, I just feel—'

'Tell me one thing, Alison,' he interrupted. 'Just tell me this. Why have you kept me waiting so long, only to tell me this now? Did you not think it might be worth telling me before?'

'But you promised to give me some time to think—'

'Which I did. In fact, I've given you more time than you deserve. Alison, I don't know who you think you're dealing with, but I won't let you keep me dangling while you make up your mind what you want.'

Alison could see he was getting himself worked up.

'Of course not, I just want to be honest with you. And that's why I came to see you—'

Alison didn't get a chance to finish her sentence as all of a sudden she was forced to step back as he swiped the glass of red wine with his backhand. Almost in slow motion, she watched it fly through the air and smash against the fridge. Streaked rivulets of ruby contrasted against the white glare of the fridge doors. His rage was palpable.

'So, let me get this straight,' he said, now looking menacingly at her. 'Here's me thinking you were coming over and everything is fine. But now you've decided that it's over. Well, here's some news for you. I decide when it's over, not you. Got it?'

He paused, breathing heavily. Alison didn't dare say a word. An eternity passed.

'So, what have you been up to while I've been giving you time?' he snorted. 'Were you waiting for Mark to get back to you? Is that it? Had a better offer?'

'Wh—'

'Don't lie to me, you little bitch!' he yelled. 'It's that guy Mark I saw you with in the coffee shop, isn't it? I should have known. How long has that been going on for then?'

Furious, Alison forgot all her fear and after months of suppression, felt her own rage, which she had ignored for so long, boil up in her.

'What are you talking about?' she screamed back at him. 'This has nothing to do with anyone else. This is about you and your treatment of me! You're a monster! You've lied to me, beat me and treated me no better than a dog.'

'And why do you think that is?' he stormed back. 'It's because you are a dog! You're a puppy looking for someone to love you. Well, welcome to the real world, sweetheart, because it's not all flowers and chocolate. When I punish you, it's because you deserve it – it's because you need to learn.'

She was crying now, her heart beating wildly with the unfairness of it all. How had she ever found him attractive? Her desire to hurt him, to emotionally, psychologically and physically crush him, tore through her.

'Well, you know what?' she screamed, wiping her tears aside. 'Maybe there is someone else, and I can tell you now, he treats me a lot better than you ever did!'

The Professor's head snapped towards her.

'You bitch! I knew it!' he said quietly in a tone she

recognised. 'I swear to God I'll make you pay for making a fool out me.'

He lunged at her and, whether it was the amount of wine he'd drunk making him clumsy or he had simply tripped over a chair leg, he came crashing down on the floor. Seeing the knife still in his hand, Alison didn't hesitate. She turned and ran for her life. Out through the kitchen and into the hallway. She could see it now – the front door was just a few seconds away. She had to get out into the street where there were other people. Her hand reached for the door handle and she yanked it hard. But it wouldn't open – it was either stuck or locked. She tried again, praying the door was just jammed by the carpet, but it didn't budge. She could see the keychain hanging on its hook to the side and made a grab for it. Shaking, she tried to find the right key from the bunch to open the door. She could hear him stumbling around in the kitchen and knew she only had seconds to spare. Hearing him coming out of the kitchen, she turned to look back. He looked deranged. There was blood where he had banged his head on the floor and as he came rushing towards her, the last thing Alison saw was the cruel glint of the Victorinox logo on the blade of the knife, and she knew everything was over.

45

Kate

Kate paced nervously, glancing at the clock. There was still an hour to go until the results came out. Her husband was making some breakfast and even the girls were quiet, aware of the tense atmosphere but unsure of its exact cause.

'Come on, love, come and get something to eat. You staring at that clock all morning isn't going to make the time go quicker,' called out her husband from the kitchen as he started to place breakfast on the table.

'This is terrible,' Kate complained. 'What if I've failed? What if the last four years have just been a complete waste of time?'

'You haven't and it hasn't. Now sit down, eat your breakfast and then we'll go, OK?'

Calling to the girls to join them, they sat at the table but Kate couldn't eat a thing. She had invested so much of herself into the course, she didn't think she could bear it if it turned out she hadn't passed.

'Don't worry, Mummy, even if you've failed you're still

the best Mummy,' said her elder daughter, and her younger child nodded in agreement.

Turning to face the girls, Kate felt a swell of pride. Both children were in school now and doing really well. They were keen learners, loved books and their teachers all commented on how polite and respectful they were. Kate never tired of hearing the praise that came her way and she sometimes wondered if she had turned into one of those mothers who bored everyone with her children's successes. Yes, they could still be mischievous when they wanted to be but all in all, she reminded herself that she had done a good job so far. Her daughter's words – so honest and straightforward in their message – brought a lump to her throat. 'Thank you, my angels,' she said, kissing each of them in turn. Picking up a slice of toast, she began to eat.

*

Arriving early at the college, Kate could see everyone had had the same idea. There was still another twenty minutes before the results would be released. Turning to her husband, she said, 'There's no point in all of us queuing. Why don't you take the girls for a walk around campus and I'll meet you back here?'

'Are you sure, love?'

'Yes, I'll be fine. Don't worry.'

Kate joined the rest of the students, taking a place at the end of the line to wait for the results. They were mostly young people but there were a few mature students such as herself. She had decided to study English and psychology. At the time, she had wondered if it would be too much, and while it wasn't easy, she had enjoyed the work. It was the counselling sessions that had helped guide her on the path of education and, ironically, Mr Barnes. She had never forgotten his theme of regret and as she talked through her various feelings with the counsellor, a number of topics had come up time and again.

'Do you think it's possible you had post-partum depression, Kate?' the counsellor, Jane, a woman in her mid-forties, had asked her. By that time, Kate had been seeing her for six weeks. Initially, Kate had had a hard time opening up. She hadn't ever discussed her feelings with a stranger and she found it embarrassing. But as the weeks went by and she got more used to Jane, Kate could feel a slight shift in herself. A sense of lightness, a feeling of hope that hadn't been there before.

'Post-what?' Kate had asked, confused.

'Post-partum depression,' Jane repeated gently. 'It's something many new mothers suffer from but unfortunately it's not widely talked about.'

Kate thought back to when her eldest was a newborn; the incredible feeling of love that surpasses everything, the sense of wonder as she was placed in her arms, the look on her husband's face, the joy of that first gummy smile. It was harder to remember this with her second child. Instead, she remembered the severe lack of sleep, the overwhelming sense of responsibility, the pain of breastfeeding. But that was what every mother went through, she thought. Casting her mind back even further, she also remembered the sadness, the mood swings and withdrawing from family and friends. She remembered crying herself to sleep each night and waking up to her younger daughter's cries with such irritability, she sometimes had to walk away. As Jane talked through some of the symptoms, Kate thought there was a possibility she may have had post-partum depression after the birth of her second daughter.

Kate and Jane talked about freedom and what it meant to Kate as a value. She talked about how she felt her freedom had been taken away from her and with Jane's help she was able to come up with ideas and solutions as to how to resolve those feelings. Kate also talked through her fears of having made a mistake marrying and having children so early and she came to understand that she still had many opportunities in life. While she was content with her children and her husband, Jane reminded her it was important that she also did things for herself outside of being a mother and a wife. As she discovered her own happiness, so, too, did the happiness in her marriage grow.

After that, Kate started writing a journal and discovered the pleasure of the written word once again. She wrote letters to her family and enjoyed receiving the responses in the post, but it wasn't enough. She had a thirst for knowledge and it was this that led her to doing some extra studying. She looked into taking a night class in typing or creative writing but it was her husband who suggested going one step further.

'Why don't you look into doing a degree course?'

Kate looked at her husband in surprise. 'Are you serious?'

'Of course I am – why wouldn't I be?'

'I don't know – you've never mentioned it before.'

'Neither have you,' he said reasonably. 'The girls are both in school, you'll have a bit more time on your hands, and with this new job being closer to home I'll be able to help out more with the girls in the evening, leaving you time to study.'

'You make it sound so easy!'

'It is. But if you're not sure, why don't you just take the

first step and pop down to the college on Monday and see what's available? You've nothing to lose.' And with her husband's support, that's exactly what Kate had done.

*

There was a flurry of excitement as a very official-looking person posted the results up on the board. Just at that moment Kate's family joined her. Her elder daughter slipped her hand into her mother's while her husband took their younger daughter by the hand, a reassuring arm placed on Kate's lower back. Moving forward, Kate felt the apprehension grow in her chest. As she reached the board, she found her name and read the result. Inhaling sharply in disbelief, she looked over at her husband, who was smiling broadly at her, his face failing to hide his 'I-told-you-so' grin. She had achieved a first-class degree.

*

Kate walked home in a trance. She had never thought it was possible that she could have achieved so much. After seeing the result, she had caught up with some of the other students on her course and gone for a drink to celebrate. Her husband had taken the girls home, telling her to enjoy herself. The atmosphere in the pub had been celebratory and Kate was thrilled with her mark. Excusing herself from the pub, she decided to head home to make some phone calls to let her family and friends know. As she came up the flight of stairs, she heard a door bang. Not sure if it was hers or a neighbour's, she quickened her steps but when she reached her door, it was closed. She felt a stab of panic at the possibility of Mr Barnes coming back. She hadn't thought about him for years. She put her ear to the door. It was all quiet. Too quiet. Quickly, her levels of anxiety rising, Kate put her key in the door and opened it up.

She jumped in astonishment as the cries of 'Surprise!' rang in her ears. As she looked around, balloons and streamers hung from the ceiling while a huge congratulations banner had been hung on the back wall. The dining table had been set with a buffet and in the middle was a huge cake, which said 'Congratulations on your degree'. Looking around her, seeing all her friends and family gathered, including her parents, and her husband coming towards her with a glass of champagne, Kate let herself be surrounded by their love.

46

Catherine

It was finally happening. Catherine's months of writing had paid off and she had agreed with Michael to meet following his release. After all this time, she was desperate to meet the man behind the letters. She had agreed to visit him in his flat in Durham at 12 noon on 15 August 2011.

Catherine had told Richard that she would be attending a series of meetings so not to bother with his normal lunchtime phone call as she may not be able to pick up. Meeting Michael at lunchtime would also give her enough time to drive there in the morning without rushing.

The night before, Catherine barely slept. She was understandably apprehensive. When she finally did drop off, it was the early hours of the morning, and by the time she woke, Richard was just about to leave for work.

'I was just writing you a note,' he said when he saw her padding towards him in her dressing gown. Slipping the note in her pocket for her to read later, he gave her a quick kiss, eager to get the day started. Catching his hand, Catherine drew him close to her and wrapped her arms around him.

'I love you,' she said simply. 'I hope you have a good day.'

'I love you, too,' he replied. 'Hope your meetings go well.' And with a last kiss, he was gone.

She felt bad for deceiving him but the stakes were too high, and after writing to Michael for so long, she needed to do this last part by herself. She knew it was dangerous meeting a convict and not telling anyone where she was going or what she was doing. But she was prepared to take that risk – had been waiting for it, in fact, for so long now. She felt ready.

She went to get dressed, carefully putting on the outfit she had chosen the night before. Despite the month of August being lovely and warm, she dressed all in black, making her blue eyes and blonde hair stand out even more dramatically than usual. In her bag, she packed all the letters she had received from Michael, as well as the address, phone number, and directions he had provided. With one last look in the mirror, she carefully applied a rich, red lipstick.

With a little time left, Catherine sat at her desk, remembering all the times she had admired the view while working. Picking up the Mont Blanc pen, she remembered how happy she had felt when Richard had given it to her all those years ago. Taking one last appreciative look of her living room, she headed to the car.

*

It was a relief to be on the road and focusing on the drive. Catherine admired the stunning scenery as she drove cross-country, taking in the majestic North Pennines. She involuntarily shivered at the thought that they were all that separated her now from Michael. It had been over ten years since Catherine had been in Durham and as she entered the city, she realised how much she had changed. She was older, wiser, more focused, and certainly more experienced. Even her hair colour and style were different, as was her dress sense. Glancing in the rear-view mirror, Catherine caught sight of herself, the red lipstick almost brazen against her cool and composed face.

She followed Michael's written directions to the flat towards the outskirts of Durham on an old estate. As it was a Monday, parking was easy. Getting out of the car, Catherine looked around her. A dog barked noisily somewhere nearby, while in front of the block of flats a large skip was close to overflowing. The block itself was made of grey stone, its ugliness somewhat diminished due to the sunny day. But there was no escaping the peeling paint, the graffiti on the stairwell, and the occasional boarded-up window. Catherine took the stairs to the seventh floor, passing a group of youths with strong North-Eastern accents. At the sound of their voices, she was instantly enveloped in a wave of memories from her childhood. She had worked hard to lose the Pitmatic, or what many mistakenly referred to as the Geordie accent, to fit in with the local accent of the Lake District, but at that moment she would have given anything to go back in time. The memories were simple but warm: chatting over tea with her parents, messing about with her friends at school, meeting her husband in the local pub. It was so long ago now but Catherine felt like it was yesterday. At the top of the stairs, she followed the flat numbers until she reached number 17. The blue painted wooden door was slightly rotting in places and the '7' of the flat number had a screw loose so it hung like an 'L'. Catherine took a deep breath and knocked.

Michael answered the door quickly. He must have been waiting for her. Catherine, knowing that the first interaction with Michael might be difficult, had prepared her first words and practised them in the car.

'Michael, hi!' she exclaimed cheerfully. 'My name is Catherine – it's good to meet you at last!' She held out her hand and Michael shook it formally.

Inviting her in, he smiled at her, showing her through to the living room.

'Thanks for coming all this way. You must be thirsty. Would you like a cup of tea or coffee or something a little cooler?'

'Thank you – coffee would be great – milk and... just milk, please.'

As he headed into the kitchen across the hall, Catherine tried to calm herself. Her anticipation was making her forget she no longer took sugar in her coffee. As she heard him preparing the drinks, she took in her surroundings.

The sofa was a two-seater – clean but she could feel a spring coming through under her left thigh. An attempt had been made at disguising the two mismatching armchairs with a throw over the back of each one. A seventies tiled fireplace was the unfortunate focal point of the room. There were no plants, just a couple of pictures as well as a small television and coffee table with some newspapers. There was a pile of books in one corner. She was just about to go over to take a closer look when Michael entered the room carrying a tray. Placing it on the coffee table, he seemed relieved to have something to do. Watching him, Catherine took in his appearance. His hair was completely grey and, while combed neatly, she could see that it needed to be cut. He wore jeans and a long-sleeved, dark blue shirt with the sleeves rolled up slightly to reveal his forearms. As he leant to pour the drinks, his sleeve moved slightly to reveal the edge of a scar. Catherine wondered if he had received it during his time in prison.

As he handed over her coffee, she noticed Michael's hand shook slightly. Catherine took the cup gratefully and they made small talk about the weather, her journey, and any other minutiae they could think of. Every so often, Catherine could sense him looking at her, slightly quizzically. As they each got more comfortable, Catherine asked how he was settling into his new life.

'I'm getting there,' he replied quietly. 'As you can see, I'm not in the best living situation but at least I have a free roof over my head and I'm not sharing with anybody. I was very specific about that – I really didn't want to live with anyone else. The rehabilitation team also advised me to take my time settling in, but I'm keen to find some kind of employment soon. I think it would help to have a bit of structure to my days.'

'Do the rehabilitation team also help you find a job?' Catherine asked, still trying to take in that a convicted murderer was able to get free housing.

'Yes, they do, to a point,' Michael responded. 'They have connections with the local community. But, as you can imagine, it's not easy trying to place an ex-prisoner.'

'I'm sure there will be something available,' reassured Catherine.

'I hope so. Unfortunately, this is often the most difficult part in the rehabilitation process. As there are so few job opportunities, boredom opens up a whole host of alternative employment, if you know what I mean.' Michael emphasised the words 'alternative employment' and Catherine, from her research, unfortunately knew what he meant. Despite huge amounts of efforts in the resettlement process, ex-prisoners often turned to other means of activity, such as drugs and alcohol.

'Well, there's time yet. It's only your second week.'

Changing the subject, Catherine asked, 'And how have you found Durham? Has it changed much?'

Michael laughed drily. 'Well, I'm not too familiar with this part of Durham,' waving his hand to indicate he was talking about the block of council flats. 'But what did I expect? It's not like they were going to put me in a penthouse in the city centre overlooking the river now, was it?'

'No, I suppose not,' agreed Catherine, not sure if he was joking or not.

'Sorry,' said Michael. 'I'm suppose I'm finding it all rather difficult at the moment.'

Catherine let him speak.

'Looking back, I think I focused so much on the actual release, I didn't give too much thought to how life would be outside. Or rather I did think about it, but I thought more about the good stuff, you know, rather than the reality.'

'Can you give me an example?'

Michael looked at her in surprise. 'You really want to know?'

'Yes, of course.'

'Well, when I was in prison I imagined going back to my favourite coffee shop and just sitting and reading.'

'And why can't you do that now?'

'Well, I tried it, but as you know, Durham's a small city and people have long memories...'

'Did something happen?' Catherine asked gently.

'Nothing I couldn't handle,' replied Michael gruffly, 'but

needless to say I don't think I'll be going there again.'

As if to avoid further questioning, he changed the topic.

'I know I've said it before, but thank you very much for all your letters. They were incredibly cathartic for me and a big help in getting me through that last year. I don't think I would have got my parole if it wasn't for those letters and your encouragement – I'm pretty sure your letter of recommendation went a long way in helping the cause as well.'

'You're welcome,' Catherine automatically responded. Still thinking about Michael's plans after his release, she asked him if he had managed to get to the sea yet.

'You mentioned in your letters, it would be one of the first things you did,' she reminded him.

'Well remembered,' Michael laughed. 'No, unfortunately not! The rehabilitation centre have kept me pretty busy but perhaps one day, we can go together?'

'That's a nice idea,' replied Catherine, non-committally.

'I have to say, Catherine, you do look very familiar,' Michael said, taking off his glasses, cleaning them and putting them back on to look at her face more intently.

'Really?' said Catherine. 'A lot of people say that to me. I think I must just have one of those faces.'

As he put his glasses back on, Michael commented, 'Many things have changed, including my eyesight – I must get new glasses.'

'Tell me about your first night of freedom,' asked Catherine, hoping the open question would distract him. 'How did it feel when those gates finally opened and you walked free?'

'Oh, well, let me tell you, it was incredible,' remembered Michael. 'One of the best days of my life.'

It had been a good question to ask, Catherine thought as he was speaking.

'The day I woke up, I thought to myself, this is the last day I'm going to be looking at this ceiling ever again. I really shouldn't have been in there for so long you know. Eleven years is a long time.'

Catherine tried not to choke on the sip of coffee she had just taken. In her opinion, eleven years was nothing for someone's life.

'It's the small things, you know? Like putting my own clothes back on instead of wearing prison uniform. In prison, they strip away your identity so putting my own clothes on was the first step to freedom. When the guard took me through the gates – he even shook my hand and wished me luck – I just breathed in the fresh air and started walking. It was an incredible feeling and I felt so lucky to have survived prison. I had to go and meet my rehabilitation officer after that. I had a lot of questions for him, which he helped me with, so that's good, but there's still so much I want to do.'

'Like what?' asked Catherine, intrigued.

'Well, I want to learn to drive again and I want to explore the Internet a little more. I also want to go and see my mum. She might not want to see me but I have to try at least. She's my only hope, really. Unfortunately my dad died when I was inside.'

'I'm so sorry to hear that,' said Catherine automatically.

'Don't be. He was a hard man but I am sorry that he died while I was in prison. It probably finished my mum off, me in prison and my dad gone.'

'And have you not seen her since…?' Catherine left the question hanging.

'Since going to jail? No, I haven't. Neither of them came

to visit me. The last time I saw them was in court,' he said sadly. 'Anyway, enough about me. How about you? How do you find living in the Lake District?'

'Yes, I enjoy it,' replied Catherine. 'It's an incredibly pretty place and a little bit warmer than the North-East!'

'I'm sure it is! Although I hear it rains a lot there.'

'It does.' Catherine wondered how they had managed to get onto such mundane topics as the weather again.

'Is there anything I can do to help you settle in?' Catherine asked. 'I've brought a few groceries for you. I don't know if that helps...' Feeling slightly ridiculous, she handed over the bag. He wasn't ill, for goodness' sake, she chided herself.

'Thank you,' said Michael. 'The supermarket is quite far from here so that's really good of you.'

Continuing, Michael said, 'I don't mean to be sexist but I wonder if you could help me with the washing machine? For some reason, I can't seem to work it out.'

'Of course,' laughed Catherine nervously, relieved to have something to do with her hands. 'What seems to be the problem?'

'Well, there's no problem, but there are just so many settings, I have no idea which setting is best. I have a few shirts in at the moment. Can you take a look?'

'Yes, of course.'

'Thanks – I'll just pop and see if I there's anything else I can add to the load.'

Absent-mindedly, Catherine took a look at the washer dials. Hearing Michael come back, she opened the washer door while he put a few more things in.

'OK,' she said. 'For shirts, I would suggest forty degrees on a spin of 600. In fact, you can probably use that setting for most loads. If you're washing towels or bedding, just increase the spin to 800 as they get quite heavy when wet. Put the tablet in the machine itself – yep, no need for powder these days – and you're done.'

'Thank you!' said Michael. 'Domestic responsibility was never my forte,' he laughed.

'No problem. Is there anything else I can do?'

'I think I've done most of it. I've put a few pictures up and tried my best to make this place homely, but it needs a woman's touch really.'

Taking her by surprise, Michael touched Catherine's arm. Without thinking, she jumped.

'Sorry,' said Michael, slightly flustered. 'It's been a long time since I've touched a woman.'

'No, no, not at all. You just took me by surprise, that's all.' Steady, Catherine, she told herself. You don't want to frighten him.

Slowly placing her hand on his arm, Catherine squeezed it as she would an old friend. 'Everything's going to be fine, Michael, you'll see.'

Looking at her for just a second longer, Michael squeezed her hand back in gratitude. Catherine felt like she had been burnt.

Breaking the moment, Michael stood up. 'Are you ready for some lunch?' he asked. 'It's nothing much, just a salad and some quiche.'

'Sounds great. Let me help – I can set the table and chop the salad.'

'There's no need—'

'I insist,' interrupted Catherine.

Walking through to the tiny galley kitchen, she got out some place mats and knives and forks and put them to one side. While Michael prepared the quiche – shop-bought Catherine noticed – she began searching for a knife in the drawer.

'The knives are in the second drawer,' said Michael. 'I like to keep them separate.'

As Catherine opened the second drawer, she chose the largest one, slipping it from its cover.

Gripping it tightly, she began to slice the tomatoes, cucumber, celery and lettuce.

'So, what plans do you have for the rest of the week?' she asked, her mind focused on the salad in front of her.

'Well, I have to check in with my rehabilitation officer each day so I usually do that in the morning,' he replied. 'Get it over with,' he added with a grin. 'And then I suppose this week I'll start job hunting.'

'What kind of job are you looking for?'

'I'm not sure really,' Michael replied. 'Maybe in a restaurant? I'd quite like to apply for a job as a chef but I suspect I'll be more suited to the role of dishwasher,' he said, with a touch of irony.

'Well, I'm sure once you've got that sorted it will give you something to focus on.'

Out of the corner of her eye she saw Michael move to the small dining table with the quiche.

'Here, Michael, let me do it. You relax and I'll bring everything to the table.'

Surprisingly, he did as she asked, perhaps enjoying being looked after, and he sat down on one of the chairs.

'You know, Catherine,' he said, removing his glasses and cleaning them again, 'I keep looking at you and, I said it before, but you just seem so familiar. I keep trying to think where I may have seen you. Are you sure we didn't know each other from when you were in Durham?'

'I don't know, Michael, what do you think?'

The knife still in her hand, Catherine turned to him, but instead of sitting down, she remained standing, letting him look at her.

Putting his glasses back on, his eyes widened in recognition. 'Kate!' he exclaimed.

As the realisation dawned on his face, he didn't see the knife coming towards him.

'Do you know what date it is today, Michael?' she asked him, unflinchingly.

Unable to respond, Michael sat there, shock and disbelief reflecting in his face. Her first wound had gone deep, and she was so close to him she could see the naked fear in his eyes. She had aimed her first blow in the centre of his chest, and she had done this deliberately to disable his movements. She wanted him paralysed but conscious.

She had imagined that first stab so many times. What would it feel like to inflict such damage on another human being? As the knife sliced into his chest, Catherine felt something release inside her – like an elastic band that had been slowly stretched to its limit and had now snapped. Pain and relief intermingled. But standing over Michael, she felt herself transformed. No longer was she powerless: a helpless mother who had been unable to protect her daughter. For twelve years, guilt had been her only companion, when all she wanted was to be alone, to heal, to grieve. But whichever way she turned, whatever she did, and no matter how busy she was, it was always there, consuming her every moment. But it would soon all be over and as she pulled the knife out, she felt herself rising to be the mother she knew she could always be.

'Today is 15 August. Does that date mean anything to you, Michael?'

As she said his name, she thrust the knife into his stomach as he helplessly clawed at her. Scrambling for something to defend himself, his hand found the edge of the table cloth, and he pulled helplessly, the plates crashing to the cheap Formica tiling.

Power surging through her, Catherine aimed for his kidney and jabbed the knife hard into his side. Michael was now making a strange keening noise and she heard gurgling coming from the back of his throat.

'Not yet, Michael. You can't go just yet. I haven't told you why today is so special. I haven't driven all this way for nothing. Today is the anniversary of my daughter's death. Her name was Alison. Do you remember her, Michael?'

As Catherine removed the knife from his stomach, Michael keeled over, blood flowing rapidly. Catherine ignored it.

'It was on this day, Michael, twelve years ago, that you – decided – to – take – her – away – from – me.' Punctuating every word with a jab of the knife, Catherine felt an almost beautiful, satisfying ache in her arm.

Standing back up and catching her breath, she asked, 'Do you have any idea what you did to our family, Michael?'

She looked at his face, thin and gaunt now, but still handsome. His eyes were still flickering. Good, she thought. He's still alive. She wiped the blood splatter from her face, streaking her red lipstick as she did so, merging the scarlet tones as one.

'And when I found out that you were Michael Barnes, the very same Mr Barnes who had taught me writing classes at the local college, I thought to myself, no, it just couldn't be. Surely fate wouldn't be so cruel. But it was. Do you remember me, Michael? Do you remember our afternoon of passion? Your Mrs Robinson?'

Catherine paused, remembering her affair with a young Michael almost twenty years ago. The hotel, their love-making, the threat to tell Richard. But that was nothing compared to what he had done to her daughter, and as she imagined this very same scene before her twelve years ago – her daughter helpless and alone – Catherine let out howls of rage, finally losing control as she brought the knife down again and again, and again, her years of pent-up anger, guilt and sadness released in the violence of the movements, until her body and soul were cleansed.

*

Later, looking at the scene of destruction, Catherine sat back, her clothes soaking up the pools of blood like a sponge. She could see it disappearing under the fridge and idly wondered who would be responsible for cleaning up her mess.

'Eleven years, Michael – that's not justice,' said Catherine quietly. 'You're a man of the law – you know that. So that's why I decided I had to do something myself.'

With the knife still in her hand, Catherine caressed the seal of the Victorinox logo with her thumb while she waited for the police to arrive.

*

Afterwards, Catherine recalled seeing the recognition in Michael's eyes of the two sides of the woman he used to know: Kate, the vulnerable young mother he had once nearly broken, and Catherine, the name she had reverted to after he was tried and convicted for the murder of her elder daughter, Alison. According to the police report, Alison had been stabbed seventeen times in the chest, abdomen, neck and face by Dr Michael Barnes. Afterwards, apparently, he hadn't even tried to escape – just sat there next to her with his head in his hands. A neighbour had called the police after hearing raised voices and shouting from next door. As the detective inspector quietly and respectfully explained these facts at 11 p.m. on 15 August 1999 to Kate and Richard, Kate knew their lives would never be the same again.

She had been Catherine for over ten years now. After the media storm of such a high-profile murder case, she had changed her name to the more formal version. Her husband believed it was to avoid being recognised, wanting to have a fresh start in the Lake District, but really it was because Catherine couldn't bear to be Kate any longer. She hated her. There had been no words to describe the loss of her daughter, but the fact that it was the same man with whom she had had an affair all those years ago, made her feel responsible and almost as guilty as Michael.

Her husband, Richard, thankfully, had never found out. Jan had seen to that. It was just one of two secrets she had ever kept from her husband, the second being her correspondence with Michael. He wouldn't have understood and she knew he would ask why she had done this. Hadn't they been through enough with the loss of one daughter? Why would Catherine do this to him? Why would she do this to Helen?

She thought of the holiday to the Caribbean. It had been so long since Catherine had shown any interest in travelling anywhere. They used to travel every year once Richard had got his promotion, to beautiful countries such as France, Spain, Turkey, Italy. But after Alison was murdered, the holidays all stopped. They never spoke about it. Richard would have felt guilty even suggesting something so enjoyable as a holiday, while his elder daughter lay dead in the ground.

So, when Catherine had wanted to go all out, telling him she wanted to make it the holiday of a lifetime and that they all deserved it after everything they'd been through, Richard was happy. He hadn't begrudged any of it. Catherine knew what Richard was thinking: that this is exactly what they needed and he should have persuaded Catherine to do it years ago.

Perhaps, she thought to herself now, she should have talked to Richard first about her plan. But then that would have put him in jeopardy and he would only have tried to talk her out of it. Besides, she needed him to be there for Helen. But whatever had happened to Alison, he wouldn't have wanted her to go this far. Catherine knew that what she had done would destroy her family even further but she also knew Richard would cope. He would have to, if only for the sake of Helen. She knew he would be angry and she knew he would think her selfish. But as she lay in Michael's blood, the knife glistening in her fingers, for the first time in twelve years, she was at peace.

Richard had practically raised Helen single-handedly after Alison died. Yes, of course Catherine had been physically present but it was Richard who had made sure Helen had someone to talk to, to sort out the problems at school, to make sure that she felt loved and supported, and to reassure her that the same thing wasn't going to happen to her. Catherine just wanted to immerse herself in being busy. There was always something to do – a school fair to prepare for, a committee that needed forming, an errand that needed to be run. She kept herself so busy that somehow the human connection between them all became so vast. So while Richard and Helen were healing, Catherine was alone with her grief. They couldn't say she hadn't tried. Counselling, therapy, group sessions, support networks, even medication – there was very little they hadn't done in the aftermath. But Catherine knew all along that the guilt would get to her eventually. While she hadn't killed her daughter directly, she had brought Michael into their lives with her actions all those years before. The loss of her daughter combined with the excruciating guilt had broken her and now, finally, it was her turn to do time.

Catherine

Picking up her pen, Catherine began her first letter to Richard. It would be the first of many, collected and sent by the prison guards. No rich, creamy writing paper with matching envelopes here. Against her fingers, the paper was practically see-through.

Dear Richard,

I know how angry and shocked you are that the terrible tragedy that took away our beautiful, precious Alison over twelve years ago has come to this. I have admired – and sometimes envied – how you have built a new life and maintained some sense of normality, if only for the sake of Helen. I am not as strong as you but I did try my best. I just couldn't carry on any longer, especially when I learnt there was a chance he may be up for parole. I felt paralysed for so long and I had to do something to avenge our daughter.

I had felt optimistic about our fresh start in the Lake District, and for a while it seemed to be working.

No longer surrounded by memories, each of us, in our own way, began to build a new life for ourselves. But while you and Helen seemed to move on, I found myself gradually sinking further and further into depression and I just ran out of energy to keep on fighting. It gave me no comfort that that man was being punished in prison. Just knowing he would be released eventually hung over me and I knew the only way to find peace of mind was death, either for myself or Michael. In the end, I chose Michael. Nothing else mattered. I was aware of the potential consequences but I had to take the risk. I do hope in time that you can – if not forgive me – at least understand why I had to do it.

I know you think it was selfish of me but I hope with time that you will come to understand that a mother's love for her child is stronger than everything.

While I know you may not visit me for a long time, I pray that you eventually come to understand my actions and take comfort from the fact that I am not suffering here. I have always wanted to come home to County Durham and while Low Newton Prison has physically captured me, my mind is now free and justice has been done. I know I don't need to ask but please look after Helen and I hope she also comes to understand one day, when she has children of her own, why I had to do what I did to finally become a good mother.

With much love,
Catherine

Acknowledgements

I would like to thank my agent Luigi Bonomi for his encouragement and optimism. To my editor, Sarah Ritherdon, who was simply amazing to work with, the talented copy-editing team, Yvonne Holland and Sue Lamprell, and the digital team, Nia Beynon and Yasemin Turan. Thank you to the whole team at Head of Zeus and Aria for believing in this book.

My novel writing journey started at the Emirates Airline Festival of Literature (EAFOL) winning the Montegrappa Novel Writing Award. Thank you to Isobel Abulhoul, Yvette Judge, and the whole team at EAFOL as well as Charles Nahhas of Montegrappa Middle East for creating such an opportunity for new authors.

To my parents, Sandra and Chris Whittle, thank you for always being there for me and supporting me in everything I do. I would also like to thank Murtaza Manji for his incredible mentorship and Tiffany Eslick for taking the time to provide so much valuable feedback. Special thanks also go to Noha Osman, Sian Fouracre, Rosalie Carlos, Samantha

Armstrong, Jessica Jarlvi, and Emma Smalls. Your support was invaluable.

To all my family and friends turned supporters, too many to name and too important not to be mentioned, every word of encouragement helped another page get written.

Finally, to my amazing husband Fahad – thank you for making all my dreams come true.

Dear Reader,

I do hope you've enjoyed *The Good Mother*. This is a very special book to me as I wrote the majority of it when I was pregnant with my second child and my first child was two years old.

The experience of motherhood was a huge part of the inspiration for this book as it brought to the surface so many new thoughts, feelings and emotions. As I write this, my sons are now eleven months and three years old and continue to amaze me each and every day.

When I was brainstorming ideas for *The Good Mother*, I also included in the list my years at the University of Durham. There were a variety of volunteer roles available for students and letter-writing to a prisoner was among them. While I never took this opportunity (I ended up volunteering in a hospital), the idea always intrigued me – what would you write to a prisoner?

By combining these two experiences, I came up with the idea for the book and from there, developed the characters. I have always enjoyed letter-writing so the letters between Michael and Catherine were definitely one of my favourite parts of the process.

I'd love to know what you thought of *The Good Mother*, so please do drop me a line or connect with me on social media.

Karen Osman
4 August 2017

An Interview with the Author

Why do you write?

I write because I can't imagine doing anything else. I've always written in one form or another, mainly as a journalist and copywriter, but never books until now. It's a different type of writing for me, which requires a lot of concentration and dedication, but the satisfaction of seeing a book come together is incredible.

Where do you write?

I'm originally from the UK, but I moved to Dubai in 2004 so most of my writing is done from here. I normally work from home but if I need a change of scene, I'll pick up my laptop and head out to one of the cafés on the beach for a bit of inspiration.

What's your writing process?

I've experimented with quite a few ways and I've found that setting a daily word target works best for me. The most important thing in the initial stages is getting the thoughts down. The editing process comes later. Before writing, I do a rough sketch of the characters and the chapters, but the characters will often develop as I write.

Who are your favourite authors?

I'm a huge fan of historical novels so Philippa Gregory is definitely one of my favourites. I also enjoy Haruki Murakami, Paula Hawkins, Annabel Kantaria, Elena Ferrante and Mary Kubica.

What were your favourite childhood books?

Enid Blyton was a huge part of my childhood and my bookshelves were filled with those stories. I was recently in the Cotswolds and was browsing an antique fair when I came across an old copy of *My Enid Blyton Book*. There's an inscription inside indicating it was a gift – a little boy called John Broad must have enjoyed the book from his Auntie Daisy and Uncle Arthur – a little piece of history right there!

What's next for you?

I'm currently working on my second novel, which will be published in October 2018. It's a thriller about a woman who grew up in the harsh environment of a children's home in the sixties, before being adopted by loving parents. The novel describes the woman in her late twenties as she tracks down her reluctant real mother. At the same time, a series of unexplained, frightening incidents befall the mother and as they gradually reunite, the mother starts to believe her daughter is secretly trying to take revenge for giving her up for adoption.